CALIFORNIA
BONES

Greg van Eekhout

A TOM DOHERTY ASSOCIATES BOOK

NEW YORK

CALIFORNIA BONES

Copyright © 2014 by Greg van Eekhout

Edited by Patrick Nielsen Hayden

A Tor Book
Published by Tom Doherty Associates, LLC
175 Fifth Avenue
New York, NY 10010

www.tor-forge.com

Tor® is a registered trademark of Tom Doherty Associates, LLC.

Library of Congress Cataloging-in-Publication Data

Van Eekhout, Greg.
  California bones / Greg van Eekhout.—First edition.
     p. cm.
  "A Tom Doherty Associates book."
  ISBN 978-0-7653-2855-7 (hardcover)
  ISBN 978-1-4299-4685-8 (e-book)
  1. Magic—Fiction. 2. California—Fiction. I. Title.
  PS3622.A585485C35 2014
  813'.6—dc23

                         2013029670

Tor books may be purchased for educational, business, or promotional use. For information on bulk purchases, please contact Macmillan Corporate and Premium Sales Department at 1-800-221-7945, extension 5442, or write specialmarkets@macmillan.com.

First Edition: June 2014

Printed in the United States of America

0 9 8 7 6 5 4 3 2 1

With respect, affection, and gratitude to my friends in the Blue Heaven writing community, and especially to our mastermind, Charles Coleman Finlay

CALIFORNIA BONES

Daniel Blackland's clearest memory of his father was from the day before his sixth birthday, when they walked hand in hand down Santa Monica Beach. That was the day Daniel found the kraken spine in the sand.

It was a slate-gray morning, and Daniel shivered without a jacket, but he wouldn't complain. The soggy air carried roller-coaster screams from the pier, and Daniel hoped for a ride. Maybe he and his father would even drive the bumper cars, teaming up to bash other kids and their parents. But then he spotted the bone splinter in the foam of the receding surf, a silvery fragment the length of a knitting needle, rising from the sand like an antenna. Years later, he would wonder if his father had planted it there for him to find, but on this day, he hadn't yet learned that level of suspicion.

The sliver drew him like a magnet. Breaking contact with his father's grip, he ran across the wet-packed sand to claim his prize. When he brought it back, his father held the spine to his long, bent nose, and his dark eyes focused like a microscope over a glass slide. He took an aggressive sniff, as though he were trying to suck the soul out of it. In his white dress shirt and gray slacks, he resembled one of the seagulls wheeling overhead, and Daniel imagined him spreading his long arms to catch the wind and take flight.

Daniel's mom once said his father was made of air. "Sebastian Blackland's not down here with us. That's why he's hard to understand. Spend too much time searching the sky for your father and you'll just crimp your neck."

Sebastian held the sliver up to the weak sun. "Kraken. We hardly ever find these anymore. Not outside of the Ossuary, anyway. But something must have dredged it up from the sea floor, and then the currents carried it here, right in your path, just for you. It's not surprising. I've used a lot of kraken in my work, so it's in my bones, and I've passed some of that affinity to you." He handed the spine back to Daniel. "The kraken used to live in the great deeps. They were creatures of storms and wind and rain and lightning. Not much in the way of solid skeletons, so their remains are rare."

He paused and looked at Daniel, and Daniel felt as though he were being measured. He held his father's gaze, struggling to triumph over squirms and fidgets.

"This is a good find, Daniel. Better than most of the La Brea fossils. The kraken is even older, with deeper osteomancy."

Daniel glowed. His father didn't lavish idle praise.

"Find me a seashell," he instructed Daniel. "Abalone would be perfect, but I'll take anything from the ocean I can use as a crucible."

Daniel raced off. He found no abalone, but from a tangle of seaweed swarming with sand fleas, he excavated half a large mussel shell. He rinsed it in the surf, dug out some stubborn sand grains with his fingernails, and rinsed it again before bringing it over for Sebastian's inspection.

"Good," Sebastian muttered. "This will be good."

They sat cross-legged on the sand together.

"Do you trust me?"

This was a serious question. An important one. Usually his father's eyes roamed when he spoke, looking at things Daniel couldn't see. Now, they saw only Daniel.

Daniel loved him with the uncomplicated desperation with which small boys love their fathers. But trust? It had never occurred to Daniel not to trust him. It was like earth. Daniel never wondered if it'd be there when he took a step. Now, the smallest of fissures opened in his unquestioning certainty.

"I trust you," Daniel said, because he knew it was what his father wanted to hear.

His father took the mussel and kraken spine and set them both on the sand. From a leather zipper case, he produced his scalpel. The handle was polished bone, coffee-stained from millennia in tar and so well used that there were indentations where his fingers gripped it. The blade was fashioned from the tooth of a *Vipera americanus*.

"I'm a powerful man," he said. It didn't sound boastful. It was a simple fact. "Some people want what I have. They're not dangerous to me, because I'm stronger than they are. But there are other people who are more powerful than me, and they're afraid I'll want what *they* have. Those people are very dangerous to me. And because you're my son, they're dangerous to you. So, I have two choices. I can keep you ignorant and weak. Or I can try to make you strong. Do you understand?"

"Not really," Daniel said.

His father's smile formed a pale seam in his face. "No, of course not. I'm not sure I do either. But you said you trust me. And there will be times when I ask you to do hard things.

Things that hurt. Things that make you cry. But I'm doing them for your own good, so that when you grow up, you'll be strong. Stronger than me. Stronger than the people who are stronger than me. Can you understand that, at least?"

Daniel nodded.

"Good," said his father.

Daniel watched his father's hands work the kraken with the scalpel, curling away shavings and letting them drop into the shell. Sometimes Sebastian spoke as he worked, instructing Daniel in the way his teachers must have instructed him. He spoke of *Elysia chlorotica*, a sea slug he'd been studying that stole genes from the algae it ate and gained the ability to convert sunlight to energy. A natural osteomancer, he called it. But sometimes his words couldn't express what he was doing. Sometimes Daniel could only watch and smell. Some of what he smelled now was earthly—the salt and mud and sour rot of things from the bottom of the sea. And some of it was osteomantic, impressions of ancient things, lurking deep, of old power, of electric anger, waiting to discharge.

Next from the zipper case, Sebastian produced his torch. In outward appearance it looked very much like a cigarette lighter of burnished copper, but it was an intricate instrument with inner workings as complex as a fine watch. Sebastian thumbed it open and dialed the flame to a precise temperature. He applied it to the bottom of the shell, and the flame changed color, fading from intense red to pale peach, and then to an invisible heat. The flame wasn't just coming from the torch. Daniel's father was fueling it, too, and his heat baked Daniel's face.

For a stretch of time, nothing happened. Sebastian remained perfectly still, holding the torch steady. Daniel's foot began to fall asleep, so he counted ocean waves to take his mind off the tingling. By the time he got to seventy-five, the kraken shavings had melted to a tiny pool of molten silver. Sebastian spit into the shell. He wasn't a tobacco user, but his saliva was the same rich brown as the tar-infused bone handle of his scalpel. The kraken shavings burst into flame, with tall flickerings of gasjet blue.

"Our bodies are cauldrons," he said, "and we become the magic we consume."

He often said things like that, things that circled around the perimeter of Daniel's understanding, sometimes veering just within reach before darting away into ever-widening orbits. Daniel could remember the names of osteomantic creatures and their properties—mastodon for strength, griffin for speed and flight, basilisk for venom—but he grew lost when Sebastian spoke of the root concepts of magic.

The blue flame deepened to a dark royal color, like the flags that snapped above the Ministry of Osteomancy building where Sebastian worked. When the flames shrank and died, he capped the torch and held the mussel-shell crucible out to Daniel.

"Drink," his father said, not in the firm tone he used when Daniel didn't want to eat his brussels sprouts, but softer, more encouraging, almost a whisper of anticipation. "Drink."

Daniel obeyed. He lifted the shell to his mouth, took a breath for courage, and touched his tongue to the fluid. His tongue blistered in an instant, and his taste buds charred and fell away. His hand jerked in pain, but his father's strong fingers steadied his wrist, and Daniel spilled no kraken.

"Drink," he said again, and maybe it was the pain, or maybe the magic, but it sounded as though his father's voice had come from the crucible.

Daniel tipped the shell back and let the scalding silver slide down his throat. At first there was only fire and searing pain. He tried to scream but all that came out was a strangled croak, and in that croak was stored not only physical agony, but deeper injuries of betrayal. His father had done this to him. He was in pain because of his father.

And then Sebastian's cool hand cupped the back of Daniel's head, as if he were an infant and his father were cradling him, and the pain went away, replaced by flavors and aromas of secret places in deep, sunless waters, and great black pressures from the miles of vertical ocean. Daniel was a skeleton swimming in the sea-water cage of his own body, and the pressure suddenly gave way and Daniel shot to the surface.

"Quick, now, Daniel. Hold my hand."

Light-headed, Daniel gripped his father's hand as tight as he could. A prickling sensation raised goose bumps on Daniel's skin. The tiny hairs on his arms stood at attention, and his blood popped like cola.

Gulls cried overhead and waves hammered the shore. Daniel looked up at Sebastian. His face was a blur, and Daniel realized his father was vibrating, and Daniel was vibrating with him.

"Don't be afraid," his father said, voice shuddering. "I'm strong."

Lightning struck. Silver-white cracking bursts. Threads of blinding light coursed over Daniel's arms and legs, snaking around his chest and rib cage and mingling with the lightning coming off his father. Pain gouged his flesh. He screamed, desperate to let the pain fly from his body, but there was only more pain. His body was a sponge for it, with limitless capacity. Pain replaced everything.

After a time, Daniel's world settled and he could once again see. Fused sand, pools of black, gooey glass, thick as La Brea tar, smoked and bubbled around them.

"The kraken was a creature of storms," Sebastian said. "It's been a part of me for a long time, ever since I consumed my first one, when I wasn't much older than you. And now it's yours. That's the osteomancer's craft, to draw magic from bones. To capture it and store it, to use the creatures' power, guided by human intelligence. One day you'll be able to use the kraken's power as you will. Understand?"

Sebastian studied him a long time. The pain was over, but the memory of it roiled inside Daniel, like smoke from a fire.

He felt strong.

"I understand."

Not all Sunday visitations were like this. There were also days at the movies, and miniature golf in Van Nuys, or at the water park in San Dimas. But by the time Daniel was twelve, the outings tapered off and weekends were spent at Sebastian's house, a warren of tilting walls jammed into the earthen gouge of Topanga Canyon. The area was popular with artists and musicians and chefs and osteomancers. Daniel didn't like their children. They had names like Aquarius or Oat and a lot of them didn't wear shoes. Daniel was jealous of them. They had time to screw around with skateboards and bikes. They had time to shoplift CDs from Rhino Records. Not that normalcy was an entirely foreign country to Daniel. Monday through Friday, at home with his mom, things were kept as normal as possible. But the weekends were marathon lessons with his dad, and that world was full of bones and oils and feathers and powders. He learned about Colombian dragon and smilodon and eocorn, the primitive New World unicorn. He learned about osteomancy imported from other lands, like abath from Malaysia and criosphinx from North Africa. And he learned to use the osteomancy already in him. He could generate sparks from his fingertips without having to consume more kraken. His father fed him a lot of magic.

On the last day he saw his father alive, Daniel watched a little nugget of bone bob in a kettle of boiling oil. Sebastian lifted it with a copper spoon and sniffed it. "Tell me what this will do," he instructed.

"I have no idea," Daniel said, giving the bone a cursory sniff. Outside was a blue sky and a warm sun and a short gondola-bus ride to the beach, where Daniel fancied he could rent a surfboard and maybe figure out a way to impress a girl. He didn't want to be here with the curtains drawn, breathing air full of dead things that stank.

Sebastian dipped the bone back into the oil. "Try, Daniel. Let it in. Let it talk to you."

His father wouldn't give up, and there was still a part of Daniel that wanted nothing more than to please him. Resigned, he lowered his face to the kettle. At first all he detected were his father's tells: There was clean sweat. Shaving soap. And tar, deeply embedded, from the marrow of his father's bones. And there was also something of Daniel. The ghosts were all mixed up, and Daniel couldn't tell where his father's smell ended and his own began.

"What is our essence?" Sebastian asked.

Daniel had answered this question a thousand times. He answered it again. "Cells."

"And what is the essence of the cell?"

"The molecule."

"Was that your mind answering, Daniel, or just your mouth?"

"Molecules," Daniel repeated, adding a touch of drone in order to make himself sound as brainless as possible. But taking the time to answer, even in his smart-assed way, forced him to concentrate on the word just enough that he involuntarily began to envision molecules, like knotted beads twisted into esoteric chains.

Sebastian smiled, enjoying his small victory. "And what is the essence of the molecule?"

"The atom."

"And the essence of the atom?"

"Electrons, protons, neutrons. And quarks."

This was where Sebastian Blackland had made his innovations in magic. He'd followed the research in nuclear and particle physics, reading papers smuggled into California from the United States, seeking to understand the fundamental nature of matter on a finer-grain level than his colleagues at the Ministry of Osteomancy. Ultimately, he felt that magic came from understanding matter, so he sought to understand matter as deeply as he could.

"What is at the heart of the subatomic particle?"

"Energy," Daniel said, his answers more than recitation now. Sometimes he felt he was coming close to understanding his father's model of magic, and that's when he felt nearest to those beach-walk afternoons of long ago. But his understanding was like a whiff of vapor that stole away on the breeze.

"What bridges energy and matter?" Sebastian continued.

"Magic," said Daniel.

"Trick question," Sebastian said, a little mischievous now. "Magic transcends energy and matter. Magic transcends the laws of thermodynamics. An osteomancer consumes a creature, and not only does he use its power, but he increases it." He stirred the pot again. "If he's any good, that is. Now. Smell the preparation again."

Daniel moved his face over the bubbling kettle. He shut his eyes and thought of chains and links and impossibly small bits of matter and impossibly huge parcels of energy.

"Well?" Sebastian whispered, close to Daniel's ear.

"It's sint holo?" The sint holo was an extinct horned serpent from the American southeast.

"Yes," Sebastian said. "And what does it do?"

"I don't know," Daniel said. "It's like something I can't hold on to. It's like confusion."

Sebastian straightened, smiling, and Daniel felt his head swim. Maybe from the fumes. Maybe from pride.

"That's right. Sint holo remains transfer properties of invisibility. It's for a weapon I'm making. Part of a sword blade. Want to see?"

Did Daniel want to see? Was he kidding? What kind of wizard's son would he be if he didn't want to see his father's sword? He'd read a book about the swords the Hierarch had used in the Battle of Santa Barbara, and he knew if he ever became a true osteomancer, he'd specialize in making magic swords.

"Okay," Daniel said.

He imagined Sebastian would take him through some secret doorway, down a passage to an underground vault, and that the sword would be displayed in a magnificent case, or embedded in a stone. Whenever Daniel heard mention of the Ossuary catacombs, where his father worked, that was how he envisioned it. Instead, Sebastian took him to a bureau in a spare bedroom stuffed with books and file cabinets. He slid open a long, flat drawer, from which he took out a towel-wrapped bundle. He set it carefully on the bureau and peeled back the terry cloth.

It looked . . . okay. The pommel was a round metal disc welded onto a bare tang, and the guard was an unadorned crossbar. The leaf-shaped blade was kind of short, a little over two feet long and in need of a polish. Running down the blade, almost from guard to point, was a sort of channel inlaid with bone chips. Many were the rich brown of La Brea fossils. Others were tan or gray or white. A few were iridescent pearl, or the rich jewel tones of a church window. Some of the chips appeared to be assembled from smaller pieces, little nuggets of bone, or teeth.

The inlay only ran halfway up the blade, indicating many more hours of toil left to be done.

"Does it have a name?" Daniel asked. All great swords had names. The Hierarch's was called El Serpiente.

"Not yet. I've been calling it the Vorpal Sword for now, just for convenience. It's kind of a joke from Lewis—"

" 'Jabberwocky,' I know. Mom read it to me."

"Ah. Good," said Sebastian. "Well, whoever finishes the sword gets to name it, because it'll have that person's essence."

Daniel pointed out the bone chips. "What do they do?"

His father's eyes shone. He somehow managed to betray giddy excitement and remain grave at the same time. "Right now, the sword does everything I do. It has kraken properties,

and firedrake. Thunder and flame. Sint holo will make it hard
to defend against. But we won't know all its properties until
you're finished."

"I'm finishing the sword?"

"Yes, that. But I also meant we won't know what it's capable of until *you're* finished. Here, look at this." His father ran
his finger along some of the inlaid chips. "These are your baby
teeth. And these threads between them are made from your
hair clippings. And these lacquered bits here? I made those from
your tonsils."

Daniel's tonsils came out when he was five. He didn't remember why. He didn't remember being sick. He just knew his
father had taken him to a doctor and then his throat hurt and
there was ice cream.

"Your magic is in this," said his father. "And you'll keep
growing your magic, and you'll keep investing in this weapon,
and in others. Using the magic brewing inside you . . . that's
deep magic. That's osteomancy." He gestured at his work counter, littered with jars and vials and little envelopes. "Everything
else is just recipe. It's so important you learn that, Daniel. It's
important you make powerful weapons. That you be a powerful
weapon."

"Why?"

"Because the Hierarch is making *very* good weapons."

He rewrapped the sword in its towel and returned it to its
drawer. Back in the kitchen, he dialed down the heat on the
boiling sint holo bone and fitted a heavy copper lid over the
kettle. "It still needs to simmer awhile. So, let's use our time
to—"

"Can we go somewhere?" Daniel interrupted.

"Go somewhere?"

"Yes. Somewhere outside? Or at least somewhere with natural lighting?"

Sebastian's gaze skated worriedly over his work counter.

"It doesn't have to be Disneyland or anything like that," Daniel pressed on. "We can even just stand out on the curb. We can gaze into the mysterious shadows of the canal and you can tell me all about the osteomantic properties of carp or canal scum or anything you want—"

"Okay," Sebastian laughed. "Okay. What do you *really* want to do?"

"Mini-golf and go-carts."

Sebastian's eyes warmed. "Aren't you getting a little old for that?"

"Also, I want to destroy you at skee ball."

"It's good to have ambition. I'll get my keys."

They left the workroom together and entered the living room, little more than a narrow pathway between teetering boxes that went almost to the ceiling. The boxes contained the books and papers Sebastian had hauled over from his Ministry office.

From outside, the sound of a helicopter rotor chopped the air. Sebastian went to the window, but came away when the phone rang. He lifted the receiver.

"This isn't a good time, Otis," he said. And then for a while he didn't speak, but only listened.

"Who else did they get?" Whatever the answer, it made him shut his eyes. When he opened them, he looked over to Daniel, and for the first time in his life, Daniel saw his father's fear.

"You'll take care of them?" Sebastian said into the phone. "Promise me, Otis. *Promise* me."

There was a short pause, and then he returned the receiver to its cradle.

Out on the canal, boat doors slammed. Sebastian pushed Daniel back into the kitchen.

"The sint holo isn't ready yet," he said, lifting the lid of the simmering pot. "But it will help you, at least for a little while."

"What's going on, Dad?"

"Wait as long as you can before swallowing it, and when you walk, make no noise. Take the sword, and go to 646 Palms Boulevard. Your mother will meet you there. Wait for Otis, and he'll help you and your mom get out of Los Angeles."

"Dad . . ."

He ruffled Daniel's hair and placed a priestly kiss on his forehead, just like he used to do when putting Daniel to bed. Then he went into the living room and shut the door, leaving Daniel alone.

Here, Daniel's memory of what happened became less clear. Mostly, he remembered noise and light. Splintering wood and boots pounding the hardwood floor. Shouts. Then, cracks of thunder, so close, like bombs detonating between his ears, the loudest thing he'd ever heard.

After that, a brief silence, followed by soft footsteps outside the kitchen.

Daniel ran to the stove, where the kettle rested over the flame of the burner. The bone still tumbled in the low boiling oil. With a pair of tongs he lifted the bone and braced himself for pain. He opened his mouth and dropped the bone in, forcing it down, tears streaking his face as the jagged nugget burned and tore its way down his throat.

The kitchen door flew open and a half-dozen cops rushed in. The gray-haired man in the lead wore the Hierarch's wings-

and-tusks emblem on his windbreaker. Daniel backed up against the stove as the man came closer, his hand extended.

The man's eyes lost focus. He blinked.

Daniel stepped around his outreached hand, avoiding contact. When he moved past the cops, they flinched as though brushed by cobwebs. He went into the front room.

Four charred bodies lay amid an avalanche of overturned boxes, yellow-edged papers and books spilling across the floor. The men's faces bubbled, black with char and red with blood. The room stank of ozone and cooked meat and kraken.

His father hadn't managed to get them all. He was on his back. Three cops were cutting the flesh off him with long knives. They'd already flayed one arm, exposing the deep, rich brown of his radius and ulna. They peeled back his face to expose his coffee-brown skull.

The man on the carpet being dissected before Daniel's eyes was no longer his father. Daniel understood that his father was gone. In the space of an instant, eternal moment, these men had taken his father away from him. They had reduced his father to a sack of magic, and now they were plundering him.

Daniel reached back to that day on the beach, six years before, when he'd found the kraken. He remembered its smell, and he searched for it in his own body, and when his fingers began to tingle, he knew he'd found it. His father had made him strong, and now Daniel would use his strength to make these men with the long knives shriek like slaughtered animals.

In the doorway stood a man. Whether it was a trick of memory or a trick of magic, Daniel couldn't quite focus on him, as if light slid off his flesh and dripped away. But Daniel caught an impression of him. A smell of deep things underground. The smell of earthquakes.

The Hierarch entered the house. The earth shuddered with each step. The pictures on the walls rattled in their frames, and glasses in the cabinets and the silverware in the kitchen drawers jingled. The Hierarch loomed over the body of Daniel's father. In his hand, something of polished metal glinted. It was a fork.

"Excuse me," the Hierarch said in a sandpaper voice. "I'll have him fresh."

Daniel did not want to see this. He wanted to run. That's what his father had told him to do, and he did not want to see this, because he knew that, once seen, he would never be able to close his eyes without seeing it.

But the sword. He couldn't leave without getting the sword. The sword was his father's magic. It was Daniel's own magic. So he forced himself to turn back to the spare bedroom, where two of the men with the long knives stood before the door. There was just enough space between them that Daniel should be able to slip past. He took a step. And then he heard something, over from the floor where his father lay, and where the Hierarch crouched. He didn't look, would not look, but the sound was obvious. The Hierarch was chewing.

That night, Daniel left the sword behind and ran. Away from the house. Away from the rotor blades and searchlights. He ran until he could only walk, walked until he could only stumble, stumbled until he could only crawl. When morning broke, he awoke in wet sand and bathed himself in the cold waves rolling in on the edge of a winter storm. He would live here, he thought. He would live here on the beach as a ghost.

He was already dead, Daniel told himself.

When the Hierarch began eating his father, he was already dead.

Ten years later, he would still hear the sound of the Hierarch's teeth grinding his father's cartilage.

Daniel caught the gondola-bus at Lincoln Station and rode it all the way to Wilshire and Fairfax, just a few blocks from La Brea Tar Pits. The gondola doors flapped open with a pneumatic hiss, and the burned-dirt stink of tar settled in the back of his head. He only realized he'd been woolgathering at the door when the gondolier growled something about schedules and people with heads lodged in their asses. Daniel stepped off into the tar-haunted air.

Delivery boats and taxis left trails through rainbow-slicked waters. After more than a century of use, the Los Angeles canals had become a swill-clogged circulatory system on the verge of seizure, not so much the quaint Venetian paradise Abbot Kinney had envisioned in the early 1900s. Daniel's father used to rant about how LA deserved a land road system worthy of the kingdom. Ten years after his assassination, roads were few and canal traffic was even worse. The Hierarch liked gondolas in his city.

Daniel climbed up the dock steps and glanced over to the community bulletin wall, where the Hierarch's authority was on display. The hands of thieves decorated one section of the wall like fish scales. Nearby, the crow-picked corpses of sub-versives hung in gibbets like wind chimes.

Entering the sprawl of Farmers Market, Daniel negotiated the maze of stands and awnings and bins and baskets where little old ladies with sharp elbows crowded the lanes. Deeper into the market he went, through aromas of charred meat mixed with garlic and cloves and ginger and grease. The market was even busier than usual, with shoppers eager to spend for the upcoming Victory Day celebrations. Dragon magicians smoked the air with flash-powder, while jugglers and snake charmers vied for space with guitar-strumming buskers whose repertoire spanned the spectrum from soulful pop to soulful folk-pop. But what Daniel noticed most was the smell of tar from parcels of gas lurking below the streets like jellyfish.

He made his way to Apothecary's Row, where the shelves bore a dizzying array of things in pickle jars: teeth, bones, penises, glands of all kinds.

"You got a problem?" said a man behind a stall. His face was creased like a cinnamon stick. "Yeah, I can tell. You got lots of problems. Fatigue, listlessness, bedroom difficulties, am I right?"

"I don't have bedroom difficulties," Daniel said, defensive. He'd passed by this stall three times this week, sniffing. He knew the apothecary's pitch. He knew there was a storage space behind the curtain at the back of his stall. He knew in which pocket the apothecary kept his keys.

The man shook a few grains of bright orange dust onto a metal tray. It looked like dehydrated cheese powder from a box of instant macaroni.

Daniel sniffed. "What's this?"

"Dragon-turtle," said the apothecary, his smile revealing

jade teeth. Jade veneers were catching on as a fad. They were believed to counteract poisons.

"Real dragon-turtle?"

The apothecary launched into an unlikely narrative about the turtle's origins. The Chinese still had dragon-turtles, he explained, living ones grown from ancient fossils, and there'd been a typhoon last week and a Chinese turtle carcass had drifted all the way across the Pacific to wash up on a San Diego beach. There, a lifeguard, who just happened to be the apothecary's brother-in-law, got to it before the Hierarch's men were able to confiscate it.

Daniel had to give him credit: It was not the worst spiel he'd ever heard.

A woman in a black peacoat stepped up to the counter and stood at Daniel's elbow. She glanced at him, her brown eyes level with his, and he took in her talcum-powder and clean-soap scent, and suddenly the thought of needing an aphrodisiac was beyond absurd.

"Are you going to try it?" the woman said to him.

"I really don't need—"

"My husband does," she said, waving her hand to show off a loose-fitting gold ring crowned with a sparkly chunk of rock. "But he'd kill me if he knew I was shopping for this kind of thing."

"There's no shame in it," Jade Teeth said, turning on the charm. "But you have to be careful where you get your magic these days. Some of the vendors around here aren't selling anything more potent than baking soda. And that only works if you want your man foaming at the mouth."

The woman laughed extravagantly and waved her hands in a gesture of careless hilarity. Her ring slipped off her finger and flew across the counter. She and the apothecary fumbled hands as they both made a grab for it, but it ended up in her palm, and then back on her finger. Daniel caught an expression of lost opportunity flash on the apothecary's face, but Jade Teeth hadn't noticed the woman's hand dip into his pocket.

"That would have been a disaster!" the woman said with a relieved gasp. "He would have just *killed* me if I'd lost my ring! I guess I should take that as a sign or something. No bedroom enhancements today, thanks."

She smiled, her nose crinkling in a way that Daniel found unbearably fetching, and with a small wave good-bye at the apothecary, she drew away from the counter. The apothecary hungrily watched her go.

"Try the dragon-turtle," he said, snapping back into sales mode, "and you might have a chance with a girl like that."

Daniel suppressed a sudden urge to punch the man in the nose. He licked his fingertip and applied it to the powder and gave it a deep, healthy sniff. Mostly flour, a small touch of sulfur, a pinch of deer horn, mixed with common herbs. Fairly harmless, and not even remotely osteomantic.

True osteomancy was scarce these days, but that didn't stop the market. People craved magic. Magic to heal their ailments, magic to boost their mental acuity, magic to put some octane in the old sex tank. And people like the apothecary were only too happy to sell them counterfeits.

Behind the apothecary's back, the curtain blocking off the back room wafted ever so slightly.

"This is not making me horny," said Daniel.

"You only had a little."

"It's not even making me a little horny. Do you have anything other than kitchen experiments?"

The apothecary squinted. "Are you a cop?"

"Do I look like a cop? I don't even have a mustache."

"I got nothing for you."

"But what about my bedroom difficulties?"

"Fuck your bedroom difficulties."

Daniel shrugged his eyebrows and moved back into the crowd.

He found the brown-eyed woman with the loose ring near the doughnut stand on the other end of the market. She handed him a small white bag. He peered inside.

"Devil's food! With candy sprinkles!" he said, delighted. He took a munch of doughnut. "So, how'd we do?"

"You tell me."

She undid the two top buttons of her coat and flapped the lapels. A sour tinge of cerberus wolf passed across Daniel's senses. Not a lot of it, and it was cut with a dozen useless compounds, but these days it counted as a decent score. Still, it rankled Daniel to be punching so far below his weight class.

Cassandra Morales rebuttoned her coat. "Don't give me that look. That's a month's rent for each of us. Beats working, anyway."

Daniel actually had nothing against working. But getting straight work in Los Angeles wasn't an option for him. Straight work meant submitting to an interview by the Ministry of Labor, which meant an hour-long interrogation, background check, peeing in a cup, letting a hound sniff your skin. It was an opportunity to slip up in the smallest way and earn a place back at the end of the line, or a flogging, or worse. And for Daniel, with his magic-saturated bones, walking into the Ministry of Labor was equivalent to volunteering for a vivisection.

Los Angeles wasn't a safe place for the son of Sebastian Black-land.

So, he was left with these petty thefts of trace magic.

"It's a lot of work for little gain," said Daniel.

"Speaking of work, you didn't tell me I'd have to break a sweat to get into the safe."

"I saw you steal the apothecary's key."

"Yeah, but there was an alarm. All you had to do was talk to the apothecary and lick stuff."

"I'm just saying this was hardly the heist of the century."

"Well, okay," Cassandra allowed, "sniff us out a better score, and we'll see what we can do."

Daniel caught a whiff of something and his mouth went dry.

Cassandra noticed. "What's wrong?"

"Hounds," he whispered.

They came from the other side of the food court: Garms, the lean, smoke-colored breed favored by the Ministry. Like hyperactive vacuum cleaners they sniffed the carpets and wares of the stalls and the shoes of the shopkeepers. Even now word would be filtering through the network of black marketers, and contraband magic was being flushed down toilets or sent off with runners.

"Go," he told Cassandra, and she trusted him enough not to argue. Daniel wasn't too worried about her, nor the cerberus wolf in her pocket. She could take care of herself. With a talent so sharply honed it might as well be magic, she melted into the crowd and was gone.

Daniel would have a harder time. The hounds were trained to detect magic, and Daniel *was* magic.

He shouldered his way past a clump of people surrounding a street performer in silver paint doing a human robot bit. Threading himself into the knot, he unzipped his black hoodie, reversed it, and put it back on, red-side out. That wouldn't fool the dogs, but if the handlers radioed in a fleeing suspect, at least the description of his clothes would be a little off. Much better, of course, if the dogs didn't pick up his scent. But a wet canine snuffle sounded from behind him. He glanced over his shoulder. The dogs were less than a dozen yards away, noses to the ground, sweeping.

No point in running now.

He came to a stop in a crowded market corridor. Sunlight filtered through the multicolored plastic canopies and bathed the space in a floral glow. The hounds were close enough to cover the distance to him in a single lunge. They strained against their harnesses, twisting, threatening to slip their restraints. Alarmed shoppers shoved one another to get out of the dogs' way. A woman dropped her purse and a man stepped on her hand as she bent to pick it up. Oranges spilled out of someone's bag, starting an argument that ended with the snarl of a hound.

Sebastian Blackland had taught Daniel osteomancy, but Otis had taught him almost everything else necessary to survive as the son of an osteomancer. He drew his shoulders in. He expanded his abdomen to create a small paunch. This wasn't magic. It was acting. He was no wizard's son now. He was no professional thief. He had no power. He was a man of little consequence. Of no interest. He was just a guy.

It didn't work. The hounds smelled the truth. They smelled it in his blood and lymph. They smelled it in his marrow. They howled as though he were a rabbit at the end of the hunt, and the handlers drew their cleaver-clubs. Daniel would have to burn them with lightning or let himself be beaten and cut and taken into custody. If he was lucky, he'd just end up with his body parts pinned to the community wall. But that was probably too good a fate to hope for. He was Sebastian Blackland's son, and the Hierarch would make a project out of him.

He called on the sint holo now. He remembered its chaotic, contradictory aromas. It was slippery, ungraspable, and he drew its memory from his bones. Most osteomancers needed constant replenishment of osteomantic materials to use magic. But there were the rare few, like Sebastian and Daniel, who retained the osteomantic properties of what they ingested. With Sebastian the ability had come from research and training. With Daniel, it had come from being used by his father as a human laboratory. He'd eaten what his father gave him, and surrendered his baby teeth and hair and nail clippings, and then Sebastian cooked the magic residue in them, reprocessed them, and fed the refined results back to Daniel, again and again until the magic embedded itself in his bones.

He became invisible now.

Glassy-eyed from sint holo miasma, the dog handlers merely looked through Daniel. But the hounds reached for him. They'd been bred to detect osteomancy, and nothing got them more excited than sniffing out magic. The hounds paused. They half turned away, then back, then away again. Addled and crestfallen, they bowed their heads and whimpered.

"What are we even doing?" one of the handlers asked his partner.

The other sheathed his cleaver. "I don't know. It's weird."

Daniel didn't stick around to see if the hounds would reacquire his scent. As quickly as he could, without running, he moved through the market. By the time he reached the docks, the sint holo had worn off, leaving him exposed. He hoped he'd fogged the brains of the hounds and handlers enough that any memories of the pursuit would be something like the sense of dread following a long night of drinking, where you could remember having your pants around your ankles at some point but not much more than that.

He raised his hand to flag a water taxi when he felt a presence behind him. He knew what was about to happen: A massive hand took hold of his thumb and pinky in a grip that threatened pain if Daniel resisted. At the same time, a white van floated up to the dock. The side door slid open, revealing two more muscle-slabbed men inside.

First cops, and now Otis's goons.

"I'm not having a great morning," Daniel said.

THREE

L et's go," said the muscle with the death grip on Daniel's fingers.

"Oh, please don't hurt me," Daniel wailed. "It's not manly to weep in public."

"Get in the van or you're gonna be crying blood."

"You know, that literally makes no sense. Did Otis tell you who I am?"

"We found you, and we bagged you. What does that tell you?"

"That he doesn't like you much. Well, okay, then."

He stepped forward and ducked into the van, where the muscle-slabs shoved him down onto a bench seat. The door slammed shut and the van rumbled into traffic and started slogging toward Culver City.

He'd learned to drive getaway in a van much like this, when he was fifteen and Otis's thugs were schooling him in the basics of thiefcraft. Daniel noted the odors of stale fast-food grease and pine air freshener, and he was getting nostalgic when he saw drops of old blood on the carpet and caught the faint tinge of urine.

The van passed beneath the shadows of RKO Studios, where chimney towers poked above the fortress walls and vented eocorn-tinged steam into the gray morning sky. Daniel usually tried to avoid steering this close to such high-powered operations, but Otis liked headquartering near them. Hiding in plain sight was one of his specialties.

The van docked behind a low-slung brick warehouse, and Otis's thugs brought Daniel out with some extracurricular shoving and a stinging slap on the back of the neck. It was hard enough to bring water to Daniel's eyes. Two of them gripped his biceps and marched him through a maze of plywood and dry-wall to Otis's office.

Otis wasn't there, but his menagerie was, housed in cages and fish tanks. The animals were oddly quiet. No ear-gouging screeches from the parakeets or cockatiels. The mice and hamsters didn't run on their wheels or gnaw their cages. Even the fish seemed spooked. The animals had been bred to detect osteomancy. They were Otis's alarm system.

"Daniel, my boy!"

Otis's mass entered the room, his arms spread in welcome, his voice booming. A pink-cheeked, carrot-haired white man, he looked like someone who could fit in anywhere. Put him in a suit, he was a lawyer. Put him behind a bar, he was a bartender. Here, smiling warmly, he could be someone's favorite uncle, and Daniel reminded himself Otis was none of these things, but was in fact a kind of monster. His goons still held Daniel fast.

"How about a drink? Horchata? I remember how much you like horchata. Boys," he called out to nobody in particular. "Can we welcome Daniel home with a glass of horchata?"

Daniel was aware of some scrambling around, as Otis's minions combed the warehouse in search of whatever he demanded.

"Hello, Otis," Daniel said. "Watch this." He reached back for the memory of kraken. The brine-and-mud scent filled his nostrils and electricity tingled through his veins. A sizzling crack of kraken energy burst from his skin.

The hired musclemen screeched like cats and leaped back.

"That's for the slap on the neck," Daniel said.

One of the men stared at him with wide "how could you do this to me?" eyes. The other sucked on his burned fingers and looked like he was trying not to cry.

"You don't send your fuck-clowns after me, Otis. I don't owe you money and I'm not your boy."

"But you don't answer my calls! You ignore my letters!" Otis was still smiling, his eyes a-twinkle. He was a black marketer, a crime lord, and also not a very nice man, and he enjoyed himself immensely.

Daniel turned to leave, and the muscle looked to Otis for instruction. They feared another shock from Daniel, but they feared their boss more.

"All right, boys. Let him go and get lost."

With great relief, the men squeezed themselves through the door and disappeared.

"I wasn't sure you still had the juice," Otis said, "which is why I told the guys they could be a little rough. I'm surprised you didn't burn them when they bagged you."

"What do you want?"

Otis smiled his avuncular smile and removed a smog-stained oil painting of a sad hobo clown from the wall, revealing a standard-looking wall safe. There was no point in spinning the dial, because the lock didn't work. To all appearances, the safe was empty. But Daniel knew better. It was lined with ground-up sint holo vertebrae and treated to bring out properties of visual confusion. Otis reached into the seemingly vacant space and pulled out a rolled sheet of paper.

"There's a job."

"I don't want a job."

Otis reacted as if Daniel hadn't spoken. He unrolled the paper on his desk. There were actually several sheets, the topmost being a basic canal map of the Miracle Mile district, encompassing Farmers Market, the banks and office buildings of mid-Wilshire, the Tar Pits, and Ministry headquarters. Otis peeled back the map to reveal a civic engineering drawing of some kind, with sewers and pump works and electrical junctions: the flayed city.

He tapped his finger on a rendering of a pipe or a tube or something. "This is the job."

"I'm not looking for a job," Daniel said, with more force.

Otis lifted the engineering drawing away to expose yet another beneath it. He liked to unveil things gradually. He liked theater.

Daniel refused to even look at it. "I don't want work from you. I don't do that kind of thing anymore. Not for you. Get someone else. Get Little Al. Hell, get Fat Al."

"The Als are dead." Otis tapped the paper again. "I need you for this, Daniel. And you need me. I know how things are. I know how hard it is. Those little jobs you and Cassandra are pulling? It's unworthy of you."

Again, Otis tapped the drawing, and this time Daniel looked. The page was blank, at least in the visible spectrum. Then, from a desk drawer, Otis produced a corked ceramic vial. Once he popped the cork, Daniel smelled sphinx. The essence of the sphinx was the riddle, and it could be used for locks, for barriers, for secrets and codes. Sphinxes had once roamed all over Pleistocene-era California, leaving hundreds of skeletons behind. Most had been taken east by Freemasons before the Hierarch came to power. Yet Otis had sphinx ink. It wasn't cheap.

He moistened a small sponge with the contents of the vial and rubbed it over the paper. A hand-drawn diagram faded in like an apparition. It was a maze of some kind. A labyrinth. A faint circle about the size of a decitusk coin sat just off center. If the drawings were the same scale and orientation, the circle would have to be somewhere beneath the Tar Pits.

Otis's smile twinkled. "I've found the Ossuary."

Daniel rolled his eyes. "Oh, kill me now."

To most, the Ossuary was a place out of legend, the vault where the Hierarch was said to store his personal stash of magic. Daniel's father had worked there, but he'd never revealed its exact location to Daniel. Thieves murmured about it with fear and longing. And there were always rumors: The Hierarch kept entire herds of mammoth remains down there, bones and beautiful ivory tusks, interwoven like mountainous baskets. Basilisk teeth and griffin claws towered to the ceilings over bog-preserved unicorn carcasses.

And there were stories about attempted heists: Tunneling and mining and armed sieges and all manner of magical infiltrations. The names of thieves who'd tried it were whispered like ghost stories. And the one thing all the stories shared in common was that they ended in executions, in dungeons, in glue factories.

"Assuming this is even a real place—"

"It is," said Otis.

"—how'd you come by this map?"

Otis paused as if weighing how much to reveal, but Daniel knew he had this entire conversation planned out from beginning to end.

"What do the greatest heists in history have in common?"

And suddenly school was in session again.

"All the thieves were caught and tortured until they begged to die?" Daniel said.

"What they have in common is that every single one benefited from having an inside man." Otis gestured at his drawings. "Same here."

"You have a guy in the Ossuary? Okay. Who?"

"Are you taking the job or not?"

"I'm not," said Daniel.

Otis regarded him for a while. Up to now, he'd been playing the role of jolly uncle and impresario. Now his eyes grew tired and wise and concerned, like the doc character in an old Western. He reached into his desk drawer and came up with a bottle of tequila and a pair of shot glasses. He filled both and slid one toward Daniel, like an opening chess move. Daniel left it on the desk.

"You can't afford to be this way, Daniel. You're all knotted up inside, racing around like a roach on the edges when you could be claiming big piles of treasure right there for the taking. What was the score on that Farmers Market job today? A few hundred? I'm offering you the biggest job of your life. Hell, the biggest job of *my* life."

"So put on some gloves and a black beanie and go get it yourself. You don't need me."

Otis took one of the glasses. He held it up to the light, as if looking for a speck of magic trapped in amber. "When your dad asked me to take you in, he didn't have a lot of options. He was a powerful man, but he was trapped in the machinery of the Ministry. I was the only one outside the system he could turn to. But I did it without exacting a price from him. I kept you away from the Hierarch. And more. I taught you everything I know about thiefcraft. About leadership. And for the things I couldn't teach you, I found people who could. I got tutors to teach you osteomancy." Otis downed the shot.

The sphinx ink began to fade, and Otis rolled up the papers. He replaced them in his wall safe, straightened the hobo clown.

"When you left, I didn't like it, but I let you be. I didn't harass you. I showed you respect. Now show me some."

Any score from the Ossuary would be huge. The Hierarch had the best magic, and the best osteomancers to refine it. A single cask of pure hydra regenerative could fetch millions on the black market.

Otis straightened some invoices into a neat pile. He folded his hands over it and looked up at Daniel. "Sleep on it and get back to me?"

Daniel turned to the door, but he knew Otis wouldn't let him go before jiggling the lure again.

"It's a sword, Daniel."

Daniel stopped but didn't turn around.

"It's the sword your father was working on when the Hierarch got him. It's the best thing your father ever made. The most powerful weapon."

And now Daniel felt himself turning back to face Otis, as if he were a compass needle and Otis a magnet.

"That sword is made of you, kid. And as long as the Hierarch has it, he's got you."

"He's had it for years. Why is this a big deal now?"

Otis tried to look grave and concerned, but Daniel knew him too well. He could see Otis's delight. The old man was enjoying his abracadabra moment.

"Because my source says the Hierarch's going to use it. And when he does, he'll be using you."

FOUR

Daniel was walking down Venice Canal, away from Otis's warehouse, when he smelled soap and talc. A quick figure darted out of an alley and blocked his path.

"You okay?" Cassandra said.

"Yeah. You?"

She nodded. Daniel wished they could linger over this moment, in which the most important thing on their agenda was making sure the other was unharmed. Some lengthy gazes into each other's eyes would have been nice. A hug would not have been unwelcome.

Cassandra pounded down the sidewalk, determined to get distance from Otis's headquarters as quickly as possible, and Daniel hurried to keep up.

"You tailed me from Farmers Market?"

"Lost you when you did your invisibility thing," she said. "But I figured if you slipped the hounds you'd end up back at the bus dock. When I saw you get in the van I hailed a taxi."

"Farmers Market to Culver City . . . that's not a cheap fare."

"I didn't tip generously. You were in Otis's place a long time. I almost went in after you."

"You think you can just break in and out of Otis's? I like your spunk. Not sure I like your delusions."

No gazing and no hugging, but Cassandra would still risk her life for him.

"There are seven entrances and exits in and out of Otis's," she said. "Otis only knows six of them."

Cassandra had joined Otis's crew when she and Daniel were both fourteen. Her parents were small-time smugglers who'd fallen into Otis's debt, and when they couldn't pay, Otis took Cassandra instead. Her parents died the next year, but the debt survived unpaid until Cassandra turned eighteen. This was a very fair arrangement, as far as Otis was concerned. He didn't mistreat her. He educated her. She learned how to pick pockets with a bell-dummy wired to buzz whenever jostled. She knew more about locks and safes than a locksmith, and as much about barriers and wards as an osteomancer. She could also fight, and she could drive, and she could shoot.

Daniel was dazzled by her. She was smart and funny and pretty, and she was kind to him when he was a short and scrawny kid with splotchy skin who was entirely incapable of arranging his hair in anything that didn't look like a bowl cut. And only a few years removed from his father's murder and his mother's defection, he wasn't very fun to be around. After a few months, they were a couple, and they had three years together, running jobs for Otis with their other friends. It was good, profitable fun, right up to the night of the Sylmar job. After that, Cassandra left Otis, and if Daniel had followed right away instead of working another four jobs for him, they might have stayed together.

At least they were still partners.

"So what did Otis want?"

Daniel told her about the Ossuary job. It took a while before the magnitude of Otis's proposal sank in. Her brown face paled.

"Jesus." She stopped on the sidewalk, staring off into space. A refuse barge chugged past before she spoke again. "What's the take?"

He nudged her back into motion. "The sword is priceless. But the cash score is actually a bundle of basilisk fangs. They're high purity and untapped. Otis figures he can sell them to his Malaysian partners for half a million, at least. If that falls through, he knows some Salvadorans who can't pay as much, but they can pay. It means he doesn't have to sit on the fangs for months and months. It's quick cash."

"Half a million . . ."

"I told him no, Cass."

"Of course you did. It's too dangerous. But, just theoretically, how big a crew would it take?"

Daniel didn't like the gleam in her eyes. But if he looked in a mirror, he'd see the same gleam in his own. For that kind of money, he could get out of Southern California. He could get away from the Hierarch's shadow. Maybe he could convince Cassandra to come with him. There'd be money left over for start-up funds. New identities. Jobs. Decent schools. Daniel pictured a house where he and Cassandra could start over, somewhere safe, clean. And a white picket fence and a green lawn and two kids and a dog named Spot and Cassandra would call him "honey" and he'd bring her breakfast in bed.

He gritted his teeth to dispel the fantasy.

But escape and safety and a chance at a life away from Los Angeles? That part of the dream was achievable. If he took the Ossuary job.

"There's still too much about it I don't know," Daniel began. "Otis isn't going to spill until he's sure I'm on board."

"Then just tell me the parts you do know. Who'd be on the crew?"

Daniel thought it over as they walked past a strip mall reeking of dry cleaner chemicals.

"An osteomancer. Not just to sniff out the targets, but to handle barriers."

"Of course. That's you," Cassandra said. "Who else?"

"Someone to handle conventional alarms and locks. And a good box man, because the sword will be protected by both the magical and the mundane."

"Bells and boxes. That's me. Who else?"

"Utility muscle. Not one of Otis's guys. They piss me off and I don't trust them. It'd have to be friends only."

"Right," Cassandra said. Her cheeks flushed and she walked faster, growing excited. Daniel tried not to notice the change in her body chemistry. It smelled too good. "What about Big Carly?"

"She's doing a two-year bit for carrying dirty labor papers."

Cassandra forged on. By now they'd both walked past their gondola stops. "How about Moth, then?"

"We're still just talking theoretically, right?"

"Of course."

"Then Moth is perfect."

Cassandra nodded, satisfied with Daniel's answer. "And a shape-changer? That'd be Jo, of course. What about Otis's inside man?"

"Otis is going to stay tight-lipped until he knows I'm in," Daniel said. "But just by showing me he knows where the

Ossuary is, he's proving he's got solid intel. I saw the drawings. They've got the whiff of truth."

"Hm."

They walked in silence for another half block.

"I don't want the job, Cass."

She studied his face. "Because of Punch? Punch wasn't your fault."

It was a warehouse in Sylmar, belonging to a man named Castillo, who fancied himself a rival to Otis. He'd taken delivery of a juvenile monocerus recovered from a peat bog, and Otis wanted the horn. Not just for its magic, but to send a message to Castillo. Daniel's crew was supposed to break in, saw the horn off, and leave the rest for Castillo to contemplate. Daniel spent three weeks planning it. Not counting the boat drive out to Sylmar, the job took less than four minutes. Until Punch decided six hundred pounds of monocerus carcass was too much magic to leave behind. Things went bad very quickly, and the job went from being a burglary to a rescue, and, ultimately, an effort to recover Punch's bullet-riddled corpse.

"Maybe not my fault. But my responsibility."

Boats continued to chug down the canal, their wakes pushing coffee cups and fast-food wrappers against the sidewalk pylons.

"But I have to take the job, don't I?" Daniel said.

"It's too rich not to."

"No, not for that reason. Otis is right about the sword. My dad put my essence in it."

"But the Hierarch's had that sword since you were a kid, and you've been okay."

"I know. It's just . . ." He couldn't find the words, because he wasn't sure what it meant, to have part of him invested in an artifact, and for that artifact to be stored in the vault of the most powerful magic user in the realm. In the years since the Night of Long Knives, he'd never stopped thinking about the sounds of the Hierarch eating his father. But he hadn't thought much about the sword. It was a part of him that was gone, like his tonsils, like his baby teeth. Now that the possibility of recovering it presented itself, he couldn't get it out of his head.

"Otis says the Hierarch's taking the sword out of storage. And if the Hierarch's wielding the sword, then he's wielding me."

Cassandra's enthusiasm resolved into something more serious.

"We'll do the job, then," she said.

Daniel didn't respond, but he was already imagining the underground world depicted in Otis's drawings. He saw himself slipping through dark places where he wasn't allowed to go, and his heart beat with longing.

That night Daniel was awoken by a wraith. He jolted up in his sofa bed and took a moment to remember where he was—a bare studio apartment in Mar Vista. He seldom stayed anywhere longer than a few months, and he'd only had this place a week. He owned a cast-iron skillet, an enameled Dutch oven, copper pots and pans, and a beautiful set of Japanese knives, a gift from Cassandra for his eighteenth birthday. The same skills that made him a good osteomancer made him a good cook, and when he thought of a life away from Los

Angeles, he pictured himself in chef whites, in the kitchen of his own restaurant. But the cookware seldom made it out of the boxes.

The TV was an old twenty-two-inch set, left behind by a previous tenant, and between the rabbit ears was perched the apartment's only personal touch, an empty picture frame. Long ago, it had held a picture of him and his mother. But Otis urged him to get rid of it. It was too dangerous to keep a piece of evidence clearly linking him to his parents. So, at the age of fifteen, Daniel had torn it up and held it over a gas burner and watched the pieces blacken and curl. He remembered a sense of icy satisfaction as the flames overtook the smiling faces, as if they could obliterate the memory of a mother who'd fled to the north when her son was hunted, who'd never come back for him, who'd never even sent word. Now, years later, Daniel understood it was more complicated than that. Now, when he looked at the empty frame, he tried to remember his mother's face without the flames. But the flames never really went away. They were more real than any memory the photo captured.

The knocking on his door was as light and persistent as the beating of a moth's wings. Daniel crept to the one window in the living room, overlooking a courtyard of jacaranda petals, and beyond that, the black ribbon of Slauson Canal. He spotted no cop boats, heard no helicopters in the sodium-orange sky. He tugged his jeans up over his skinny hips and went to the door. A dreadful face looked back at him through the peephole, gray and smudged as a kneaded gum eraser.

He opened his door.

The wraith was a boy of ten or eleven, with underfed arms

sticking out from a billowing men's undershirt. His hair was a colorless tangle, his sockless feet swimming in battered sneakers. His birdlike eyes darted in deep hollows.

"Pier Four, Broadway Canal, Chinatown," said the boy, the night air turning his arms to goose skin. He passed on a few instructions, then turned and walked back down the cement steps to the courtyard.

Daniel fumbled for a moment, thinking he should give him something to eat or a jacket or a pair of socks, but he knew the boy wouldn't eat anything offered, and any clothes would be quickly shed and abandoned. He was a wraith and would only accept what his keeper gave him. He could go only where his keeper told him to, and could say nothing except what his keeper told him to say. And if he were followed, he would drown himself in a canal before bringing unwelcome visitors home. That's what made wraiths useful messengers, and that's why Otis kept them.

Daniel locked his door and turned on the TV and watched infomercials until the sun came up. Today, he'd be meeting Otis's inside man.

He cut a path through the scents of ginger and deep-fry grease and spotted a tall white woman leaning against a concrete fu dog. Late forties, her chestnut hair streaked with silver, she struck a smart figure in a camel-hair coat and a red scarf. Daniel stopped in front of her and stared openly until she looked up. She held an unlit cigarillo tucked between two slender fingers. He smelled tobacco and vanilla.

"Got a light?" she asked. Her accent reminded Daniel of the

posh BBC programs his mom would sometimes pull down on the shortwave radio at night.

"I don't smoke," said Daniel.

Her eyes crinkled with amusement. "That wasn't the signal."

"I know. I'm not much into cloak and dagger."

"Spoil my fun, then." The cigarillo went into her pocket. "Let's get some tea."

She had a favorite place a few blocks away, and they sat at a banquette of pink vinyl repaired with duct tape. Daniel was dubious until he tasted the Oolong. It was a rare delicacy in Los Angeles these days, and Daniel was glad she was paying.

"What do I call you?" she asked.

"Today? Daniel Torres. And you?"

"I'm Emmaline Walker. I go by Emma. That's my real name, and you're welcome to keep using it for as long as we're acquainted."

Daniel clinked his cup into Emma's a little harder than cordiality required.

"You live around here, Emma?"

"I do."

"A woman in your occupation, you could live anywhere. I'd think you'd have a nice beach house, or a place in the Golden City. Beverly Hills, Bel Air . . ." Otis said his inside man—woman, it turned out—worked for the Hierarch in the Ossuary, which meant she was by definition a person of high rank and privilege.

"I have a few residences. But I do like Chinatown. Nostalgia, mostly. Chinatown used to be the heart of osteomancy in Los Angeles. In fact, the only licensed apothecaries are still here. Also, the best restaurants. And the tea, of course."

"How do you know Otis?"

"My memories of Otis go back from . . . well. From before. Good days, I recall. It was like a big social club back then. Pool parties, dinners out, nightclubs, a lot of fun. Until the night things went ugly. But you know all about that."

There was nothing flippant or mocking in Emma's demeanor.

"I respected your father," she added.

"Emma, right now there's only one thing I want from you: I need you to answer a question. And I actually need an honest answer before I agree to work with you."

"I treasure honesty, Mr. . . . Torres. Ask away."

"You already have position and money. Why risk that? What's in this for you?"

The obvious answer was even more money, and Daniel was prepared to accept it.

Emma poured more tea for herself and Daniel. "Do you read any of the older Chinese script styles? It was a required subject when there was still a school for osteomancy in Los Angeles. The most important texts were written in Chinese, and many of them haven't been translated. Much has been lost." She sipped tea. "In any case, 'Oolong' is a word from the Min Nan. It means 'the black dragon.' The black dragon is not only a potent creature—"

"An extinct creature."

Emma paused, neither agreeing nor arguing. "—but also a creature with cultural associations to kings. Specifically, kings who dwell in the depths of mysticism."

"I'm not following."

"Very rare these days, Oolong. But down in the catacombs,

beneath Ministry headquarters, where I work? Why, I've seen bales and bales of it, hoarded away, drying out, unused. I have seen things down there. I've seen what the Hierarch keeps."

"You want to rob the H-Bomb . . . because he's got too much tea."

"Southern California is a lie, Daniel. And Los Angeles is the heart of that lie. People came here for land and for weather. They came to build their little garden cities, and to pick oranges as bright as miniature suns. They came for oil and opportunity. And many of them came for magic. That's what they were promised, and that's why they came from the east, because this was billed as a newer land, and a richer land, and a more bountiful land. And there should have been magic enough. It came from the ground, and up from Mexico, and from across the Pacific, and Los Angeles should have been the paradise they painted on the orange crate labels. But for the Hierarch, it would be."

"So, you're not happy with your cut?"

She pressed her pale lips together in a tight smile. "It's funny you should use that word, 'cut.' In the Hierarch's realm, we're all human resources, from the highest osteomancer, to the average citizen, to the wraith-slave. It shouldn't require too much imagination to see why someone might have a problem with that." She set down her cup and dabbed her mouth with her napkin. "It's been a real pleasure to meet you," she said, standing. "I hope you've used our brief time together wisely, and I look forward to seeing you again soon."

She gave him a jaunty little salute and was out the door.

Daniel lingered over his last sip of Oolong, which was too good to waste. He dropped Emma's teacup into a plastic freezer bag, and the bag went under his jacket. In a moment he was back out on the pier, and then behind the wheel of a Ventura two-seater from Otis's boat fleet.

Without breaking laws, he passed several slow-moving boats and made it just past a traffic buoy before it turned red.

He got the walkie-talkie out of the glove compartment and keyed it. "Hey, Cass, you still got our guy?"

"Affirmative, yessiree," came Cassandra's fuzzy voice. "She's in nice boat, a totally sweet cherry Kuai, and driving like someone used to getting out of traffic tickets. She just passed Spring and Ord."

"Keep up with her, but don't tip her with your driving."

"Dude, I'm in a pizza delivery boat. I could ram a pontoon bridge and nobody'd even blink."

"Do not ram a pontoon bridge," he said.

He tightened his seat belt, took a deep breath, slalomed around a bus and a cargo tug, and accelerated down open water to catch up to Cassandra.

Daniel keyed his handset. "I'll take up the tail for a few blocks, then you take it back."

"Roger, over, delta-foxtrot, breaker-breaker."

Sometimes, Cassandra was a clown. He would not tell her that to her face.

Emma's route took her past payday loaners and pawnshops and boarded-up businesses west of Chinatown, then through the trendy clubs and galleries of Silver Lake, eventually coming down Third Canal, and west to Hancock Park. Through binoculars, Daniel watched Emma glide up to the guard gate and have a brief and seemingly cordial exchange with security. The iron gates opened for her, and Emma was in the Golden City, where Daniel could not follow.

"Okay, pull over," he said through the walkie.

At a parking dock a few blocks away, Daniel joined Cassandra in her van. He produced the freezer bag containing the teacup.

"This is Emma's," he said. "I slipped her some lamassu when we clinked cups."

"What's a lamassu?"

"Avian-mammal from the Middle East. I think Otis brings it in through some Panamanian contacts. Anyway, it's got useful psionic qualities. If Emma left essence, I might be able to pull something out of her head."

"Essence?" Cassandra said. "You mean . . . ?"

"I mean spit."

Cassandra made a face, but he could tell she was impressed, and he liked the feeling.

"Your dad taught you lamassu osteomancy?"

"Well, no."

"One of Otis's tutors?"

"Not exactly."

"By which you mean not at all, you've never used lamassu, you're about to mine into a stranger's thoughts, and you have no idea what you're doing."

"If I die, please sprinkle my ashes at Tito's Tacos," he said.

Cassandra gave him a hard look. "Not funny."

He licked the inside of the cup, stretching his tongue to get all the way to the bottom. An experienced osteomancer might be able to pick up a strong impression of his quarry's emotional state from this, maybe some image flashes of important places or objects or people, maybe even some distinct thoughts. Daniel entertained no such expectations. A general impression of honesty or deceit would be enough.

He didn't taste much in the cup other than bitter tea dregs and the slightly metallic flavor of cheap porcelain.

Then he fell.

Right through the floorboards of the van, into the canal water, through the algae and mud of the canal bottom and through clay and stone and magma and fire, all the way through the earth.

He awoke with his cheek in wet beach sand, body chilled and clothes stiff with salt. He lifted his head with a groan, remembering everything. He remembered the bare bone of his father's cheek, and the scrape of knives as the Hierarch's men stripped away flesh and fat and muscle from his father's cheekbones. He felt as if they'd spooned out his own insides. He didn't know where his heart was.

He considered dropping his head back in the sand and letting the tide drown him, but his father had sacrificed his life to give Daniel time to escape, and he would be angry if all his efforts were wasted.

Daniel stood, brushed the sand off, and turned his back on the sea.

There was a safe house, Daniel remembered. His father had told him to go there, one of the last things he'd ever said. His mom would be there, waiting. He reached for sint holo invisibility, but he couldn't sense a whiff of it. He didn't even remember what it smelled like. So, exposed, he hid from sirens and searchlights. He hid from the drum of boots on pavement. In Mar Vista, he cowered in an alley behind a trash bin as flashlight beams probed the shadows.

At last he found his way to the yellow house with aluminum siding in Venice. He climbed front steps of sloppily troweled concrete, rising from a patch of dead grass. The door opened for him. His mother threw a protective arm around him, and she swept him inside.

On the beach, Daniel had felt hollowed out, like a husk of skin. Now, with his mother's solid presence, he felt real. His father was the magician in the family, but his mother was always the strength.

And yet, she was a secret. She taught Daniel how to fight with his fists. She taught him how to fire a gun. She taught him how to spot a plainclothes cop, and how to know he was being followed, and how to forge a signature. Daniel didn't know why she knew these things.

She held his face in her hands and stared into his eyes. Somehow Daniel felt there was only one possible thing to say to her now: "It's me. I'm Daniel. I'm your son."

"Were you followed?" Her voice carried a brittle edge, as though it might crack apart into a million shards and cut him bloody. Daniel had never seen his mother frightened of anything. It was always the opposite. When his parents were still together, at dinners and backyard parties, his father's colleagues from the Ministry always treated her with careful deference. She was not an osteomancer, she held no position at the Ministry. Officially, Messalina Sigilo Blackland was a wife and a mother. But people seemed to know she was other things as well. She was a mystery, a foreigner who'd emigrated from Northern California during a very brief truce between the two California kingdoms. If people didn't know quite what to make of her, they were at least certain that she was a quietly concealed threat, like a sheathed knife. But wielded by whom?

"I wasn't followed."

She checked him over to see if he was hurt.

"They killed Dad."

"I know, Daniel."

"Are they coming for us?"

He so desperately wanted her to say no, even if it was a lie. But she'd never lied to him. She'd never even softened a truth.

"It's a purge," she said. "The Hierarch is killing anyone he thinks is disloyal, or a threat of any kind. He's arresting the families, too."

He remembered the glint of the Hierarch's fork. He would pick Daniel apart if he found him. The Hierarch would dissect him, and he'd feel the Hierarch's teeth sinking into his muscles.

"They won't find you. I won't let them. Do you trust me?" Her voice sounded empty of emotion, as it did whenever she hurt most.

"I trust you," he said.

A noise came from the front door, and suddenly there were two guns in his mother's hands leveled at Otis's face. He stood in the doorway, still as a wax figure.

"Easy, Messalina, it's me."

"Were you followed?"

"No."

"Are you sure?"

"Of course I'm sure—"

"Are you *sure*?"

"I wasn't followed, Messalina. I was careful. Let me in."

Only then did she lower the guns. Otis came inside, shutting and bolting the door behind him. He was not alone. He had a kid with him. Or a thing.

The thing looked almost exactly like Daniel. Its hair was a little longer. It was dressed in one of his shirts. It was wearing his other pair of sneakers. It made dull eye contact with Daniel, then looked at a table lamp with the exact same degree of interest and comprehension.

"What's this?" Daniel said when he found his voice again.

"It's nobody," Otis said quickly.

"This is something I have to do," his mother said. "To protect you. You can't understand now, but later—"

"I can't understand what you won't tell me," Daniel said.

His mother held his shoulders. She scanned his face, as if trying to memorize it. She was crying now, something Daniel had never seen before, and it horrified him.

"You're my son, and I love you, and I will always love you. Never believe anything else."

Otis put a hand on him, and too late Daniel realized it wasn't for comfort, but to restrain him as his mother and the vacant thing that looked like him, that wore his clothes, that held his mother's hand, headed out the door.

That was the last time he saw his mother. Later, Otis told him she went north, over the Tehachapi mountains and into the Central Valley, trying to get to the border of the Northern Kingdom. She was supposed to bribe the border guards and make contact with friends in San Francisco, the city of her birth. But the bribe must not have been good enough, because the guards killed her. Then Otis told Daniel he'd take care of him, that things would be okay, that he knew he couldn't replace Daniel's parents, but he could be his friend.

Daniel rocketed upward, through the strata of earth, through the scum at the bottom of the canal, and he gasped for air, coming back into himself in the boat, next to Cassandra.

"So? Getting anything?" she said. She hadn't changed position. Her facial expression hadn't changed. No time had passed.

Daniel's belly felt scooped out. Emma's teacup contained

everything: the emotions of those early bad days, with the crunch of cartilage and watching his mother get into the boat without him and his dull twin looking back at him and listening to Otis telling Daniel he was alone.

"I think I may have just gotten a little too much."

Gabriel Argent rode the private cable trolley from the foot of Mount Hollywood to the flattened hilltop and arrived at Griffith Observatory. The house's size was deceptive, for much of it was hidden underground, but even the aboveground parts impressed the visitor. Built of white stone with three symmetrically placed domes of patinated green copper, the building was a masterwork of Art Deco elegance.

Standing outside the house on the railed mountain ledge, Gabriel could see almost all of Los Angeles, from the lit downtown towers to the twinkling pinpoint lights of the harbor, and all the gridded golden sparkle of the canal system between. This was not the entirety of the Hierarch's realm, but it was its heart. The house belonged to the leader of Los Angeles and Southern California, possibly the most powerful magician in the Californias, and certainly one of the most powerful in the world. He used it for parties.

Gabriel, the Hierarch's grandnephew, was feeling neither awed nor powerful as he circulated through the evening garden-party crowd. It was a glamorous affair, the city's elite gathered to celebrate the eightieth anniversary of Southern California's independence from the United States of America. The clothes were expensive and the crudités traveled on silver trays.

Gabriel suffered a few exchanges of riskless conversation, but mostly he tried to keep to himself. Nobody was willing to say anything that could be interpreted or misinterpreted as seditious or disrespectful here. Which was fine with Gabriel, except people insisted on making strained conversation anyway. He watched his various cousins doing the rounds, speaking to the right people, saying the right things in hopes of making an impression that would earn them a place more central to the regime's inner circle. There was his cousin Connie, wrapped like a deli sandwich in a peach designer dress, trying to hold the attention of General Ramirez. She was wasting her time. The Hierarch didn't trust his relatives and few of them ever rose high. But that wouldn't stop her from nattering about some actress caught stumbling from the Viper Room with her panties around her ankles. All the trust-fund kids, actors, aristocrats, glittery things, and cousins here tonight made Gabriel miss his desk at the Ministry Office of Accountability.

Why can't we few hundred guests enjoy some good, companionable silence? he thought, pursuing a servant and his tray of tasty little cheese puffs.

"Gabey!"

A rush of red silk and oleander perfume took him in a surprise embrace. He tensed at first, then relaxed and returned the hug.

"Apple," he said, with real pleasure.

Abigail "Apple" Sandoval, née Argent, was one of the rare cousins Gabriel liked. As kids they used to hide at family gatherings under the inevitable grand piano and stick gum to its underside.

"Oh, god, Apple, are you wearing a tiara?"

Indeed, she was wearing a circlet of silver encrusted with fossilized smilodon chips. Gabriel did a quick mental calculation and estimated its worth as roughly that of his condo.

"Why not?" she said with mock haughtiness. "I am, after all, a baroness now."

She'd married Orlando Sandoval earlier in the year. He was an old man with no magic, but he kept the Mojave territories secure, and the Hierarch rewarded him richly for it.

"It suits you," Gabriel said. "Palm Springs treating you well?"

She shrugged. "Well enough. Tennis keeps me in shape, and I'm catching up on my reading. Speaking of boredom, where's your date?"

Apple seldom approved of his girlfriends, who were always careful, studious young women whom she deemed joyless.

"I came stag. I'm just here to be polite. Then, home, paperwork, maybe a glass of milk."

"Joyless," said Apple. "But I have exciting gossip. Want to hear?"

"Is it juicy? What am I saying, of course it's juicy."

Her mouth quirked in a mischievous smile. "He's going to make an appearance," she whispered. It took Gabriel a second to realize who "he" was.

"Seriously? When?"

And now Apple's smile became devilish. "Here. Tonight."

He looked around the grounds, with the Chinese lanterns like fairy orbs, the elegant waiters and their trays, the fluttery sparkle of Los Angeles aristocracy . . . none of it made sense.

The Hierarch hadn't been seen by anyone outside his inner-most circle in six years. There were rumors—always expressed in terms of love and concern for the realm's dear leader—of illness, of feebleness, of his more than nine decades as ruler finally catching up to him. And Gabriel believed them. He knew very well how magic was being acquired and spent. He saw the meager resources, both magical and otherwise, going into the basic upkeep of the city. It was the little things. Public bakeries going dark because nobody was maintaining the wind farms. Schools switching to a recitation curriculum because paper shortages meant they couldn't afford books. Hospitals losing patients because their pharmacies couldn't get magical stock. Sometimes it seemed like nobody was running the kingdom.

Apple's face flashed with alarm, looking over Gabriel's shoulder.

"A word with you, Mr. Argent."

Gabriel turned to find himself staring down into the face of a shrunken little man swimming inside a gray business suit. Disney's blue eyes retained some of their merry shine, but everything else about him was ancient. His gnarled brown hand almost blended into the knotty wooden knob of his walking stick.

"Come with me," said Disney.

Gabriel looked to Apple, but she was already a retreating figure in a shiny red dress. His beloved cousin had abandoned him. So much for pianos and chewing gum.

Gabriel followed Disney into the house, past the giant Foucault pendulum knocking over pegs in the foyer, and down a corridor guarded by guys in immaculate black suits who admitted them into a book-lined parlor. A guard shut the door and left the two men alone.

"It's cold in here," Disney said, sinking into a plush red chair. "I suppose your uncle doesn't get to this part of his house much."

"I'll build a fire." But Disney motioned him to take a seat. Gabriel settled into a chair much harder than Disney's and withstood the old man's baleful glare. He stifled the urge to fidget.

The glamour mage was one of the Hierarch's most successful projects. Starting in the 1920s, Disney's "Imaginancers" began developing a potent distillation of osteomantic intoxicant, and once they started misting it into movie theaters, they acquired an audience of happily addicted consumers who kept coming back for more. The Hierarch had been sufficiently impressed with Disney to grant him resources suitable to his ambitions, including an entire theme park built over an expanse of orange groves, where Disney constructed gussied-up roller coasters and whimsical dark rides and a replica of Mad King Ludwig's castle and pirate-ship tableaus and a haunted house to gently satisfy macabre urges, all in an ingeniously engineered miasma of osteomancy that kept visitors feeling like they'd come to the happiest place on earth.

But the magic was going dry, and Gabriel guessed that was the subject of this meeting.

"It's his damn war," the glamour mage blurted without preamble. "He can't take his eyes off San Francisco long enough to see that without people like me, he'll have a war right here in his own city."

Gabriel weighed how to respond to this openly seditious statement, made within the walls of the Hierarch's own house. Of course he would not in any way voice agreement with Disney, but neither did he want to provoke the old mage's ire. It was said the Mouse had its own enemies list.

"I'm certain he has nothing but the utmost respect for the contributions of your art, sir."

Disney made a sour face. "Art? I never called it an art. Entertainment is a business, and it's one of the most important businesses a man can devote his life to. I have lived a very, very long life, Mr. Argent. I was around when the Ministry was just a squabbling cabal of cutthroats, and the citizens of this kingdom were no better. Southern California was not a happy place back then. I helped make it a happy place for business. And now the Hierarch is taking a grand crap on my happiness."

"Maybe we should lower our voices, sir."

But Disney gnat-waved Gabriel's caution away. "We're down to two hundred pounds of eocorn. One hundred forty pounds of parandrus. I haven't seen an ounce of sint holo in years. My theaters and park serve a critical function, and if I don't have enough bone to run my operations, everyone will discover just how critical."

"Sir—"

"Yes, I'm talking about unrest. Protests. Riots. That's what happens when people aren't happy. The idiots will burn their own neighborhoods. You get the reports, the ones that don't end up in the *Times*. You know the insurgents are making gains. This kind of thing catches and it'll be a conflagration. You have to soothe them, don't you know. Rock them like babies. Any idea how much magic that takes in a kingdom the size of Southern California? I could show you spreadsheets."

"I'm sure if you spoke to the Hierarch . . . You're old friends. I'm sure he'll listen . . ."

The glamour mage's trim mustache twitched in irritation. "Oh, he's far too busy for me. I can't get into his chambers.

I'm not one of the Six. You must convince him for me. You must convince him to grant me audience."

Gabriel almost laughed. "I'm flattered you think I have that kind of influence."

"Mr. Argent, I despise insincerity. You are the Hierarch's nephew."

"Grandnephew. The Hierarch has a lot of grandnephews. He's sired a pretty large brood." Gabriel wondered if Disney was putting each and every one of his cousins through a meeting like this. Maybe Apple was next on the list.

"The Hierarch was fond of your mother," Disney said, as if that were the capstone to some well-constructed argument.

Being related to the Hierarch just meant you were a little closer to his dinner table.

Gabriel did his best to murmur and nod politely at the right times as Disney subjected him to another half hour of complaints.

In truth, Disney's grievances and warnings were legitimate. Southern California's easily accessible natural supply, the resources the Hierarch used to establish his rule, had been mined decades ago. The stuff remaining was scant and difficult to obtain. There were still imports from Mexico and Central and South America and the Far East, but those had slowed in the last several years. Gabriel wasn't privy to the reason why, but he understood how fragile those trade relationships were. From his knowledge of smuggling operations in the north, he knew San Francisco must have some osteomancy left— historically, the north's supply came from the Siberian steppes, where entire mammoths and griffins could be found preserved in the permafrost—but nothing could change the simple fact that there wasn't enough bone to go around.

Disney rose from his chair. He leaned on his walking stick, gripping it with both hands and driving it into the Hierarch's carpet. "I hope you've been listening, Mr. Argent. And not just to my petition. Ask around. Talk to Mulholland. Talk to Weinstein. Go see Baron Doheny. Go see Baron Chandler. The powers that run this kingdom have huddled in the Hierarch's shadow for a long time, but they won't do so forever."

Gabriel could not let a declaration like that stand unanswered.

"The Hierarch runs the kingdom, sir."

The mage smiled, revealing a ghost of the comforting presence he still managed to project when he hosted his TV programs.

"Even the most powerful engine needs fuel," he said. "And this time, the osteomancers won't sit idle while the Hierarch grinds our bones for it."

Gabriel stayed behind once the mage had left the room, giving Disney time to get some distance. Then he rubbed his temples and rejoined the party. A fog had come in off the sea, a ghostly electric haze lit orange-yellow by thousands of canal lights.

Apple and her red dress came out of the mist in a rush to besiege Gabriel. She clutched his arms and leaned in conspiratorially. Gabriel assumed she wanted the skinny on his meeting with Disney.

"I don't want to talk about it," he said, but she shook her head.

"You almost missed it. He's about to show."

She towed him around to the front of the observatory, where a great clot of party guests stood, gazing up at a balcony. The music had stopped, and all conversation fell to whispers. The moan of a barge horn came from somewhere down the mountain, but all other sound from the outside world was swallowed in the thick, wet air. French windows behind the balcony opened, and there was a collective gasp as Fenmont Szu stepped around a silk screen and stood at the balustrade. Tall and thin in a blood-red suit so luxurious it made Apple's dress look like a valentine card, he directed a withering smile at the gathering. Five others came around the screen to join him. The Alejandro. Mother Cauldron. Madeleine Sing. Sister Tooth. Mr. Butch. These were the Council of Six, the Hierarch's adjudicators, enforcers, ministers of fear and discipline. Powerful osteomancers, all. Seeing them together at a celebratory gathering such as this, attended by a crowd whose competence lay in spreading gossip, sent a clear signal: The people of Los Angeles had been acting as though they'd forgotten what fear was. It was time to remember.

Fenmont Szu said some words in praise of the Hierarch's long-ago victory of independence, and then he announced the Hierarch. The silk screen at Szu's back flared with red light, as though a fire had been lit behind it. And then, like a Balinese shadow puppet, a silhouette appeared, an almost skeletal figure. Servants removed the screen, and there stood a thing. It was hard to make out, exactly. Maybe it was the red light. Maybe it was the fog. Maybe it was because the Hierarch's magic distorted perception. Even if he was sick and ancient, even if he was no longer human, even if he was mostly constructed of dead things, the Hierarch was still terrifying.

He raised one arm in salute, the light died, and he was gone, and the Six returned inside the house.

The partygoers clapped dutifully and returned to conversation and crudités in a nervous chill.

"Well, that was anticlimatic," said Apple, snatching a drink off a passing tray.

"That wasn't a climax," Gabriel said. "That was a beginning."

This time when Daniel went to see Otis, nobody put a hand on him. The muscle-slabs who'd bagged him at Farmers Market cut off their conversation about last night's Angels-Padres game and tried to find something to do with their bandaged hands.

"No hard feelings, guys," Daniel said. And he meant it. He didn't regret kraken-burning them, but they'd only been following Otis's instructions.

They nodded as though they understood.

Daniel found Otis at his desk, working numbers with an abacus.

"How'd your meeting with Emma Walker go?" Otis said, not looking up.

"Why does she know about my mother?"

Otis took off his glasses, deliberately folded the temples, and set them on his desk. "What are you talking about?"

"I slipped her lamassu and ate her memories. They were of me. Of when my mom went North with the thing that looked like me. Who is she, and what's she got to do with me?"

Otis clucked his tongue. "You used lamassu. That's tricky

stuff. You probably tried to drink up her memories but ended up regurgitating some of your own. Brain magic is complex, Daniel. Memories get mixed up. Maybe you somehow picked up some of your mom's."

"All of a sudden you're an expert in osteomancy."

"I've been around it all my adult life," Otis said, jollier than ever. "I've dealt it by the ton."

"Otis . . ."

"Listen. Truth. This is what I know about Emmaline Walker. Born in London, came to California by way of Hong Kong, very quickly put her talents to use at the Ministry. For the last twenty years, she's worked in the catacombs on special projects. She came to me eight months ago and asked me how to get into the Ossuary's primary vaults. She provided intel, and drawings, and she has an intimate knowledge of the layout and protocols of the catacombs, and if you're going to infiltrate the Ossuary, she's the one who can get you in there."

"You trust her?"

"Trust?" He rocked his hand in a fifty-fifty gesture. "I know she's useful."

That meant something to Daniel. He knew Otis didn't invest in jobs he couldn't profit from. Nor in people.

"What's her score?"

"From the Ossuary? She won't say. And I worked her really hard on that. It's not treasure. It's something more personal. The good news is that she doesn't want a cut of the basilisk fangs, so more profit for us."

"I don't like it."

"Look, it's not the fangs, it's not the sword. There's no job without her, so I'm giving her just that much privacy." Otis moved a bead on his abacus. "My advice, Daniel? Use Emma.

But don't trust her. Build your crew around that idea. Take Cassandra. You know she'll have your back. And take whoever else you want. Your father gave you osteomancy, and I gave you thiefcraft. But those aren't your most powerful weapons."

"And what are those?"

Otis didn't hesitate to answer. "Your friends. Whoever has the skills, whoever *you* trust. Get Jo. Get Moth."

"You don't like Jo and Moth."

"I don't have to like them. It's your call. And you know why?"

Daniel waited.

"It's because I trust you, Daniel."

"Oh, shove it, Otis."

Otis put his glasses back on and returned to his abacus, and Daniel made for the door.

"The thing," he said, before leaving. "The boy. The one my mother took North. You really don't know what it was?"

"What did I tell you, Daniel?"

"You told me it got shot along with my mom when she was trying to cross."

"And it looked like you, right?"

"Yeah."

"And it made the Hierarch think you were dead, right?"

Daniel didn't say anything.

"Then it doesn't matter what it was," Otis said. "It worked just as your mom and dad intended."

SEVEN

Daniel asked around for the whereabouts of his friend Josephine, and the answer led him to Douglas Fairbanks Jr. Or, more precisely, to Douglas Fairbanks Jr.'s brass star in front of a yogurt shop on Hollywood Boulevard.

Daniel edged near a group of pedestrians clustered around a man barking a sales pitch. Under a fedora that looked like it had been well chewed by a bullmastiff, his sun-speckled face showed evidence of many naps on park benches.

"I can see you're pooped by the way you droop and stoop! By the lack of pep in your every step! Well, what if I told you this: an opportunity you just can't miss? A simple stone, a piece of bone, that you could have for your very own, that will give you something greater than wealth? A Peruvian carbuncle, to restore your health!"

After suffering the pitch man's rhyme, Daniel wanted a carbuncle to restore his sanity.

Peruvian carbuncles were toadlike creatures whose heads grew deep red gemstones. The skull stones possessed osteomantic healing properties, and amulets made out of them were the thing among the Golden City crowd.

Beside the pitch man, on a square of black velvet draped over a folding TV tray, was a copper bracelet set with some small red stones. He held it aloft and crowed, "Who wants to feel better right now?"

A couple of hands went up. The salesman picked a drab-looking woman out of the crowd. Her sweater was the color of grass in need of fertilizer.

"You, miss! Forgive me for saying, but you look like you could use a little magic."

The woman was jowly and turkey-necked, with bags under her eyes. When the pitch man stepped forward to take her arm, she made a show of demurring, but she relented without too much struggle.

"Now, I'm too much of a gentleman to ask your age, miss—"

"I'm thirty-seven," she said, with a self-conscious giggle. Actually, Daniel knew she was only twenty-two.

The hawker patted her arm. "And what do you do for a living?"

"Well, I'm unemployed right now, but I'm a nurse."

"Always sacrificing your back and your arches and your sleep to take care of others. Well, maybe it's time to take care of yourself. What do you say?"

I bet she'll say "yes," thought Daniel.

"Oh, I don't know. I suppose . . . Okay."

In a manner that was equal parts doctor and suitor, the pitch man took her slender wrist and clasped the skull-stone bracelet around it.

"From the high mountain peaks to the lush rain forests of

Peru, the indigenous men and women of that pure country keep magic close to the skin."

While he barked, the woman's posture subtly changed. Her shoulders straightened. Her paunch vanished.

"They bask in the radiance of native osteomancy, to heal their ailments, to thrive with the vitality of the ancients." He rested a hand on her shoulder. "How do you feel, miss?"

"My skin is tingling." She ran her hands over her neck and kneaded her cheeks and rubbed her eyes. "It's wonderful."

"Now, some of your skull-stones, I am very sad to say, are little more than paint and epoxy. Don't be fooled, people. Don't part with your hard-earned wages and give your hope to charlatans and thieves. Demand evidence! Demand proof! And that's what I'm giving you right now. What do you say, miss? Are you a believer?"

Gently, he took her hands away from her face. The bags beneath her eyes were gone. The jowls were smooth, the flesh of her neck taut.

As the hawker began struggling to manage the fistfuls of cash people thrust at him, the woman made her way through the crowd, out onto open sidewalk.

Daniel followed.

"So, you're a thirty-seven-year-old woman now?" he said, drawing up even with her.

"I've been a woman before."

"Well, okay, but last time I saw you, you were a sixty-year-old dude, so . . ."

"You know me. Whatever the job requires." A police cruiser puttered down the canal, and Daniel turned his face away. But Jo Alverado didn't have to worry about being recognized. She could always change her face again.

"You call this a job?" Daniel said, once the cruiser turned onto Vine. "Why are you hanging around a low-rent grifter like that anyway?"

"You don't have to insult Fargo."

"Mr. It-Slices-It-Dices? Nothing against him, but with your talent, you should be doing jewelry stores and banks. Hell, you could be stealing real skull-stones."

"How do you know they're not real skull-stones?" she said, stepping around Shirley Temple's star.

Daniel tapped his nose and sniffed conspicuously. "Look, I didn't come here to question your life choices. I have a job."

"Oh?" She looked up at him, curious. She'd given herself a very cute nose and a sensuous mouth, and Daniel reminded himself that the last time he'd seen her, she was a dead ringer for W. C. Fields. "Lucrative?"

"Remember the warehouse in Rosemead?"

"With all the griffin claw?"

"That's the one. This job is worth, oh, sixty times that."

She stopped dead on Alan Ladd.

"It's not an Otis job, is it?" she said.

"What if it is?"

"I don't work for Otis anymore. I'm not one of his."

Daniel smiled his most confident, convincing smile. It was the one she'd taught him. "And that, Jo, is exactly why I need you on my crew."

Tommy's, Big Tommy's, Original Tommy's, Tom's Number 5, Tomy's, Big Tomy's. And there were more, spread all over Los Angeles and beyond, from Simi Valley to the San Gabriel

Valley, all the way down to San Diego. The burger joints
shared two things in common: the oddly compelling generic
meat flavor of the chili, and the ubiquitous presence of his
friend Moth, whose lifelong meal plan consisted of a circu-
itous pilgrimage to every one of the Tommy's variants.

Daniel caught up to him near closing time at the Big Tomy's
in West LA, at Pico and Sawtelle. Moth was just about to tuck
into what was probably his third or fourth or seventh chili
burger of the day when he saw Daniel approach and rose to
engulf him.

"Man, I've missed you," Moth purred, like the lowest note
on a cello. "But you gotta fuck off."

"Well, aren't you Mr. Hot and Cold. What's up?"

"I'm meeting people in ten minutes. Working a deal."

"Here? What happened to not shitting where you eat?"

"Not *here,* here," Moth said. "But close enough I don't want
you around."

It was then that Daniel noticed the plastic lunch cooler on
the cracked tile floor.

"What's in the box?"

"Ah, you don't want to know." Moth wouldn't meet his
eyes.

"Moth? What's in the box?"

Moth blew out a puff of air. He looked around to make
sure nobody was eavesdropping. "Okay, fine, it's a kidney. I'm
selling a kidney. Are you happy?"

"Please tell me it's not your kidney?"

"Well, fuck, who else's kidney would I be selling?"

Daniel buried his face in his hands.

He'd first met Moth on an asphalt basketball court at Venice High, a school neither of them attended. They'd been on

opposite teams for a pickup game, and Moth had used his superior size to foul Daniel on every possession, whether or not Daniel was driving with the ball or stopping to tie his shoe. When Daniel finally had enough, he charged Moth with fists windmilling in a suicide bid for vengeance. Moth easily absorbed Daniel's blows and sent him sprawling on his ass. But he was impressed by Daniel's recklessness and declared that he was switching teams to Daniel's side. He'd been on Daniel's side ever since. They'd had a lot of good times, Daniel and Cassandra and Moth and Jo and Punch, graduating from junior-varsity store break-ins and home burglaries to warehouses and secure storage facilities and jobs that could properly be called heists.

But at the end of those years, things were different. Daniel and Cassandra were no longer a couple, Jo was out of the business, Moth was changed on a cellular level, and Punch was dead.

"Moth, I shouldn't have to keep saying this: It's just not healthy to be selling your own kidneys."

Moth sat back down and took a massive bite out of his chili burger. "I know, but my 'Hey, there's a finger in my soup' scam is played out. And a man's gotta earn a living."

"Not this way. I have a job for us."

Moth chewed. "What is it?"

"Let's get out of here, and we can talk about it."

Moth made a paper napkin translucent by wiping orange grease off his lips. "First I finish my deal, and then we can talk about it."

"Who're you selling to, anyway?"

He hunkered down, as if by doing so he could make his broad, six-foot-six frame less noticeable. "Sawtelle Boys."

"Are you fucking crazy?" Daniel whispered. "Because the Sawtelle Boys are."

"Aw, they're not so bad, once you get to know them."

"I am never going to get to know them." The Sawtelles were leeches. They acquired bones and organs and corpses of magic users and leeched whatever osteomantic residues they could recover for resale. Daniel really, really didn't like these guys. "Moth, listen. The job. It's the Ossuary. It'll pay way better than whatever the Sawtelles are paying for your kidney. Let's just go. I'll take you to Original Tommy's, I'll lay out the details, we'll—"

Moth jiggled the ice in his soft drink cup and slurped on his straw. "I'm receptive. But I have to finish this little deal first. Because I said I would. So, how about I meet you at Original Tommy's in an hour, and you can give me the whole pitch. I gotta go now."

Daniel wanted to scream.

"Fine," he spat. "Fine. Sell your stupid kidney if you have to, but I'm coming with you."

They had a good, long stare-down. Moth's stare was definitely more frightening than Daniel's, but Daniel wasn't going to let Moth deal with the Sawtelle Boys without backup. In the end, Moth said nothing. He picked up his cooler and headed out the door, and Daniel followed.

They walked several blocks beneath the 405 flumeway without talking, the sounds of rushing water and boat engines mixing into a white-noise roar over their heads.

The Sawtelles had sent five guys. They slouched around a support column in their red bandanas and voluminous khakis. Dirt crunched beneath Moth's and Daniel's shoes as they approached.

"Who's the gristle?" one of them said, tilting his chin at Daniel. He was short and pudgy, and his sleeveless T-shirt revealed little muscle. Nothing about him suggested leadership qualities. But since he'd spoken first, Daniel decided to watch him closest.

"Just a friend," Moth said, clearly annoyed at Daniel. "Is it a problem? 'Cause you got four other guys with you, so."

Short-Pudgy grinned jade teeth and laughed as if something funny had just occurred. "I don't care, everyone needs backup, and we're all carrying." There were a lot of hands in pockets. "You got the meat?"

Moth set his cooler on the ground and popped it open. Short-Pudgy took a couple of steps forward and leaned over. Sealed in a plastic sandwich bag and packed in ice was a bloody purplish shiny thing, shaped like a flattened potato.

"Okay," Short-Pudgy said.

Moth shut the cooler and began a sentence that was probably about the money when the guns came out and the shooting started.

The Sawtelles were such fuckers.

Daniel didn't see much, because Moth had thrown him to the dirt. He landed facedown, and when he rolled over onto his side, it was a storm of muzzle flash and gunshots. Daniel screamed as a spray of something struck his cheek, but it was only gravel from bullets striking the ground. Moth wasn't so lucky. Blooms of red appeared in his side and back as bullets tore through him, but the gunfire tapered off as he reached the shooters, and then the sounds became high-pitched screams and snapping bones. Moth laughed hideously, which meant he was hurt and in pain and also really angry, and by the time Daniel managed to reach for smell-memories and bring a fuzz of kraken electricity to his fingers, the five Sawtelle Boys were sprawled on the ground, cradling broken limbs. Short-Pudgy shrieked like a tropical bird and stared at the white, splintered bone emerging from his calf. The shrieking died in a gurgle of pain as Moth jostled him, searching his pockets for money.

"I don't think they have any." Daniel got back to his feet.

"I know, but I at least need to check," Moth said, somber.

"I could have told you it would play out like this."

"D, I'm shot. Like, a whole bunch of times. So let's not do I-told-you-so."

"Okay, I'm sorry. But can we go? In case of cops?"

The Sawtelle Boys, those who could still move, rolled in the dirt, groaning or weeping. Moth gave up on his cash and picked up his cooler with a bleeding hand.

"Total waste of a kidney," he said.

"You'll grow an even better one," Daniel soothed.

They turned and walked away and left the leeches behind.

"How're you feeling?"

"Enh," Moth said. "Hurts like a meanie, but I'm healing pretty good. New one should be ripe in a few hours."

"I meant the bullets."

Moth grinned like a maniac. "Little bullets," he said.

When they reached Daniel's boat, Daniel tossed Moth a towel from the trunk. "Still up for Original Tommy's?"

"Let's make it Tom's Number 5, and I'll hear you out about this job."

Daniel opened the passenger door and let Moth squeeze gingerly onto the seat.

"I've missed you, buddy," Daniel said.

"You, too," Moth said. He set the cooler containing his kidney on his lap and buckled in.

EIGHT

Daniel could tell Otis was serious about security by the number of guys standing watch around his warehouse, and by the armed guys outside the door to his office, and by the wraiths milling around, prepared to throw themselves in the line of fire in the unlikely event the Hierarch's cops showed up and Otis needed time to bail.

His office was outfitted with a folding picnic table, chairs, a chalkboard on a rolling stand, and a big bucket of fried livers from Pioneer Chicken. Moth and Jo were bonding over some bootlegged Broadway musical Jo had acquired, while Emma sat a few chairs away, observing them. Cassandra leaned against piled sacks of birdseed. She observed Emma.

Daniel took a seat.

"You've all met," Otis began, taking a position in front of the chalkboard. "But let's do formal introductions. Moth is our utility muscle. Josephine is our shifter. Cassandra is our yegg—"

Emma raised her hand. "Excuse me, I'm somewhat new to this. Yegg?"

"Can-opener, peterman, boxman, safecracker," Jo cheerily provided, "and all-around thief."

"How delightfully colorful," said Emma. "My apologies."

"Daniel is our osteomancer and field leader," Otis went on. "And Emma will be our guide."

Otis handed Emma a piece of chalk as if passing a baton and yielded his position at the chalkboard.

With a courtly little bow, Emma began. "You've all worked together, whereas I am new to your enterprise. An unknown quantity, and one about whom you are rightfully suspicious. I have no magic words that will make you suddenly trust me. What I have, instead, is invaluable knowledge that will make you all fabulously wealthy."

Moth popped a chicken liver in his mouth. "It's a weekday. Did you call in sick? Nobody at the Ossuary is missing you right now?"

"I'm not the kind of person who has to punch a clock," Emma said. "I won't be missed."

Moth chewed, unconvinced.

Emma flipped over the board to reveal a chalk-drawn map of Westside Los Angeles and drew a circle where the Santa Monica and Wilshire canals split off, and from there, a line to Rodeo Canal.

"This will be our breach point: Cross and Carsson's."

Daniel already had an obvious objection, but Cassandra saved him the trouble of voicing it. Cross and Carsson's used to be an osteomancy boutique, right in the heart of Beverly Hills' most famous shopping district.

"There is no Cross and Carsson's," Cassandra said. "Not anymore."

"Yes, the earthquake. Well, the shop is naught but swept rubble, but the vault below remains intact. Of course it is well guarded, above by human security, and below by Hyakume eyes. Also, the vault door . . . Well, we'll get to that later. Moving on, things get more difficult."

Jo snorted. "More difficult than Hyakume eyes? Have you ever tried to walk past Hyakume eyes, Emma?"

"No, and nor could I. Because I am not a brilliant thief, unless you count the chocolate bar I nicked from Sainsbury's when I was six. But you are all brilliant and I assume you have the skill to get past Hyakume eyes. From here," Emma continued, unperturbed, "we will have to travel three-point-six miles by way of a decommissioned subterranean utility canal. The canal is sealed by a two-foot-thick concrete wall. We'll have to find a way through it. From there, through the catacombs, and finally to here." She tapped a spot near the La Brea Tar Pits, site of the Ministry of Osteomancy's headquarters. "More precisely, eight levels below, which is where we will find the Hierarch's Ossuary."

She flashed a happy smile, her eyes crinkling.

"The Ossuary is guarded by enhanced sentries," Emma continued. "Their senses are heightened with cerberus wolf. Their fighting skills are lethal. Included among them are the most aggressive Garm hounds bred in the Hierarch's kennels. And there are passive wards as well. Sphinx riddles. Confusion spells. That's in addition to conventional surveillance and alarm systems."

Daniel still said nothing. He allowed his friends go through their own thought processes.

Cassandra walked up to the chalkboard. She studied it silently for a solid minute. Then, "What's the out?" she said.

That was always the question. Getting inside a secure facility was one thing. Getting out was another.

"I don't have an answer for you," Emma said, amiably enough. "I'm sure you'll generate some ideas."

"Basically, this is an unbreachable fortress," Moth said.

Otis stood. "No, it can't be. The Hierarch still acquires new materials and uses the Ossuary to store them. You can't have an unbreachable fortress if it also takes deliveries. You can't have an unbreachable fortress if personnel go in and out. Every building has an entrance and an exit. Every building has to breathe. Every building is a system. And there are essentially two ways to enter, move through, and exit a system. One requires force. It is loud, action-packed, violent, and, in this case, suicidal. The other method requires traveling through the system like an undetected illness. The victim only knows he's sick when he discovers he's been robbed. We will pursue this method."

"And how are we going to do that?" Cassandra asked.

The chalk-drawing began to fade, ghosting out to a faint trace of dust, then vanishing completely. Emma sniffed her stick of chalk and smiled. "Why, by magic, of course."

NINE

T he mammoth was always dying. Mired to her shoulders in the lake of tar, she reached out with her trunk to the dry-grass shore where her mate and calf remained frozen in horror. The La Brea Tar Pits were a place where the skin of the world broke open to reveal the magic underneath, and the life-sized plaster mammoth sculptures emphasized a very important message: Do not fuck with the tar.

Not that there was much incentive to fuck with the tar these days. The Ministry had long ago excavated every visible fragment of mammoth, mastodon, wyvern, hippogriff, saber-toothed sphinx, and three-headed wolf. These days, the Hierarch's paleomancers had to sort through tons of tar with tweezers, looking for bone bits the size of sesame seeds.

Tar bubbles expanded and deflated like the throats of bullfrogs as Gabriel crossed the bridge over the lake to the Byzantine sprawl of the Ministry of Osteomancy headquarters. He glanced only briefly at the mammoths. Displays of power and terror annoyed him. He believed in competence, thoroughness, conscientiousness. People would do good work if you motivated them with reasonable reward. Read your reports, and not just the executive summaries. Do your damned job. Great civilizations might be born from guns, germs, and magic, but it was bureaucracy that kept them going.

The route to Gabriel's office took him through a gauntlet of security guards, clerks, assistant clerks, accountants, gossips, goldbrickers, backstabbers, flirts, and brown-nosers. Gabriel acknowledged each according to his estimation of them, favoring the competent with a by-name greeting, and offering the rest at least a courteous nod. He didn't feel like stopping to talk. Last night's party at Griffith Observatory had bugged him, the forced chatting, the threat of the Six, the rare appearance of the Hierarch. And then there was Disney's talk of rebellion. These were not safe thoughts. And once a thought took root, it was only a matter of time before it found its way to your tongue, and then your tongue found its way to being nailed to a wall. Today's schedule included Gabriel's weekly briefing with the senior minister and deputies, and it was a very inconvenient time to be thinking tongue-nailing thoughts.

He changed direction and headed outside to see the kennels. He liked the dogs. The dogs were his favorite colleagues. They just did their jobs.

Crouching before one of the chain-link enclosures, he reached his fingers through a gap to scratch the ears of a young, floppy-eared Garm. The dog sniffed his fingers and its tail got happy. It was probably smelling Disney on him.

"Good girl. They should give you a promotion."

He rose and continued through the kennels. Turning a corner, he nearly collided with a leashed Garm, leading its handler at a pace too quick for the narrow aisle. The Garm went straight for Gabriel's fingers, sniffing and barking and twisting in its harness to get its handler's attention. This was not the reaction of a well-trained hound, at least not here at Ministry headquarters, where you didn't want the dogs going after everyone who'd handled osteomantic materials.

"Stella! Ut!"

The dog withdrew at its handler's command and sat at his knee.

The handler looked mortified. Partially due to his dog's behavior, but also because he no doubt recognized Gabriel. Relatives of the Hierarch made people nervous.

"I'm sorry, inspector. I don't know what's gotten into her these past few days."

Gabriel smiled reassuringly. "That's okay. I was in contact with some strong stuff last night." He watched the dog fidget with little telltale ear twitches and shudders. "You say she's not acting like herself?"

The handler's stiff posture relaxed a little, like someone relieved to unburden himself. "She's been antsy ever since we did a sweep of Farmers Market."

The public markets weren't among Gabriel's responsibilities. They fell under Minister Watanabe, a man with more ambition than diligence, and also kind of a jerk.

"You found something there?"

"No," the handler said. Then, reluctantly, "Well . . . it seemed for a few seconds like maybe she'd caught a whiff of something, but then it was like she wasn't sure. Or like she couldn't trace it, or . . ." Gabriel saw something in the handler's eyes. A glazed look. Confusion. "It was weird," he finished weakly.

Gabriel watched the dog twitch. Maybe she was picking up her handler's unease. Or maybe it was the other way around. Something about that Farmers Market sweep had affected both of them.

"She's a good hound," the handler added, as if he feared Gabriel would take his dog away, or worse. Some people in the Ministry were like that. Watanabe was like that.

"It takes young dogs a while to get used to working crowded places like Farmers Market," Gabriel said. "Lots of smells and distractions to confuse them. Give her some extra time in the yards and I'm sure she'll work it out of her system."

The handler broke out a grateful nod. "I'll do that, inspector. Thank you, sir."

Gabriel stepped aside and let him and his Garm squeeze by.

He found the kennel master inside one of the cages, brushing the hair of a gray-muzzled Garm. Gabriel waited until she gave the old dog a rough petting, creaked to her feet, and turned to see him standing there. She was an ancient woman with a neck like juniper bark.

"What?" she said, holding the wire brush like she'd strike him with it if he wasted a second of her time.

"I'd like to requisition a hound."

She scowled at him. "They're not pets, Inspector Argent."

"Matilda, I'm serious."

The woman's face softened, but she didn't lower her brush. "What for, Gabriel?"

"I think there's some stray sint holo out there."

"Sint holo . . . ? There hasn't been any of that on the street for fifteen years. We don't even train the dogs to detect it anymore, because we can't."

"I know. I don't need a dog. I want the other kind of hound."

"Oh," said the kennel master. And then, fully understanding, "Oh."

She let a thick moment go by as she considered Gabriel's

request. Then she withdrew jingling keys from her coveralls pocket.

She took him around the back of the dog cages, down a covered walkway, and through a locked green steel door set in a concrete wall. They left behind the bark and bustle of the kennels and stepped into cool shadow, where the only sounds were the occasional soft snuffle, a mewling, the soft clink of a chain. The air stung with the scent of cleaning fluid.

As Gabriel's eyes adjusted to the dim light, he took in the enclosures, each only a little larger than the dog kennels, and each outfitted with a stainless-steel toilet and a cot bolted to the floor. The men and women inside were naked and clean. They wore only soft leather collars from which dangled rings for their leashes. Their teeth and hair and skin were cared for by the attendants with sponges and buckets and brushes and picks. The attendants were gentle eunuchs. There was no mistreatment here, no rape, for these hounds were the Hierarch's property, and mishandling his property would result in a torturous death.

"Gabriel, I know you're a big boy, but this isn't your area. You're a paper pusher. Anything that involves taking hounds out into the field is Watanabe."

"If I file a NRT-3070—that's a Necessary Resources Transfer authorized by a deputy-minister-level signature—I can requisition any—"

"I know you know your paperwork, Gabriel. I'm not sure how much Watanabe respects your paperwork."

"Don't worry, Matilda, if he has a problem with this, I'll make it clear you were acting under protest, on my orders."

The kennel master waved all this away. "I'm old and I've

survived a few purges. But I know how it is with you fellas near the top. Your kind eats its own."

"I'll press down really hard when I sign the forms."

He followed her farther down the corridor. At the end was a single enclosure, a little smaller than the rest, and darker. Matilda flipped a switch on the wall, and the enclosure flooded with light from a yellow bulb behind wire mesh. The man inside the cage threw an arm over his eyes. He coughed a noise. It might have been a curse. Two places on the top bar of his cell were stained dark, as if with human oils. The stains were spaced the right distance if he were using the bar for pull-ups. The side of the metal cot had two similar stains. Triceps dips, thought Gabriel.

"What's his story?"

"He's scheduled to be put down on Thursday," Matilda said, unlocking the enclosure. "That gives you two days to work with him."

"He's being executed? What for?"

"We don't call it 'execution' here, Gabriel."

A muttering noise from the hound. Definitely a curse.

"Why, Matilda?"

"If they can still smell, hounds are put down for only one reason, and you know what it is." She watched Gabriel carefully. Matilda was always willing to let her superiors make their own mistakes. "Do you still want him?"

"Yes."

"On your feet, Max," said Matilda. "It's time to earn your keep again. This is Inspector Gabriel Argent. He's a bright boy in some ways, and a complete idiot in others."

"You're too kind," Gabriel said.

"He's after sint holo, and you're going to help him." She opened the cage, and Gabriel stepped inside.

The hound drew his arm away and squinted up with eyes that revealed nothing. One of his ears was a rough clump of red flesh. He'd taken a beating or two over the years.

Gabriel put out his hand. "Hello, Max. I'm Gabriel. You're my new partner."

Maneuvering through Farmers Market was easy when holding a hound's leash. People were quick to give way. They moved their shopping carts from the path and restrained their children. They hunched their shoulders and dipped their heads, trying to make themselves smaller. Gabriel's hound moved deliberately through the crowd, probing with keen eyes, sucking air through his narrow nostrils.

More than watching Max, Gabriel watched the crowd's reactions to him. Gabriel couldn't tell if the attention bothered him. He'd never worked with a human hound before. In the kennels, they were kept naked to make it easier to keep them clean and less likely to bolt. In the field, they wore gray coveralls, collars to attach leash and identity tag, and rubber slippers to protect their feet. Like Garm dogs, they were highly trained, valuable animals, but this one didn't act like an animal. He held his head high. When he looked at Gabriel, he made eye contact.

"Picking up anything?"

The hound crouched to sniff the bottom of a trashcan near a doughnut stand. Then he straightened and turned to face Gabriel, his head cocked to the side. "I'll let you know if I do."

The hound stood there, waiting for something, his eyes locked on Gabriel's. There was nothing extraordinary about the color or shape of his eyes, but there was a strange combination of confidence and wariness in them that held Gabriel transfixed. Garm hounds could look fierce, but usually they were just so eager to please. Here, with this human hound, Gabriel felt less like a handler and more like he was being handled. He decided on the spot that this hound was a person. Gabriel knew how to deal with people.

"What's your name?"

"They call me Max."

"I meant your real name."

"It's my name."

"What was your name before you were made a hound?"

"Max is my name now, inspector."

Shoppers shuffled cautiously past them, parting as though they were an island in a stream.

Gabriel had done a little bit of digging into the records and learned that Max was brought into the kennels when he was seventeen, a late age for a hound. He'd served the kennels for a decade and a half before turning on his handler and beating him to death with a trashcan lid.

Gabriel made some calculations on his mental abacus. He predicted transactions of favor and obligation he'd have to perform, and he came to a decision.

"Max. Well, okay, Max. We took you from your parents, stole your dignity, unmade you so we could make you something else. We use you, and when we're not using you, we keep you in a cage. I understand. I've worked in Ministry human resources, so I've seen it. We kill what you were because it's not convenient to keep it around. But you're different. You're prouder than most. Or more reckless."

Max didn't betray even a flicker of having been touched.

"If it sounds like I'm threatening you," Gabriel went on, "I apologize. What I'm asking is for you to deal with me as though I were an intelligent adult. Do that, and I'll deal the same way with you. Fair?"

Max said nothing.

Gabriel stepped up close to him. He reached for his neck. "I'm not going to hurt you," he said, unnecessarily perhaps. Max made no movement. Gabriel unbuckled his collar. "Shall we continue?"

Max's throat moved as he swallowed. "They'll make you put the collar back when you return me to the kennels." Then he turned and resumed sniffing.

They passed through the food court and the toy market and the clothing market without pausing, but after a circuit around the candle market, Max wanted another go 'round.

"Is there something here?" Gabriel asked.

Max looked sharply at him, as though surprised he was still there. "It's better if you let me work without talking."

"A concentration thing. Okay."

"Not so much concentration as . . . When I'm sniffing, I'm in a different place. Talking brings me back to *this* place."

"Sorry."

After a few minutes, Max came to rest before a stall of votive candles. The shopkeeper broke out in a terrified sweat, but Gabriel ignored him.

"It's faint, but there's magic here," Max said. "It's something designed to defy detection. It's designed to confuse, or . . ."

"Render invisible?"

"Yes," he said. Maybe Gabriel was only imagining respect in the way Max looked at him now. "It's faded and subtle, but . . . well, it's hard to guess."

"Go ahead," Gabriel said. "It's okay to be wrong."

"I think it's sint holo. But there's a lot more magic, too. Whoever came through here was lousy with magic." He seemed certain now, almost defiant.

"Can you trace it now that you've got the scent?"

"Yes."

Max took a route that included some dead ends and turn-arounds, but when he brought Gabriel to the apothecary's market, things began to feel right. Gabriel did not consider himself an osteomancer, but his training and exposure to osteomantic material sometimes gave him a sense for when he was in the presence of power. And there was definitely the buzz of something here.

"Our sint holo user?"

"Yes," Max confirmed.

"Can you tell where he went from here?"

Max looked like a man resigned to something horrible.

"It's okay if you can't."

"I can't," said Max.

Gabriel stepped away to look for a police call box, but when he spotted a patrolman leaning against a post eating a papaya spear, he called to him. First annoyance and then menace crossed the patrolman's face as he swaggered over, hand on the pommel of his cleaver-club.

"What?"

Gabriel displayed his ID tag, and the patrolman straightened. "May I help you, inspector?" he amended.

"Yes. Please take every apothecary in the market to Ministry headquarters."

"Every one . . . sir?"

"Yes," Gabriel said, more sharply. "Bring them to Section D."

"Yes, sir. I'll need the reason we're apprehending them, sir. For the paperwork."

"Questioning," said Gabriel.

G abriel installed the apothecaries in a conference room. It was a nice room, with dark oak wood paneling and a long mahogany table surrounded by good, leather-upholstered chairs. Each chair had a green-shaded brass lamp set before it, and beneath the lamps had been placed yellow legal pads and color pencils. On the wall hung an oil painting, six feet across, of the Hierarch on Mount Wilson, depicting his famous victory over a squadron of American B-29s. He stood on the mountain's peak in silhouette, his sword raised overhead and crackling with lightning as bombers fell in flames and oily smoke.

The apothecaries were brought cookies, coffee, tea, cola, lemon-lime, water, wine, or beer, according to each one's desire. A functionary explained to them that the Ministry was seeking a sint holo user whose presence had been traced to their sector of the market.

Gabriel watched the apothecaries through a two-way mirror. They'd been understandably terrified when first brought in, but now, after Gabriel had established a nonthreatening tone and shown them hospitality, most of them seemed to have relaxed. A few even summoned outrage at their continued detention.

"Why bring them in when I could have sniffed them at the market?" asked Max, pulling at the collar of his coveralls.

"I wasn't expecting you or the Garms to find anything. Honestly, tracing our sint holo user to a specific quarter of the market makes you a hero."

"Are you going to torture them?"

"I'm trying something else first," said Gabriel.

Max accompanied him into the conference room.

"How much longer is this going to take?" one of the apothecaries demanded as soon as Gabriel crossed the threshold. "I've got a business to run." He was a smallish man with jade teeth.

Emboldened by his outburst, a few of his fellows nodded and made supportive noises. But others seemed to remember where they were and remained stiffly silent.

"No more than an hour, I think," Gabriel said, addressing the room rather than the outspoken apothecary. He was no fan of giving grease to a squeaking wheel. "But that's largely dependent on you and the rate at which you metabolize osteomancy."

Rather than paying attention to Gabriel, three of the apothecaries were sketching feverishly on their legal pads. One was working on a landscape, another rendered a still life of one of the green-shaded lamps, while the third was doing some kind of abstract.

"What's that supposed to mean, metabolizing osteomancy?" spat Jade Tooth.

Another apothecary began sketching so hard she snapped her pencil. She snatched neighbor's pencil and resumed drawing a very credible giraffe. Gabriel had no idea why a giraffe, but she was clearly inspired.

"I'll explain myself," he said. "Your beverages were laced with an old preparation that was popular with artists in the 1920s. It's called Muse. It enhances your ability to translate thoughts and memories into two-dimensional images. Muse improves hand-eye coordination and fine motor control. It also enhances other, more ineffable qualities that, for lack of a better term, we'll call the 'artistic impulse.' And it increases recall to the extent that one's observations become sharper in retrospect than they were at the time the observations originally occurred. It should work its way out of your systems within a few hours."

Most of the apothecaries were now sketching away. Gabriel would have to call for more paper and pencils.

"What I'd like you all to do now is draw for me every face you encountered in the market the day before yesterday. Everyone you sold to, talked to, or even just caught sight of in passing. That should be several hundred drawings for each of you. When you're done, you will be returned to your businesses."

He leaned over the pad of an apothecary who was still drawing a tree. "If you'd rather work on another project, I'd ask that you postpone it until you've met my request. If you find you can't, I'm afraid I'll have to send you to one of my interrogators who uses pain instead of osteomantic assistance."

The tree-drawer paused, his hand shaking. Then he turned the page and began sketching a face.

The next day, Gabriel visited the morgue, a sunless, stone-lined chamber in a subbasement of the Ministry of Osteomancy. There was no particular reason why it had to be kept so far out of sight, except the specialists who worked here weren't particularly pleasant to be around. Gabriel descended the long flight of stairs with Max trailing him. Max moved tentatively.

"You're used to leading, not following," Gabriel said.

Max looked at him.

"You can walk ahead if you want."

"I don't know where I'm going," Max said. "If you're not going to keep me on a leash, you could at least tell me where we're going."

"Fair enough. But can you tell me one thing?"

"I can tell you if I know it. I don't know much. I'm a hound."

"Why did you kill your master?"

Max's answer came without a moment of hesitation. "I wanted to die."

Gabriel found himself frozen, halfway down the stone steps. In the dim light, Max's eyes were the brightest things in the stairway.

"Why, Max?"

"I thought I already said, Inspector Argent. I'm a hound."

"Do you still want to die?"

"Not before I've had a chance to pee," said Max.

Gabriel nodded. "Then you have something to live for. Come on."

They continued down the stairs and came to a room the length of a high school gym. Technicians sat on benches behind long tables, piled with file boxes and folders. There was no conversation, no music, only the shuffling of paper, the soft noise multiplied by volume and repetition into a mechanical crackling. The air smelled of paper dust and ointment.

"Who are these people?" Max whispered, as though they

were in a library. It occurred to Gabriel that Max hadn't been in a library for a very long time.

Almost all the workers were stoop-shouldered old men and women with failing eyes and sun-starved flesh, sorting through old crime reports, mug shots, and composite sketches of criminal suspects, subversives, and insurgents. Younger workers lugged file boxes between towering shelves and the worktables.

"Our memoraticians," said Gabriel. "They're fed a mix that enhances memory, concentration, and facial recognition."

He approached Station 21-A, where a man in a sweater vest sat with his back to him. Gabriel watched him work for a few minutes, sorting through piles of photos with lists of physical descriptors at his elbow.

Once it became evident that the man was never going to acknowledge his presence, Gabriel coughed into his hand. "Excuse me, you're the supervisor down here?"

"I'm busy," the man said, continuing to sort.

"Which is laudable. I'm Inspector Gabriel Argent."

No reaction from the man, but Gabriel thought he detected a hint of a smirk on Max's face.

Gabriel tried again. "I brought down a sketch of the sint holo suspect at Farmers Market. I heard you were able to ID him."

The memoratician stopped and turned around. Gabriel was surprised to find him grinning.

"Oh, that one. Yes, yes, I have something to show you. You'll find it quite interesting."

The man sprang up and led Gabriel and Max on a near chase through a labyrinth of shelves, over to a corkboard. There, partitioned off by a border of yarn, was a sketch of a narrow-faced man, brown-skinned, probably some Hispanic in him, with unruly black hair. Gabriel put him in his late teens to early twenties.

"We ran the sketches from the apothecaries you brought in. Eight hundred seventy-three in all. Of those, five had criminal records, all for minor offenses. I had them sent up to your office." The memoratician's eyes sparkled like a dog playing fetch. He pointed at the drawing of the narrow-faced man. "Now, this one is different. Look at the photos."

Two prints were pinned below the sketch. One of them of them was a group shot taken at a backyard party. A red pen circle had been drawn around a woman holding a piece of cake on a plate. There was some resemblance to the narrow-faced man in the sketch. The skin tone. The eyes.

Max edged closer to the corkboard, sniffed, perhaps instinctively, and turned away in dejection.

"You don't recognize her, do you?" said the memoratician.

"No," Gabriel admitted. "Should I?"

"That's Messalina Sigilo. Born in Northern California."

"Illegal immigrant?"

"No, she came over legally during the Pax Monterey, but there are notes in her file about suspicions of espionage. Never confirmed. It's believed she tried to return to the Northern Kingdom ten years ago. She didn't make it. And her son, Daniel, was killed during the crossing. This is all in her file. I've sent everything relevant up to your office."

"Thank you. And what about the man?" Gabriel pointed to the other photo, a formal portrait of a gray-haired Anglo, mid-forties. He did look familiar.

"That's Sebastian Blackland."

"Blackland. The osteomancer?"

"One of the Ministry's top R&D men," said the memoratician. "An intimate of the highest echelons. Married to Messalina Sigilo. He was taken in the Third Correction."

Nothing unusual about that. Few high-level osteomancers
survived the Hierarch's purges.

"What's their connection to my sint holo suspect?"

"They're his parents," said the memoratician.

"So the boy who died when Sigilo was crossing the border,
Daniel . . . that was my suspect's brother?"

"No, they only had one child." The memoratician withdrew
another photo out of his file. It was a grainy blowup of a boy,
sitting on the edge of a palm planter, balancing a piece of cake
on a paper plate. "This is a zoom from the Sigilo picture. We
use over seventy different measurements of shape and pro-
portion for facial recognition. It's Daniel Blackland, age six.
And this," he said, indicating the apothecary's sketch, "is him
at age twenty-two. Daniel Blackland. Son of a spy, son of an
osteomancer, presumed dead, but, apparently, still alive in Los
Angeles."

TEN

Emma set a chip the size of a postage stamp on the conference table. "A fossilized scale from a *Draconis colombi*. That's a Colombian dragon, or firedrake, for you nonmagicians." She winked at Jo, Moth, and Cassandra, who stood around the table. "This is the first significant osteomantic obstacle we'll be facing. Harder than steel-reinforced concrete. Pressure-rated to over seventy-two hundred pounds per square inch. A six-thousand-degree acetylene torch won't even give it a rash."

Daniel picked up the scale, shocked at its heft. No bigger than his thumbnail, it must have weighed five pounds. He dropped it on the table with a *thunk*.

"This is just a sample sliver I smuggled from the catacombs," Emma said. "The vault door below Cross and Carsson's is made of this, and it's two feet thick."

Most heists were actually just strong-arm robberies. Walk into a jewelry store with guns drawn, holler a lot, in and out in a few minutes. Even an elaborate job, like the Kent depository, the biggest cash robbery in the history of the United Kingdom, was essentially just a tiger kidnapping: Abduct the manager and the manager's family and hold them at gunpoint until the manager gives you access to bales of money. Daniel's personal favorite heist was the Isabella Stewart Gardner Museum job in Boston, in which the robbers disguised themselves as cops and convinced the security guards to let them in. They'd worn fake mustaches. Fake mustaches! How could you not love it?

Fake mustaches, however, would not get them into the Ossuary.

"So how do we breach it?" Cassandra said, squinting at the scale chip.

"Seps venom is the only thing I know that burns through firedrake," Emma said.

Daniel had never worked with seps, but he knew it was one of the most corrosive substances in existence. The Hierarch used it to destroy an entire armored tank division in the Death Valley Standoff. Sometimes archeomancers uncovered a bit of it, but seps venom hardly ever left European shores. Finding it in Los Angeles wouldn't be easy.

Daniel turned to Otis, who'd been watching the meeting from the back of the room. "Got any seps in stock?"

"Afraid not."

"Surprised. You've been handing over bone like it's Victory Day." Otis was coy about how he'd come into grootslang and gorgon blood. Even for him, this stuff was hard to get. But he'd clearly tapped into some good treasure, and he wasn't afraid to spend it.

"I don't have seps," he said, uncrossing his arms. "But I know who does."

Five days later, Daniel had his crew prepped to go get it. This would be a good test. If they couldn't handle a residential burglary, then no way could they pull off the Ossuary job. Better to find that out now.

He still couldn't believe he was going to break into the house of a Los Angeles god. Not that anyone else on the crew considered Wilson Bryant a god, but his father would go on for hours about the mystical brilliance of the music he made as leader of The Woodies, especially on their breakthrough album, *Animal Talk*. To which Daniel's only ever response was, "The cow goes moo."

Bryant lived in a two-story Malibu beach house elevated above the surf on pylons. A lot of celebrities insisted on living in this pretty part of town, and every few years their houses were swallowed by the sea or consumed by fires in the canyons, or swept down the hills in mudslides. They would come on television, looking stylishly disheveled, and proclaim how they weren't going to let misfortune break their spirits, and how they were going to rebuild, and Daniel would throw a shoe at the TV.

But Daniel liked the location. Bobbing offshore in a rigid inflatable boat with his crew, he scoped out the house through binoculars. All visible windows were barred. There was a swiveling security camera on the roof, another on a second-floor balustrade, and a stationary camera over the door. Several alarm company placards were displayed like hexes. A glow in one of the upstairs windows suggested someone was home.

Daniel maneuvered the boat to avoid the pools of light cast by flood lamps on the roof. He killed the outboard motor, and rode the surf up to the iron mesh skirting the barnacle-encrusted pylons. Cassandra and Jo made quick work of the mesh with bolt cutters, and Moth paddled the boat under the house. Daniel tied off on one of the pylons and took a good sniff. Brine and sphinx-lock and a tinge of cannabis.

There was just enough space overhead for Daniel to stand. He played his flashlight over the web of support struts and spars, hoping to find an easy entrance—a rubbish chute or something. But no such luck. They'd have to cut through the floor.

Cassandra lifted an eighteen-inch, four-horsepower chainsaw. Hefting it in one hand, she smiled like a murderer.

This was going to be noisy. Daniel hated noise. He held up a finger before Cassandra touched the pull cord. With a rubber bladder, he squeezed out a few puffs of fine yellow sand. Ancient Egyptians had constructed myths around the snake personified by the cobra-goddess Meretseger. Her name meant "she who loves silence," and it made sense to Daniel that pyramid builders revered her, since any moment of silence amid the clang and crack of hammers and chisels must have been a huge relief.

Daniel gave Cassandra the nod. She yanked the cord of the chainsaw. Muffled by the meretseger dust, the blade cut through wood, no louder than an electric razor. Less than eighty seconds later, Cassandra had sawed a gap in the floor big enough for everyone but Moth to climb through. They donned ski masks, and Daniel and Cassandra and Jo went up.

They found themselves in a dark hallway hung with framed gold and platinum records. Daniel noticed Jo's acquisitive gaze, and he shook his head no. Sometimes the hardest part of a job was leaving good treasure behind, and he didn't want a repeat of the Sylmar job with Punch and the monocerus.

Without speaking, they moved from room to room, ready for bodyguards. Bryant lived well. Given all the shiny trophy records on the wall, he could afford to. In the living room, a white grand piano rose from thick, soft carpet like a gleaming island. From the panoramic windows, one could look out to sea, and on a clear day, you'd be able to spot Catalina Island. Down the coast, candy-colored lights twinkled from the Santa Monica Pier, where Daniel had found the kraken spine a lifetime ago.

The house was set up like a museum, with glass display cases stuffing entire rooms. Daniel lost count of the Grammys and Los Angeles Arts Medals and the dozens of other industry awards and civic honors on show. When they came to a room housing Bryant's comic book collection, Daniel reflexively began to add up values. He stopped before a case containing a crisp, clean first issue of *Lord Lightning* and swooned. Cassandra had to drag him away.

There was a room of baseball cards, and two rooms of guitars, and judging by the aromas permeating the carpet and walls, a sizable store of marijuana somewhere. Mostly Daniel smelled a rich miasma of osteomancy, but only recreational magic. Not the seps he was looking for.

He had to admit he was having fun. This felt good, being with Cassandra and Jo, knowing that Moth was keeping watch outside while they snuck through a place forbidden to them by law and economic status. Even more than using magic, this was when he felt powerful. If he wanted to, he could strip the house of all its gold and platinum and vintage Fender Stratocasters and pristine comics. Bryant was rich, which meant Bryant was powerful. Yet Daniel could take his power.

He gave a hand signal and the crew crept upstairs. More shiny metal records on the walls and pungent osteomancy. The room with the light was down the end of a corridor, and if Bryant had bodyguards, they'd let Daniel get unforgivably close. Either that, or they were waiting behind the double doors of the lit room. The doors were thick wooden things, carved in high relief with a surfer dude riding a longboard.

Cassandra counted on her fingers. When she reached three, she and Jo shoved the doors open, poison-tipped needle guns drawn. Daniel came in behind them, electricity on his fingers.

If the piano downstairs was an island, then the bed in the center of the vast bedroom was a continent. It rose on a mound of beach sand. The headboard was a cabinet towering to the ceiling, the shelves cluttered with more trophies and memorabilia, including photos of Bryant with Hollywood luminaries and members of the Council of Six, and more guitars, and even a surfboard. And propped up on pillows sat Wilson Bryant himself, bearded, huge, and barely contained by a white silk kimono. Yellow legal pads and In-N-Out burger wrappers lay scattered on his lap. Beside him was an acoustic guitar, half covered by a sheet like a sleeping lover.

He squinted at Daniel with red-rimmed eyes. "Oh, wow," he said. "You are made of love."

Odd reaction to three strangers in ski masks bursting into his room.

Daniel shrugged at Cassandra and Jo.

"You know us, Mr. Bryant?"

"I know you," Bryant said, a beatific smile lighting his face. "I mean, not *you* you, but the you you are."

"Which is . . . ?"

"You're incandescent, man. You're like the sun. You're like a firedrake in first bloom."

"I like his lyrics about surfing better," Jo said.

This was just a weird situation. Daniel decided to roll with it. "That's sweet of you to say, Mr. Bryant—"

"Mister? Oh, man, I'm not a 'mister.' I'm just me. Just flesh and magic. We're brothers. Brothers and sisters, all of us." He laughed a stoner laugh and spread his arms as if he wanted to hug the world.

"That's really brilliant," Daniel said. "You're such a creative guy—"

"A genius, actually," Cassandra said, helpfully. Her gun was still aimed at him. Jo turned her head so Bryant couldn't see her rolling her eyes.

"Such a genius," Daniel went on. "And this room . . . It's a really inspiring space."

"I used to have to go outside to feel the beach," Bryant said. "But then I saw the difference between outside and inside was a totally artificial barrier, so I brought that barrier down."

"Yeah. That's good," Daniel said. "That's really good."

Bryant's round head bobbed in an enthusiastic nod. The stoner laugh bubbled up, but then abruptly died as he screwed his face into an approximation of focus. "You're made of love, man. But there's something off about you. Like you're the wrong kind of love. Like a false prophet. You know, like in my song 'Unicorn Tears'?"

"I'm not familiar with that one."

Bryant sniffed, a little bit hurt. "It was a B-side. It's about making people love you. Do people know about you? How you make them love you?"

Daniel didn't like the way Bryant was looking at him now. He wasn't funny anymore. He didn't like the way Cassandra was looking at him either.

A subtle change in Jo's posture drew Daniel's attention. He followed her gaze to a shelf in Bryant's massive headboard. There, inside a two-foot-tall jar, was a snake's skull the size of a basketball, floating in bluish fluid. No wonder Daniel couldn't smell any seps. It was sealed in osteomantic preservative.

"Say, would you mind if we had a look around?" Daniel asked.

"In order to radiate more," Jo supplied.

"Sure, brother, of course. *Mi casa es su casa*. But, hey, can I sing you a song first? I just wrote it, so it's still all locked away inside me. Music is light, and you can't keep light shut in or else it'll start to burn." He laughed his stoner laugh.

"We'd be honored," Daniel said.

"Hell, we'd be irradiated," Jo said.

The stoner laugh.

Bryant reached beneath the covers for his guitar, and his hand emerged holding a handgun with a bore the size of a golf hole. The goofy, enraptured smile was gone.

"What the fuck are you fuckers doing in my fucking house? Fucking thieves! Fucking spies! *You're not going to steal my fucking light!*" His glassy eyes searched for something to aim at.

Daniel flicked his index finger in a barely perceptible signal, and Cassandra and Jo pulled the triggers of their guns. There were four puffs of air, and four needles in Bryant's chest. His gun hand sank to the mattress, and he sagged back into his pillows. He snored and was smiling beatifically once more.

J o lay in the bathtub, cheeks puffed out, her face three inches under the water, with a clip pinching her nostrils shut. Part of the Ossuary job required underwater work, and Daniel had cooked a mixture of kolowisi, bagil, and panlong to give his crew the powers of aquatic creatures, at least for several minutes. It was Jo's turn to get used to the sensations of being submerged without having to breathe, and she was doing great. Daniel waved a thumbs-up over the bath, and she returned it with her own thumbs-up, stretching the web of skin between her thumb and forefinger. She'd grown webbed fingers and toes as a joke, but Daniel thought they might prove useful.

"You're a champ!" he screamed into the water over her face. She beamed happily.

"No way she's beating my record," Moth said from the bathroom doorway.

"She's at seven minutes, and your record is officially a sad artifact of your former glory."

"I miss my former glory," said a morose Moth.

"Keep an eye on her for me while I go check on Emma?"

Moth sat on the edge of the tub with Daniel's stopwatch. "Hey, Jo. How're your lungs feeling? Kind of bursty? Good old oxygen, your gassy friend."

Jo's middle finger emerged from the water like a periscope.

Daniel found Emma in his workroom, examining a military-surplus folding shovel. An earthy aroma hung on the air. Without putting much muscle into it, she stabbed the blade into the wall, and the concrete flaked away like talc, scattering into motes that vanished before reaching the ground. The shovels were like an all-access backstage pass. With these and the seps venom, the crew would be able to breach walls, dig tunnels, go wherever they wanted.

"Good job getting the grootslang to adhere without dissolving the metal," she said, handing him the shovel. "I was worried you might be more of firework than osteomancer."

"I can go boom if I need to. But I can also measure stuff out and stir things."

"You're being modest. I'm told you're actually quite a talented cook."

"I know what most of the buttons on the microwave do. It's been days since I burned popcorn."

"You don't take compliments well. Power and skill don't always come in the same package. They do in your case. You're a true osteomancer. And I wish we had time for me to tutor you. It would be a privilege for me, and it might help elevate you closer to your father's ambitions."

"Ambitious and dead are synonymous in my dictionary, Emma. But I'm glad you're happy with my shovel. I'm going to go back to work now."

He left her alone with the gouged wall.

Things were falling into place. His crew was well equipped and prepared, and he knew they could work together. Except for Emma, they were family.

There was one last ingredient he required, because they still needed an out from the Ossuary, and for that, Daniel had decided to make an earthquake. So he went alone to Dogtown.

Tucked between Santa Monica and Venice, Dogtown was a dozen blocks of shops with boarded windows. Frayed wires jutted from decapitated streetlamps, like pistils and stamen from shattered glass globes. The slender moon cast just enough light for Daniel to spot the occasional shadowed figure making a furtive dive into a building. Incoherent mutterings and laughter and moans filled the salt air. Sounds that started as screams faded into silence or quiet weeping.

Daniel walked along the dry-weed banks of the old canals

and tried to decipher the graffiti slathered on the peeling stucco walls of the shops. He spotted some V13 tags, some Venice Shoreline Crips, the fish symbol of the long-gone St. Mark's Parish, and the skeletal glyphs of the Dogtown Leeches. But this place belonged to no one in particular. He kept kraken electricity at his fingers and held his leather messenger bag close.

He turned seaward, to the burial grounds of Pacific Ocean Park. Through the roar and rumble of the surf, he thought he heard the grinding sounds of skateboards on concrete, but it was probably just rocks rolling against the stubs of the old pier. He was spooking himself. He crossed a belt of weeds and entered the amusement park.

The steel arches of Neptune's Courtyard curved over him like the limbs of a monstrous starfish. A few bathyspheres swayed overhead, creaking on their skyway cables. Rats chittered from the dark recesses of the Davy Jones Locker funhouse.

Daniel found the man he was looking for at the seal pool, a drained concrete pit filled with tall, yellow grass. Sully chopped mackerel on the wall bordering the pool. He was a handsome man in his seventies, thick silver hair neatly combed, just a few age spots marring his good cheekbones. He had the jaw of the hero in an old war movie. In fact, he had played a bit part as a heroic submarine commander in *Siege of the Catalina Island*. But his wardrobe was all wrong today: an oil cloth apron over a stained white T-shirt and greasy khaki trousers. He didn't look up as Daniel approached, just kept on cutting the mackerel into bits.

Who could the fish possibly be for? Daniel spooked himself again, contemplating ghost seals, but then he heard rustling in the tumbleweed and smelled cat piss. There was a yowl.

"Don't mind the bad man," Sully crooned into the pit. "He'll be leaving soon. Were you followed?"

"Come on, it's me," Daniel said. "Of course not. You got my message?"

"Your wraith delivered it last night."

"Not my wraith. The wraiths belong to Otis."

Sully shrugged, as if the distinction made no difference. "Do you have the thing?"

Daniel patted his messenger bag.

"Okay," Sully said, hurling the fish bits into the pit. "Let's go to my house."

Leaving the sounds of scrabbling cats behind, Daniel followed Sully down the promenade, beneath the dark skeleton of the Sea Serpent roller coaster. On either side of the walkway, gutted and collapsing buildings gave little indication that, for a short time, this had been Southern California's most popular amusement park. When it opened in 1959, Pacific Ocean Park did better ticket business than Disneyland. And that's what doomed it. In the fight between Disney and Ocean Park, the Hierarch sided with Disney. Storms, fires, dwindling attendance, and neglect had all done their damage, and now this was a place of rubble and rust. Nobody claimed responsibility. In these latter days of the kingdom, that's how things went. Disasters and entropy served as the Hierarch's disciplinary tools.

Past the buildings housing the Enchanted Forest, the House of Tomorrow, and the Flight to Mars, they came to the oldest structure in the park, the Fox Dome Theatre. In the dark, with mist crawling up the pier, it was easy to imagine that the hundred-foot domed roof was still intact. But Sully cleared a mess of wooden pallets and rusted barrels concealing a doorless back entrance and they went inside. The illusion vanished. A few weak lights revealed the fallen-down palace.

The collapsed balcony of the two-thousand-seat theater left a jumble of wood and plaster and concrete and rotting velvet seats. The projection booth had come down with it. In its place, Sully had propped a salvaged projector on a ladder.

He slipped on a pair of white cotton gloves. "Let's have it."

Daniel handed Sully a metal film canister. Like a kid opening his Victory Day present, Sully pried off the lid and carefully removed the film reel inside. He extended a foot of film to the light, squinting, and beamed with movie-star teeth. Biting his lip with concentration, he mounted the reel on the projector and began threading the film through the puzzle of gates and sprockets.

"Slow down, Sully. This is a transaction. You know how these things work."

Frustrated by the interruption, Sully dug into his apron pocket and tossed a plastic baggie at Daniel. Inside was a small quantity of dark red flakes. Daniel opened the bag and had a sniff of sulfur and molten earth.

"What's your source?"

"Is that your business?" said Sully, returning to the job of threading the film.

"Yes, it is my business. The time you sold me Etruscan leo-kampoi? Turned out to be eighty percent catfish."

"I let you smell it before you paid for it, didn't I?"

"I was thirteen. I didn't know what I was doing."

Sully looked sad. "I know, kid. I shouldn't have encouraged your delinquency. But I liked your old man and I figured I was doing you a favor."

Daniel faltered. "I didn't know you did business with my dad."

"Oh, sure. The last time I saw him, I sold him eocorn essence, some terratorn coprolite, and some high-quality *Panthera atrox*. Pure stuff. Your dad could tell the difference."

Horn from a Pleistocene unicorn, fossilized condor crap, and American lion essence. That didn't form any combination Daniel knew about.

"What was my dad cooking?"

"Didn't say. But those are love potion ingredients."

"He didn't do love potions."

Sully wasn't going to argue. "He was a high-level osteomancer. Who knows what he could cook?"

Daniel shook the baggie at him. "Where'd you get the beetle?"

"Guy I know who used to work special effects at Universal. You ever see *Earthquake*?"

"Charlton Heston. Yeah."

"This is what they used for the earthquakes."

"If it's not," Daniel said, "I'll be back."

"Good. Bring me a burrito, too."

Sully flipped a couple of switches on the projector. The lens cast a dusty cone of light, and wheels turned, clacking. A blurry image appeared on the screen. After Sully turned the focusing ring, his own youthful face looked back at him, and the steely-eyed submarine commander confidently barked orders at his crew. He was only on-screen for a dozen seconds before the clip looped back to the beginning. Again and again, Sully embodied the handsome submariner. Maybe it was a trick of flickering light and shadow, or maybe it was the osteomancy used to develop the film, but the age spots on Sully's cheeks seemed to fade, and a few strands of dark hair appeared in the combed silver.

Daniel secured the baggie in his messenger bag. He picked his way across the debris and found the door, and he was almost outside when Sully called back to him.

"You know this is just a down payment, right? I did you a favor, and now you owe me one. That's the way these things work."

"Yeah," Daniel said. "I know how things work. Take care of yourself, okay, Sully?"

"I will, kid. See you next time."

The twelve seconds of the Sully's youth continued to shine in the dark.

"Next time," Daniel said.

Daniel's workshop was a plywood propped on sawhorses in the back of Otis's warehouse. His shelves were boards and bricks, and he stored his osteomantic materials in a mechanic's tool chest. Otis would have provided furnishings worthy of great magic if Daniel had asked, but Daniel didn't want anything more from him than was absolutely necessary.

He was supposed to be working with the seps venom, but instead he sat, contemplating a jar of dusky, oily fluid: the lamassu extract he'd spiked Emma Walker's tea with in Chinatown. It hadn't worked on her, but it had worked on him, unlocking memories of the last time he'd seen his mother. Not really unlocking the memories, actually, so much as amending them.

He picked up the jar of lamassu and held it up to the buzzing fluorescent bulbs overhead. Even without unscrewing the lid, he could smell the ancient oil. It smelled like revelation. Like the flare of a lamp in a room best left dark.

It'd been a long time since he'd been scared of magic.

He set the jar aside and turned his attention to the seps venom.

The snake's skull looked as fresh as if it had been bottled yesterday, but if Daniel removed it from the preservative, it would crumble to ash in seconds. The jar was coated in finely ground firedrake scales, the only substance known to withstand seps venom, but even so equipped, there were a lot of ways he could screw this up. Spill the venom and it would eat through the jar, the worktable, the floor, the foundation, the fabled dragon heart at the center of the earth, and probably shoot up in an acid geyser on a quiet residential street in China. So, you know, thought Daniel, don't spill the acid.

From an awkward standing position, he worked a hand drill through the left maxilla and stopped when the drill bit neared the fang. The snake's venom sacs had decomposed thousands of years ago, but if any osteomantic essence was left behind, Daniel would be able to cook it into a weapon.

He smelled vanilla and tobacco.

"Hello, Emma," he said, without turning around.

She dragged over a stool and sat beside him. "I'm going to try again. You have all the makings of a very good osteomancer."

"Enh. It's like making brownies. Anyone can follow a recipe."

She shook her head, frustrated. "You're planning to use the venom of a seps serpent. But you could *be* a seps serpent, just like you *are* kraken. It's not a thing you do. It's what's in you. It's what you are."

"You're not the first osteomancer to take an interest in

what's inside me, once you've seen the actual insides of an osteomancer, it's hard to take it as a compliment."

"Understandable. I'm sorry." Emma peered at the skull through the glass. "I think you could be one of the greatest osteomancers ever."

He went back to drilling. "I don't need to be great. I'll settle for alive."

She examined his osteomancer's torch, a contraption of copper and brass and knobs and valves. "Living is good. But since my interests coincide with yours, I'd like you to be the most effective osteomancer possible. Your kraken is a good weapon, and your sint holo is a good defense, but you're capable of more. I can smell your magic. You're redolent with power, but you don't realize it."

Daniel was content to let the grinding of the drill speak for him.

"Do you have any idea how much magic there is in Los Angeles?"

"Clearly not enough," Daniel said.

"Aha. See, that's what everyone thinks. But not so."

Daniel stopped drilling. "If you know about secret caches of osteomancy, that's generally the kind of thing I'm interested in."

"Greedy lad, it's an open secret. You're breathing osteomancy. You're bathing in it. It's concentrated in bones, but the essence is everywhere. It's in the soil and the air."

"Trace residues? Yeah, the world is magic, every particle of it. But there's not a flame hot enough to cook it out."

"You're the flame, Daniel."

"You sound like my dad."

She looked off in the distance, wistful. "If only. I heard he was working on concepts of direct absorption, taking raw magic directly, with no need of recipe at all. We all lost a lot when he died."

"I know. I never even learned how to fasten a necktie properly. Tried a half Windsor the other day and almost broke a finger."

"You're not taking me seriously."

"I'm taking you more seriously than you might be comfortable with. Can you tell me anything useful about direct absorption, Emma? Any practical advice? Anything that's going to help us get in and out of the Ossuary?"

She smiled, as if caught cheating at cards. She was a smiler. "No," she conceded.

"Then you're just teasing me."

Osteomancers loved to trade in secrets, whether or not they actually possessed them. He went back to drilling.

"Otis told me about your lamassu vision," she said after a while. "You think I'm responsible for it."

He pulled the drill out of the jar. "It came to me right after I ingested your essence."

"Lamassu is a finicky magic. It's easy to misunderstand and misuse."

"Otis told me that."

"But you don't believe him," Emma said. "What do you believe, Mr. Blackland?"

"I don't know," he said, honestly.

"Then I don't know how to help you," she said, standing. "I don't know how to convince you that you can trust me, that I mean neither you nor your friends any harm. I am Emma Walker. I work beneath the Ministry, and I want to help you get into the Ossuary, where you will find your sword. If you discover I'm lying, I know you'll kill me or have one of your friends do it. That's the risk I take, working with you. It comforts me to have that knowledge out in the open. I'm sorry I cannot provide the same comfort to you."

She smiled warmly and rested her hand on his shoulder for the briefest of moments, and as she walked away, Daniel listened to her footsteps fade, much sooner than her scents of vanilla and contained magic.

He fired up the burner and reached for the jar of lamassu. With a pair of tweezers, he removed a small wad of paste. He let it heat over the flame, and when he smelled something like hot sand and olives and puzzles, he deposited the lamassu on his tongue.

He was standing in a field with his mother. Several yards away was a bug-spattered car with the doors, trunk, and hood open. Cars were rare in Los Angeles, and Daniel found himself fascinated by the odd vehicle. It looked neither fast nor comfortable. A box on wheels. Three other cars surrounded theirs. They were on a farm of some kind, a space more vast than any in Los Angeles. The air smelled of freshly turned soil and strawberries.

Men in uniforms crawled through the car's interior. Another threw a suitcase out of the trunk. It landed in the tan dirt and popped open. A pair of jeans spilled out. They were Daniel's jeans, softened by wear, but Daniel had never worn them. He was confused and wanted to cry, but his mother's firm grip on his fingers wouldn't allow it. Things would be all right. His mom was here. She would keep him from floating away.

All the uniformed men had holstered guns. One man, who stood just a couple of yards away, also had a rifle trained on his mother's head. Another man had a Garm hound by the leash. Its slobber foamed on his shoes. And there was also a woman, interrogating Daniel's mother.

"How did you get across?" she said. Beneath the cap of her uniform, her hair smelled of rose hips and jojoba shampoo. She'd had eggs and green chile for breakfast.

"I've told you six times already," said Messalina Sigilo Blackland, incautious and angry. "When your man comes back—"

"When my man comes back from the guard station, he'll either bring word that you're telling the truth, and I will apologize for my discourteous treatment of you. Or, he will bring word that you're lying, and I will belly-shoot you, and you will die, moaning in the dirt."

"I got through by bribing the Southern kingdom guards," Daniel's mother said, her jaw tight.

"I think our Southern counterparts are more loyal to their Hierarch than that."

"Anyone can be bought."

The woman looked as if she'd just heard a mildly amusing joke. "Are you offering me a bribe?"

Daniel's mother spat on the ground. She was not herself. "That'll be the day."

"Maamah," said Daniel. His voice was slurred.

"Tell it to be quiet," the woman said.

His mother looked at him oddly, with a mix of familiar love, but also something else. Fear. Or maybe revulsion.

"Hush," she said.

Down a dusty track, a rooster tail of dirt clouded the air, and soon another car drove up and came to a stop. A uniformed man got out and jogged over to the woman who smelled of rose hips. He spoke some words in her ear, too low for Daniel to hear.

"Stand down," the woman barked, and the man with the rifle lowered it. The Garm hound was led away to piss. The woman called out some more orders, and everyone started getting into cars. "You'll ride with me," the woman said to Daniel's mother. "I'll leave a detachment behind to watch over that." She looked at Daniel when she said "that."

"He belongs to me," his mother said. "He's too valuable to be left with your guards."

The woman shook her head. "It's Southern magic. We don't know what it is or how it works, so arrangements will have to be made to bring it to San Francisco. It stays behind."

"He's not dangerous," his mother said. "I can control him."

"It'll have to be examined by guild osteomancers while you're being debriefed. If it turns out there's no reason to keep it separated from you, it will be returned."

His mother was dirty and tired. Her hair hung like wet yarn in her face. Only now did Daniel register the scratches on her face, the torn skin on her knuckles. However they had gotten here from Los Angeles, there'd been costs. And Daniel saw in his mother's face that there was only so much fighting she was willing to do to keep Daniel with her. He didn't understand.

"Maammah," he said.

What was wrong with him? Why couldn't he speak normally?

"Maammah?"

Uniformed men closed in around him as his mother got into the woman's car, and her door was shut, and his mother looked at him one last time through the window, and what he saw in her eyes wasn't love. Pity, maybe. Regret. But not love.

He watched the car recede until it faded in its own dust cloud, and then he looked down at the shoes that fit him but were not his, and he was alone with the uniformed men.

"How do we want to do this?" one of them said.

"Make it quick," said another. "I mean, Jesus, he *looks* like a kid."

One of the uniformed men came to stand in front of Daniel. He was a little older than the rest, and his face was kind.

"Son, we're going to check to make sure you weren't hurt during your trip," he said. "We just need you to kneel for a second."

"Maaamah?"

"She's fine, son. Just kneel. It won't hurt. Trust me."

Daniel gazed up into his face. He was smiling and kind. His gun holster was unsnapped.

Daniel knelt in the strawberry field.

ELEVEN

R eal estate listings called the cabin-style house a "charmingly eccentric handyman's special." Gabriel would have called the place a haunted wreck. Cobwebs laced the weathered gray plywood boards over the windows. Orange-brown pine needles carpeted the cedar shingle roof. Someone had hacked at the weeds enough to form a path from sidewalk to front door, or maybe it was the work of deer and rabbits. No one had lived in Sebastian Blackland's house since the Hierarch's purge ten years before.

"Smell anything?" Gabriel asked, following Max up the walk.

"Raccoon urine and coyote scat. Some marijuana, but that's probably from the neighbors. And somebody's cooking tomato sauce down the canal."

Gabriel tried the front door. Locked. He spent a few minutes with his lock picks and pushed open the door. Afternoon sun spilled onto the scuffed living room floor. The stale odors of wood and plaster and dark mold wafted out.

"How about now?"

Max shook his head. "You weren't really hoping to find magic after all these years, were you?"

Gabriel stepped into the house. "No."

He'd read the post-arrest report, which consisted mostly of inventory. The Ministry had carted off Sebastian Blackland's possessions and torn up the carpet and stripped the walls of paint. They'd taken his books and tools and bottles and jars. Anything osteomantic had been sorted and processed and either consumed or taken away to storage. Including Sebastian Blackland's body. Carbon. Calcium. Phosphorus. Potassium and sulfur and sodium and magnesium. Copper, zinc, selenium, molybdenum, fluorine, chlorine, iodine, manganese, cobalt, iron. Trace quantities of lithium, strontium, aluminum, silicon, lead, vanadium, arsenic, and bromine. Also, sint holo, kraken, firedrake, aataxe, abassy, abada. Criosphinx. Hippogriff.

Notably absent from the inventory were the unauthorized weapons he'd been working on, ostensibly the reason for his arrest and summary execution.

Max paced the walls, sniffing. "If you were hoping you'd find Daniel Blackland here, you're going to be disappointed. I could have told you that without even needing to make the trip."

"How's that?"

"I've tracked a lot of fugitives. They don't stay close to home. And they don't come back to places they're associated with. The only thing they want is a hole to hide in or a place to run. Every twenty-four hours they survive with their bones still inside their skin, they're happy."

No, Gabriel thought. Not always. He'd survived a bad night when he was about the same age Daniel must have been on the night of his father's death. He had lost a parent. He'd moved on, learned to survive. But he still couldn't go a night's sleep without smelling freshly spilled magic.

Daniel didn't need to come back here. He'd never really left. Max took this in, his face unreadable. "So what do we do now?"

Gabriel breathed in the stagnant air of a cold trail. "Just our jobs," he said. "Let's just go do our jobs."

A re you fucking my hound?" Gabriel didn't like meetings. He particularly didn't like the kind that consisted mostly of his boss screaming from across his desk with spit-inflected profanity. Watanabe was round of shape with a peculiar pointy head and a face that reddened with anger. He resembled a radish. Like Gabriel, he came from a family of osteomancers, and he'd gained his position in the Ministry by turning in his own parents on the night of the Third Correction. He might have risen even higher had he not run out of relatives to betray.

"No, sir, I'm using Max for an investigation. I filed an NRT-3070—"

But Watanabe didn't want to hear about paperwork. In fact, Gabriel wasn't certain the man could read.

"The hound was supposed to be put down this morning. I went to the kennels myself to supervise. I woke up early for it. And when I got there? No hound."

What kind of man, Gabriel wondered, liked to start his day by watching something die?

Gabriel opened one of the file folders he'd brought with him and placed the sketch of Daniel Blackland on Watanabe's blotter.

"Who's that?"

"Daniel Blackland, son of Sebastian Blackland and Messalina Sigilo."

Watanabe stared at Gabriel as though he were a piece of dry toast.

"Sebastian Blackland was an osteomancer, specializing in munitions," Gabriel pressed on, dauntless. "He was taken in the Third Correction by—"

"Does this have anything to do with my hound? I asked you where my hound is? Are you fucking my hound?"

Gabriel closed his eyes. "No, Minister Watanabe, I am not fucking your hound. As I indicated in the NRT-3070."

"I don't have time for his, Argent. Wilson Bryant is missing a seps head, which you'd know if you weren't so busy fucking my hound."

"If you'll just hear me out—"

But Watanabe didn't want to listen to anything other than his own invective. While he railed at him, Gabriel kept his cool with visions of strapping Watanabe to a rock and letting condors eat his intestines. They were pleasing visions.

Knowing Daniel Blackland remained alive was either a gift or a curse. It was the kind of information a savvy person could manipulate for their own gain. Bring in Sebastian Blackland's son after all these years and you were a hero. It was the kind of knowledge some might kill for, just so they could claim credit themselves. Gabriel had taken a risk, coming to Watanabe with this. Maybe it was a good thing that Watanabe was too stupid to see what Gabriel was trying to give him.

Watanabe caught his breath. He wiped spit from his lips and straightened his tie. "You have until five o'clock to return my hound to the kennels, Inspector Argent. Fail to deliver, and the hound might not be the only thing around here getting a lethal injection."

Gabriel plotted the Hierarch's assassination. The first obstacle was determining his location. He maintained multiple residences: Griffith Observatory, his castle in the Hollywood Hills, a penthouse suite in the Jade Tower downtown, not to mention a royal yacht and several bunkers serviced by the civil defense tunnels he'd built during his war with the United States.

"But assume I could fix him to a single location," Gabriel said, leaning over the city map spread across his desk. He kept his voice low and his office door locked.

Max bit into an apple. In the kennels, hounds were fed a nutritionally balanced slurry. He chewed the apple as though it were the best apple ever to fall off a tree. "You're making a big assumption."

"I know, but just go with it. Say a bodyguard or attendant or, I don't know, a Council member was unhappy enough with his working conditions. Enough to betray his master."

"An insider? Why go through the risk and trouble of contracting an assassin? Why not just kill him yourself?"

"Come on, Max, you know the answer to that."

Max chewed. "Because you'd need someone with enough power to face the Hierarch without getting turned inside out."

"Exactly. So you've got an inside man taking out a contract and giving you necessary intel."

Max wiped juice off his chin with the back of his sleeve. Gabriel's sleeve, actually, since he'd given Max the spare shirt and trousers he kept in his office. Max wore the outfit with no tie and the shirt untucked. He wore it well. Maybe that's what I'd look like if I wasn't always such a tight ass, thought Gabriel.

"You'd still need a different plan for each of his residences," Max said. "That's hundreds of obstacles and hundreds of variables."

"Then we simplify," Gabriel said. "Let's limit the possible sites to one of his bunkers. That's where he probably spends most of his time anyway."

"You're picking the best-guarded, most difficult option."

"Good. If we can work out the most difficult case, then we can certainly work out the easier ones. So, the Hierarch's underground. He's got guard units and surveillance, maybe miles of it. But who cares, because you've got sint holo and you can slink right past it."

Max cocked his head. "I didn't know you could use sint holo."

"Me? Well, I can't, of course," Gabriel said, taken aback. "I'm talking about Daniel Blackland. We're assuming this is what Daniel Blackland might do."

"Oh." Max bit his apple. "Okay. Go on."

"Jesus, Max, did you think I was planning to assassinate the Hierarch? Me?"

"We're locked in your office, contriving a plan to do just that. So, yes, that's what I thought you were planning to do."

"And you were helping me?"

"Why not? I'm overdue for my own execution, anyway."

Gabriel rubbed the bridge of his nose. Knowing Max would actually assist him in planning the worst crime imaginable was both disturbing and interesting.

In fact, Gabriel *had* once planned out the Hierarch's assassination. He'd done it a lot after his mother's death. Never with magic. He always imagined rifles, bombs, garrotes. Then he grew out of it and replaced childish revenge fantasies with hard work and study. Government employees usually lived longer than vengeance-obsessed sons. Government employees had a better chance of getting a pension.

"I'm talking about Daniel Blackland," he said. "He has sint holo. So he can get past the guards and the eyes, right?"

"I can't be the only hound in the kingdom who can nose sint holo. The Hierarch's got to have others like me."

Max was probably right, but Gabriel refused to surrender. "So if you can't maneuver in a guarded place without being seen, you'd have to maneuver in a place where nobody's watching."

He imagined what the defense tunnels might look like, envisioning a network of passageways below the city. Maps of the tunnels—assuming such things existed—had to be among the kingdom's most closely guarded secrets. He traced his finger along his own city map. "What if you could dig your own tunnel?"

"You'd have to do a lot of mining," Max said. "And not just through earth. There'd be concrete, steel, possibly dragon scale."

Gabriel sighed. "Yeah. This is starting to look hard."

Voices from outside drew Gabriel's attention. He couldn't make out words, but one voice rose above the rest, and it sounded angry. Shadowed figures paraded past the frosted glass of his door.

"Is my time up?" Max asked. "Are they coming for me?" He still didn't seem to care much if he lived or died.

"They better not be. I filed all the right paperwork. You just stay here and keep working on our problem while I see what's going on."

Max chewed apple.

"And if anyone asks, we are doing *anything* other than contemplating the death of our leader."

"What leader?" Max said.

"Good . . ."

Gabriel checked himself. He'd almost said, "Good dog."

"Good," he said again, shutting the office door behind him.

The flutter of activity was like a henhouse where a fox had come calling. Heads poked from offices and phones rang and people of all ranks bustled through the hall. Gabriel spotted a pool of calm in the storm: Hazel, one of the old hands in the secretarial pool. She observed the chaos from the water cooler.

He made his way over to her.

"A god walks among us," she said, while a deputy minister roared for someone to find soy milk for the visitor.

"Which one?"

She fanned herself with her hand. "Wilson Bryant."

"The baseball guy?"

"No, you ignorant boy, Wilson Bryant from The Woodies. Do you even listen to music?"

Down at the end of the hall, a retinue of attorneys and entertainment industry functionaries and personal assistants and stoner hangers-on escorted the recording giant to Minister Watanabe's offices. Bryant was a tall man whose hair lacked acquaintance with a comb. His white belly spilled from an unbuttoned Hawaiian shirt. His beard contained multitudes.

"What's his story?"

"Last night someone pulled a B and E at his beach house. He was home at the time, and now he's rather agitated."

"I imagine so. Any good leads?"

"No, he was drugged and has little actual memory of the events. He did say the thieves wore wool faces and one of them was made of bad love."

"Wool faces? Does he mean ski masks?"

Hazel poured Gabriel a paper cup of water and handed it to him. She was always concerned that he keep himself hydrated. "Your guess is as good as anyone's. And I'd say 'made of bad love' implicates my ex-husband, only he's dead."

Gabriel hated working celebrity-god cases almost as much as he hated Watanabe, and he feared his boss would pass Bryant down to him.

"What'd the thieves get?"

"A snake's head," Hazel said. "You know what seps venom is?"

Gabriel reached back to his early days in the Ministry libraries, pouring over Chinese texts and alchemical grimoires. He had to fight for the privilege of reading those volumes, and his simple presence in the reading rooms was enough to make enemies out of licensed osteomancers who didn't understand why an unpowered clerk should have access to their secrets. But he withstood their machinations long enough to gain a familiarity with the osteomantic bestiary as comprehensive as that of any state sorcerer.

"Seps," he said. "Very rare. The venom is one of the most corrosive substances on earth. It can eat through concrete as though it were cheese. It can eat through steel, through . . ."

Gabriel dropped the cup, splashing water on his shoes, and ran back to his office.

"Max—"

The hound was sitting in Gabriel's desk chair, hunched over the city map. "I think I figured out a way he could get to the Hierarch," Max said. "Even if he were deep underground."

"Seps venom." Gabriel was breathless.

Max looked up, pleased and surprised. "That's what I was going to say. What do we do now?"

Gabriel thought of his radishlike boss down the hall. He performed some mental calculations. He didn't mind other people taking credit for his work. But neither did he want to die for the privilege of helping others.

"I think we need a new boss," he said.

TWELVE

A t 12:13 P.M. on a Tuesday lunch hour, Moth peed on a statue. It wasn't just any statue. This was a statue in Burbank of an anthropomorphic mouse, wearing a belted robe and a tall, pointy hat, commanding an army of brooms with which the mouse was cleaning the tiled floor of a gurgling fountain. Moth's urine splashed against the smiling wizard mouse and blended into the water.

Workers on their lunch breaks gaped. A few children giggled. And three cops swarmed on Moth with their cleaver-clubs at the ready. Moth surrendered without resistance and allowed his hands to be cuffed behind his back. He was loaded into a van and taken away.

Daniel, watching from a nearby bench, dropped a decitusk into a pay phone. Cassandra picked up on the other end.

"It's on," Daniel said, and hung up.

By 4:41 P.M. that afternoon, Moth had been booked, charged, and sentenced. At some point a public defender might have been involved. Moth was taken to Century City Plaza, where a permanent scaffold abutted a twenty-five-foot-high wall of yellow limestone and steel-reinforced concrete. This was the Golden Wall, the western border of Beverly Hills. As office workers in suits and ties and skirts streamed from the glass and steel towers to claim their boats from the dockhouses and catch gondola-buses and taxis, Daniel watched marshals lead Moth and two other criminals from a police wagon in chains. The marshals wore the special black uniforms of Justice Dispensation, which came with visored helmets to protect their anonymity.

The prisoners were herded up the scaffold steps and arranged shoulder to shoulder in a line facing the crowd. The scaffold was equipped with a whipping post. There was also a set of iron rings bracketed to the wall, where sometimes prisoners' hands were bound for garroting. A set of nooses dangled from a crossbar.

A marshal with a bullhorn addressed the crowd. She called out the names of the prisoners, as well as their offenses and punishments.

Raul Ortega. Armed robbery. Death by hanging.

Patrice Beaufort. Grand theft larceny. Death by hanging.

Thomas Frasier. Desecration of the people's interest. Death by hanging.

Thomas Frasier was the name on the identification papers Moth carried at the time of his arrest.

Down below, shoes clopped on the pavement as people crossed the plaza, heading home, heading to dinner or to the bars. Some bought empanadas from a cart and went on their way. Some paid attention to what was going on up on the scaffold. One elderly couple held hands and wept. They bore a family resemblance to Raul Ortega, Daniel thought.

The condemned weren't given hoods. There was no priest to hear a confession or give a last rite. The marshals laid the nooses around their necks like garlands and jerked the knots tighter. For Moth, the marshal had to stand on a box.

Daniel liked to think the men and women who performed this task suffered hauntings by merciless ghosts. He liked to think of them screaming from nightmares, or developing habitual tremors and perforated ulcers. He liked to think of them sinking over the course of long lives into miserable graves. He wondered what became of the men who'd dissected his father right before his eyes. He often looked into the ruined faces sleeping in alleys, or under trees in the park. He looked into their sick, undernourished eyes and hoped to recognize one of his father's murderers. And if he did, would he kill that man? Would he torture him? Or would he be satisfied that their entire life was punishment enough?

He never did recognize one of those wings-and-tusks knife men. He feared they lived out quiet lives, seldom thinking about that day.

The drum of heels on the plaza quieted. At the empanada cart, the vendor clutched a customer's change and stared at the scaffold. The weeping couple held each other. With no more ceremony than flushing a toilet, a marshal pulled a lever, and the trapdoors beneath the prisoners' feet swung open, and the prisoners dropped.

The fall was not long enough to break their necks. Instead, they strangled, jerking like landed fish. Moth broke the zip-tie binding his ankles and danced.

Daniel had intended to time the entire hanging, but he'd forgotten to start his watch. He clamped his jaw tight and forced himself to keep watching. When Moth finally grew still, Daniel unclenched his hands. Half-moon cuts in his palms seeped blood.

The bodies were left to custodial staff. They snipped the prisoners' zip-ties and with ropes and pulleys, hoisted the dead to the top of the Golden Wall. There they hung, upside-down from the ankles, like holiday ornaments.

Daniel walked two blocks to a side canal, where Cassandra and Jo waited in a plain white van. Cassandra raised her eyebrows in question, but he just shook his head. He didn't want to talk about it. He settled in the back of the van, leaned against the side panel, and closed his eyes. Images of his father being cut open and Moth jigging on the end of his rope blended in a fevered loop.

At 11:17 P.M., he took up a pair of binoculars and peered out the back window of the van. He watched Moth reach up over his feet and grasp the rope he was dangling from. He climbed hand-over-hand until he was upright and without resting, continued to climb until he reached the wall's summit. He unfastened the loop around his ankles, tossed the rope over the wall, and climbed down the other side. He was now inside Beverly Hills, the Golden City.

Daniel lowered his binoculars.

"We're in."

Daniel led Jo and Cassandra into "Little" Santa Monica, a decommissioned canal that wasn't much more than a muddy trench. Under cover of overgrown willow arroyo, they tromped through mud to a steel door set into the limestone face of the Golden Wall. The door stood twelve feet high and eight feet wide. There was no keyhole, no combo pad, no visible latching mechanism. It could only be opened from the inside, and it had been at least twelve years since anyone had reason to do it. Neglected infrastructure could be a thief's best friend.

A rusty screech set the neighborhood coyotes off into a cascade of howls. With a swirling cloud of desiccated plant particulates and cobwebs, the great door cracked open just enough to allow Daniel and crew to slip through. Once they were in among a nest of high weeds, the door shut, and Jo threw herself on Moth.

"Be professional and curb the goopiness," he rasped. "I'm okay."

A ghastly welt ringed Moth's throat. Daniel raised his eyebrows at him.

"I want another ten percent of the cut," Moth said.

"You can have mine. You got balls of steel, buddy."

"Then they should have hung me by my balls."

Yeah, Moth was okay. Daniel handed him a Department of Water and Power tool bag. Rolled up inside was an XXXL-sized version of the blue-and-gray DWP coveralls Daniel and Cassandra were wearing. Moth nodded his thanks, and fresh guilt lanced Daniel.

Moth had died for him. And now he was saying thanks for being handed something to wear other than the clothes he'd died in.

A light pressure squeezed his arm. Cassandra's touch was so brief he thought he might have imagined it, but then she said,

"Any one of us can bail on this job. There's still time to say fuck it."

Her message wasn't for Jo or Moth. It was for Daniel. They were with him because they chose to be. Every risk, every sacrifice, was by choice. Nobody bailed. They gave this to Daniel freely. It'd never really bothered him before.

"Six hours till sunrise," he said. "Time to hunker down. I'll take first watch."

Los Angeles Police sergeant Hank "Ballpeen" Hammer was a man of habits.

He began his every morning by parking his black-and-white police stiletto in the valet spot in front of Esclusivo on Rodeo. The day manager would come out with a smile glued to her face and hand him a complimentary cappuccino, and Ballpeen would add a slug of something from a steel flask while frisking her with his eyes. He'd haul his lumbering bulk from his boat, and commence his beat on foot, oblivious to the Esclusivo manager's daggerlike glares.

Emma Walker had observed this routine for three consecutive weekdays before fishing his coffee cup from the trash and identifying the contents of his flask: tequila.

Who the hell put tequila in their coffee? It was disgusting and obscene, and it made everyone on the crew feel better about what they were going to do to Sergeant Ballpeen.

Ballpeen maintained his uniform nicely and afforded himself good haircuts. Still, he stood out among the posh like ketchup on a pearl necklace. He enjoyed being conspicuous, blustering down the sidewalks, making solicitous noises at the wealthy patrons and flashing his bully's smile at the shop clerks and prep cooks and janitors.

On Thursday, after the Esclusivo manager handed Ballpeen his cup and smiled her way back into the restaurant, Jo Alverado used a sphinx-key and slipped into the passenger seat of the police boat. Before Ballpeen could react, she blew a strawful of hypnalis dust in his face. She took the cup from his hand before he could drop it and dumped tequila from his own flask all over his sleeping form. She reclined his seat and covered him with his jacket, then stripped off her own overcoat to reveal a loose, black LAPD uniform, identical to Ballpeen's, right down to the badge number.

The uniform inflated as Jo assumed Ballpeen's form. After a quick check of herself in the rearview mirror, she was walking down the sidewalk with Ballpeen's customarily jaunty gait.

Daniel watched all this from a white service van across the canal. He put down his binoculars.

"Onward," he said.

He and Cassandra, Moth, and Emma, whom they'd collected upon arrival, exited the van, all dressed in Department of Water and Power coveralls, complete with official DWP tool bags. They caught up to Ballpeen-Jo at Rodeo and Brighton, and headed north, past the De Beers diamond store, past the Sergé shop, where the mannequins in the window wore nothing but thousand-tusk scarves, and up to a chain-link fence and gate. A green canvas curtain blocked view of everything behind the fence.

Daniel tried to give Jo a look that said, "You're doing great, you're an incredible actress, I'm proud of you, and I know you're going to get us through the next step of the job."

Ballpeen-Jo barely flicked a glance at him. She was in character.

She banged on the gate with her cleaver-club. A chain rattled on the other side, a key turned, and the gate opened on a pink-faced young man in Ministry security blues. One hand rested on his holster. The other held an emery board.

"Hey, sarge," he said, pocketing the emery board. His nails gleamed.

"DeSoto," Ballpeen-Jo growled. "Open up and get out of my way."

DeSoto didn't take Ballpeen-Jo's manner personally. He swung the gate open and stepped aside. Ballpeen-Jo moved past him with the rest of the crew in tow.

The fence enclosed the site of Cross and Carsson's. Customers from the richest enclaves once came here for refined La Brea magic, and for potions and elixirs imported from all over the world. Now, the shop was a fifty-foot-deep crater. Twenty years ago, the owners fell into some kind of tax dispute with the city, and the Hierarch brought down the shop with an earthquake. Nobody knew exactly how he'd done it. Possibly he'd used namazu, the gargantuan catfish. Maybe Jinshin-Mushi beetle. More likely, Daniel thought, he'd simply declared the area a disaster zone and ordered his police to shut down the neighborhood while a crew bulldozed the shop. You could get away with that sort of thing when you controlled all the newspapers and radio and TV stations. Daniel supposed the power to control what people believed was its own kind of magic.

"These guys are DWP inspectors," Ballpeen-Jo barked at Officer DeSoto. "They need to do some work here."

Emma had a clipboard with official-looking paperwork, and she made a point of not bothering to show it to DeSoto.

Daniel was satisfied with how nervous DeSoto had grown. There were many powers in Los Angeles—the Council, the Ministry, LAPD—but none held a jurisdiction as nebulous as the Department of Water and Power. They fell under William Mulholland, and if the Hierarch was the kingdom's number one, then the ancient water mage was number two. Maybe even one-A. Four DWP workers and one corrupt police sergeant versus one cop? Daniel liked the odds.

"Take a hike, DeSoto."

"I'm not supposed to leave my post, sarge."

He wasn't weak. He was fed a diet of ground cerberus wolf and could see without light. He was as fast as a greyhound. He could pulverize a brick in his left hand. And he wasn't surrendering.

"Do him," Daniel said.

Cassandra squeezed the trigger of her gun, and a narcotic dart struck DeSoto's neck. He raised his hand, as if to pontificate on some important point, and then collapsed in the dirt. Moth collected him and stuffed him inside the portable toilet, where he would finish out his shift.

Daniel let himself breathe.

"Good job, Ballpeen," he said.

"Enh," Jo said, always her own harshest critic. "He wasn't very intimidated."

"What about me?" Emma asked, securing a loose wisp of hair back in her bun. "How was I?"

"You haven't made a fatal mistake yet," Daniel allowed.

They picked their way down the sloping wall of the crater, careful not to slip in the loose dirt. At the bottom, Daniel kicked away a layer of earth and revealed a piece of what Officer DeSoto was there to guard: a solid slab of concrete roughly the area of a two-boat dockhouse.

The crew donned goggles and filter masks. From his DWP toolkit, Daniel removed a carved-bone vial.

"Stand farther back, guys," he said, voice muffled by his mask. "Seriously, you don't want to be in the splash zone."

He unstoppered the vial and let its contents dribble onto the slab, then leaped back to stand with his crew. Tendrils of seps vapor curled in the air. The surface of the concrete sizzled like hot grease, and a web of cracks formed, accompanied by the sounds of breaking molars. The concrete flaked away and fell like snow down a manhole-sized gap.

"Cowabunga," said Cassandra, impressed.

Daniel grinned. He liked impressing her.

"'All my being,'" Emma whispered, "'like him whom the Numidian seps did thaw into a dew with poison, is dissolved, sinking through its foundations.'"

"That's from a poem," she said with some despair to the crew's stupefied expressions.

"Yeah, Shelley," Moth said. "It's just we usually don't do poetry during jobs."

When the concrete stopped bubbling and the cracking sounds dwindled, Daniel tiptoed to the edge of the void and aimed his flashlight into the darkness. The beam revealed a shattered floor of white and black checkerboard marble, about twenty feet below.

At Daniel's go-ahead signal, Moth dropped one end of a

chain ladder into the hole and hooked the other end over the edge of the pit. Daniel climbed down.

He did a flashlight sweep of the vault when his toes touched the floor. It was a dusty space, not much larger than his tiny apartment. A round vault door dominated one wall. Cross and Carsson's used to receive deliveries directly to this vault from the Ossuary's distribution annex. It had been a very secure system, safe from aboveground armored boat robberies. But everything of value was stripped from the shop when the Hierarch shut it down. Only the vault door remained.

Daniel flashed the light three times up the hole to signal the others to come down.

In the Golden City, standing before the vault door. Step one of the Ossuary Job, done.

Cassandra commenced step two.

With a flashlight and jeweler's loupe, she examined the towering slab of Colombian dragon scale like a mother counting her newborn's fingers and toes. A labyrinth of hair-thin grooves was etched into the vault door's surface.

She turned to Daniel. "Sphinx riddle?"

Daniel put his nose up to the door. He smelled the scent of whispering sand, blown by hot desert wind. "Yeah."

They both took a step back and sighed.

"What's the problem?" Moth asked, stretching out his calves. "I thought we stole the seps venom so we could burn through shit like this."

That was the idea. But the grooves were impregnated with sphinx oil, and sphinx was the substance of riddle. Fail to solve the riddle, and the dragon scale might explode and impale the crew with thousands of shards, or topple over and crush them like bugs, or vaporize into a cloud of poison.

"Sphinx makes it more complicated," Daniel said. "It's kind of an impenetrable wall, plus a death trap."

"That Emma completely failed to warn us about," added Jo. "I thought she was supposed to be our inside man." Jo had shifted back to her own face and body and was shedding her cop's uniform, down to a black T-shirt and pants. The look on her face was deceptively dangerous, like someone attending to a few last-minute matters before committing a murder.

"You know I've never been on this side of the door," Emma said to Daniel. "I'll be of more use to you once we're in." She gave a winsome smile and crossed her heart. "I promise."

"Wouldn't be a good heist without some surprise hurdles," Daniel said to Jo. "And if it turns out you're lying, Emma, I'll electrocute you until your eyes melt."

Emma took this in with silent equanimity.

Cassandra continued to study the grooves.

"What do you think?" Daniel asked. He didn't like to rush her, but if she couldn't get through the door, the job was off, and the sooner they knew that, the sooner they could get out of here and limit their losses.

Cassandra smiled in the dark. "Rich people's things are so adorable. I'm going to need my ears."

She tilted her head to the side, and Daniel brushed a few stray strands of hair away from her ear and leaned in close. He smelled her clean-sweat scent and became very conscious of his own breathing, and of his heartbeat. He'd kind of forgotten about this part of working with Cassandra. He was supposed to be the leader of professionals and Cassandra was the most professional among them, and they didn't sleep together anymore, and, anyway, she probably didn't like him literally breathing down her neck.

He squeezed three drops of fachen oil in her ear, then the other.

"I need everyone to shut up now," she said.

Ear pressed to the scale, Cassandra ran a glass key over the grooves, using it like a phonograph needle to coax out the sphinx's voice. She followed the grooves along their intricate routes, backing up, pausing, starting again, and Daniel didn't realize he'd been holding his breath until Cassandra finally held the key aloft like a sword, as if she'd just slain a dragon.

Whispers rose in the vault, at first a soft chorus of sighs, of things coming awake after long sleep, and they grew louder and more distinct. The voices resolved into language, seducing and taunting with their riddle.

Some kind of Afro-Asiatic tongue, but not one Daniel understood. Fortunately, Cassandra did.

"'Who is the great one that glides over earth?'" she said, translating. "'Who swallows both waters and wood? The wind he fears, but creatures he does not, and he seeks to kill the sun.'"

She uttered a word in the sphinx's language, and the voices drained away like water.

"The answer was fog?" Emma asked.

"How did you know?" said Cassandra, surprised. She inserted foam plugs in her ears to muffle uncomfortable noise until the eardrops wore off.

"I'm not just a pretty face, dear."

The next part of the job, burning through the dragon scale with the stolen snake venom, would be fairly mechanical. This was the kind of magic Daniel liked. No guards to get past with shape-shifting and social engineering, no traps set with pseudo-sentient oils. Just osteomancy and small explosives. As he set venom charges around the door, the familiar pleasure of being somewhere he was not supposed to be and doing things he was not supposed to do returned. He was still having fun.

THIRTEEN

Gabriel cooled his heels in Fenmont Szu's fifty-fifth-floor reception hall and tried to calm himself with math.

In a glass case, four hundred tri-faced cerberus wolf skulls rested on shelves, silhouetted in orange backlight. An osteomancer could cook night vision out of a skull, or speed, or acute smell, or predatory instinct, and skulls like these were responsible for the lethality of Los Angeles's Strategic Magic Assault Command squad. Each skull was as valuable as a Fabergé egg. To maintain maximum effectiveness, a SMAC team member required half a gram of cooked skull a day. Take the magic yield of each skull, multiply by the number of skulls in the Hierarch's stores, divide by the number of cops on the SMAC team . . . So that was about thirty-seven days of operation.

Once the skull supply was used up, Fenmont Szu would still have a few options. He could import skull from his Mexican and Asian trade partners. He could convince the Hierarch to go to war with Northern California in hopes of claiming their stocks as his spoils. Or, he could cannibalize his SMAC team veterans, leeching cerberus wolf residue from their bones and feeding it to younger men and women. Gabriel suspected this tactic was already in play.

"Are you sure I can't get you anything, Inspector Argent?"

The receptionist glared at Gabriel from behind the mahogany plateau of his desk. He was a man of about fifty with a nose sharp enough to use as a letter opener. Behind him, guarding Fenmont Szu's inner sanctum, stood six guards with manticore lances.

"Thank you," Gabriel said. "I'm fine."

"Perhaps you'd like to walk your hound? The courtyard is rather spacious . . ."

"Do you need air, Max?"

Seated beside him on a leather couch, Max flipped through a *Sunset* magazine. On the cover, a glass and stone Palm Springs palace stood against painfully blue sky and sharp rocks.

"There's air in here. It's what I'm breathing."

"Thank you, we're fine."

A full half hour later, someone finally emerged from the room guarded by the manticore lances. Max's head snapped up from his magazine. His nostrils twitched. To him, Fenmont Szu must absolutely reek of magic.

Back at Griffith Observatory, standing on the balcony to honor the Hierarch, Fenmont Szu had seemed a demonic presence. Closer up, he was more human, but still intimidating, with a tan face as hard and smooth as driftwood. His black business suit drank light.

Szu regarded Max with cold curiosity and then turned a smile on Gabriel.

"I'm so sorry to keep you waiting, Inspector Argent."

"I'm grateful you could see me at all. And I apologize for not going through customary channels, but my business is urgent."

"Why don't you come with me?"

Gabriel gathered the few file folders he'd brought with him. "Max, will you be all right here for a while?"

Max flipped a page. "I know how to stay."

Gabriel followed Szu into the dark regions beyond the reception hall. A wood-paneled hallway was lined with oil paintings of Los Angeles's early glamour mages: Loew, Mayer, Selznick, Chaplin. The portraits were the equivalent of mounted heads in a hunting lodge. He wondered who'd fed on Chaplin.

Szu installed Daniel in a library-sitting room, cool and dark despite a broad sweep of windows. Outside, beyond the neighboring office towers, the snowcapped San Gabriel mountains looked like a matte painting on this rare clear day. Gabriel had been named for those mountains. His parents had loved hiking in the pines and staying in the lodges. He had a very dim memory of a spacious log cabin with a crackling fire, and a white-gloved butler carving a roast at the table. The lodges were gone now, the mountains declared off-limits for reasons unknown, and Gabriel's mother had been killed, butchered, processed, and her osteomantic essence reallocated.

"How can I help you today, inspector?"

"Ordinarily I wouldn't bother a Council member with something like this, but my boss—"

"Minister Watanabe. He reports to my brother on the Council, the Alejandro."

"Yes. I haven't been getting very far with Minister Watanabe lately. I'm in his doghouse."

"I'm familiar with Watanabe," said Szu. "He's not the sort of man who would work for me. So I understand that you might, on occasion, need to maneuver around him for important matters. Is this an important matter, inspector?" Szu's teeth showed the rich brown of La Brea magic.

"I'm tracking a fugitive." He showed Szu the sketch of Daniel Blackland.

Szu reached out and examined it.

"Should I know this person?" he asked after a time.

"No, sir, but you would have known his mother, Messalina Sigilo. And his father, Sebastian Blackland."

Szu's lips parted. "Their son—"

"Daniel. Daniel Blackland."

"—is dead. Shot, when his mother defected to the northern kingdom."

"No," said Gabriel.

"There was a body. It was recovered from the North and examined."

"Here, in Los Angeles? By qualified experts? Or just by field agents?"

Szu considered the sketch. "Tell me what you know."

Gabriel told him everything, starting with his chance encounter with the handler and nervous hound in the kennels, and his search with Max of Farmers Market, and of the sint holo, and the theft of the seps serpent from Wilson Bryant's house.

"Neither Farmers Market nor Wilson Bryant's house are your jurisdiction, are they?"

"No, sir."

Szu looked pleased, as if he'd tasted something agreeable.

"You don't have a reputation as a particularly ambitious man, Inspector Argent."

Gabriel bristled. He knew what happened to the ambitious. Some rose to great heights, like Fenmont Szu, who'd attained his position by challenging other osteomancers, killing them, and eating their remains. Other fates awaited the ambitious but less successful. They could end up ground to powder and smoked in the Hierarch's pipe.

"Sint holo for stealth," Gabriel said. "Seps venom to burn through barriers. And the son of a potent osteomancer who's been clever enough to operate for a decade without us even knowing he's alive. Put it all together, and it adds up to a serious security threat."

Szu surveyed Gabriel's face with a long, cool stare.

"A security threat to what, precisely?"

"To the Hierarch, sir. I believe he intends to assassinate the Hierarch."

Szu regarded the sketch of Daniel Blackland, turning his head sideways as if trying to understand a piece of modern art.

"That's a broad leap."

Gabriel swallowed. This is where things would get sticky.

"It's what I would do if I were him, Councilor Szu."

This got no reaction from Szu, which was somehow worse than the one Gabriel was expecting.

Gabriel threw himsef into the void. "As I'm sure you know, my mother was an osteomancer. And she was taken in the Third Correction. It was hard. She was my mother, Councilor Szu. If she'd imparted powers to me, if she'd trained me to be an osteomancer . . . fed me like an osteomancer . . . I'd be a different man today. I'd be Daniel Blackland."

"And you would . . . ?"

"I'd want to eat the Hierarch's skull, sir."

"I see. Yes, of course."

"If I could just have access to some resources . . . some uniforms who don't answer to Minister Watanabe, some hounds . . ."

Szu stood. "Thank you for bringing this matter to my attention. I will confer with my brothers and sisters on the Council to see how best to proceed, but don't worry, your involvement is inescapable."

"And if I could get some schematics of the catacombs and Ossuary, I might be able to predict where Blackland will attempt his breach—"

"You'll have everything you'll need. I'll see to it personally. We'll be in touch."

Szu offered his hand. Gabriel took it. He could almost feel the power vibrating in Szu's grip.

"Inspector Argent, you took a great risk to give me insight into Mr. Blackland's psychology. Please rest assured, your service to the Hierarch is appreciated. I will make sure he knows."

That did not make Gabriel feel good at all.

He gathered his file folders and retreated, tracing his way back through the hallway of dead glamour mage trophies, and into the reception hall.

"They're fake, you know," Max said, when Gabriel rejoined him.

"What's fake?"

Max pointed at the skulls in the glass case. "The wolves. They're made of plaster. For show. They're fake."

On the elevator ride down, Gabriel recalculated the life expectancy of a SMAC team veteran. Bloody days ahead.

———

The parking garage was a warm, moist place. Reflections from fluorescent lights wriggled in the black waters. A valet ran off to fetch Gabriel's boat.

"How did your meeting go?" asked Max.

"I think I gave Fenmont Szu a nice prize to bring his master. He'll be rewarded. Not sure how. When you're already at Councilor Szu's level, I don't know what else he could want, besides the crown."

"What about you? What do you get out of it?"

"Maybe they'll throw me a bone. That's not what I came for. I discovered a security threat, and I brought it to the attention of people who have the power to deal with it. I'm satisfied."

Max scratched an itch behind his ear as the valet pulled up with Gabriel's boat. "You're not very ambitious."

"Thank you."

Gabriel reached for the ignition and Max grabbed his wrist.

There was a frantic, angry look in the hound's eyes. His lips curled back in a grimace, showing his white teeth. Gabriel had just told the hound that they were likely off the Blackland case, which meant Gabriel didn't have any more use for him, which meant Max would be going back to the kennels, which meant he'd be tranquilized and strapped down to a steel table and injected with lethal toxins, for the crime of killing his master.

"Max, I—"

"Get out of the boat."

Max didn't wait for Gabriel to comply. He grabbed Gabriel by his shirtfront and pulled him out of his seat. Gabriel's hands scrabbled over Max's face, his nails raking across his nose. He'd never been a fighter, but he could gouge out an eye as well as anybody. His fingers ended up in Max's mouth, and Max bit down as he hauled Gabriel out the passenger side. They dropped into the water, and before Gabriel could scream or grab a breath, the hound dragged him below. By now, Gabriel knew what was going to happen. If Max was going to kill him, he could have done it in the boat. The wild expression on his face hadn't been murderous rage. It had been terror.

Gabriel broke free of Max's grip so they could both swim unencumbered. With a muffled boom, a pressure wave smashed into him.

Gabriel's head cracked against the dockhouse canal bottom. A flood of water polluted with diesel fuel and motor oil filled his mouth and throat. Blood clouded from his nose. Disoriented, he turned his body until his stinging eyes sighted the surface. Fragments of his boat swirled in the bubbling water. A roiling carpet of flame bloomed above.

Fingers wrapped themselves around Gabriel's ankle. He didn't fight them, but let Max's powerful strokes tow him beyond the flaming gasoline and oil above, and back to the surface. Gabriel coughed and choked. Between gasping spasms, he managed to suck down small gulps of hot, bitter air.

"Firedrake bomb," Max said in his ear. "Smelled it just before it detonated." His face was blackened with canal sludge. A gash over his eye bled.

"Out," Gabriel managed to croak. "Get us out."

Max snatched hold of Gabriel's jacket collar. He swam through billowing smoke and raining water from the fire suppression system until they reached the boathouse exit. Gabriel forced himself up the iron rungs of a maintenance ladder, up to the sidewalk, where he refused the help from a few passersby. He and Max jumped into the boat of a gawking taxi driver, and Gabriel dug out his ruined wallet and shoved a wad of bills at the driver. The money was soaked and it stank of fuel and oil and firedrake, but it was money, and the taxi driver made it vanish.

"Where to?" the driver said, already pulling into traffic. Sirens wailed in the distance.

Fenmont Szu had tried to kill him. Why? Because he'd admitted he'd wanted to kill the Hierarch when he was ten years old? That didn't add up. And Szu didn't have time to rig a bomb between Gabriel's admission and when the bomb went off, anyway. No, Szu or someone else must have planned to kill Gabriel even before Gabriel came here.

So, Gabriel wasn't supposed to know about Daniel Blackland, then. Why not?

"Where to?" the taxi driver repeated.

Gabriel didn't have an answer, but he'd find one.

FOURTEEN

A broad arch of jagged stone towered over Daniel and crew like a mouth of broken teeth. Daniel aimed his flashlight down a long passageway. Odors of patient vigilance told him he'd come to the right place. Daniel couldn't see them, but there were eyes in the walls. They looked for intruders, and they never blinked.

Cassandra unpacked the pieces of her rifle and screwed the barrel into the action.

"One hell of a circus shot," Jo said skeptically.

"Well, Cassie's one hell of a clown," Daniel returned.

"Bet you a taco she doesn't make it."

"Bet you two tacos she does."

Ignoring them, Cassandra attached a reel of galvanized steel cable to the rifle. She affixed a disc the size of a poker chip to the end of the cable and smeared it with epoxy from a tube.

"Okay, Moth," she said. "Hoist me up."

Moth kissed her on the cheek for luck and let her climb on his shoulders. Then he rose to his full height, providing her with a tall but ungainly sniper's nest.

The things I make my friends do, Daniel thought. But if Cassandra had any misgivings, she wasn't showing them. Instead, she peered down at Jo.

"I'm getting all the tacos."

She braced the rifle against her shoulder and clicked on her targeting laser. A filament of green light penetrated the dark and made a spot some four hundred feet away.

"Steady?" Cassie asked Moth.

"Like a rock," he said, and Daniel felt a wave of affection wash over him. Moth was a self-mutilating, self-regenerating half-mad man, but he would hold Cassie as still as a granite mountain. And Cassandra, without the benefit of magical assistance, was about to make a ridiculous shot. Daniel would have bet a thousand tacos on it.

She licked her lips. "Take a breath," she said, and when Moth did, she squeezed the trigger. The cable shot out, and the sound of the disc hitting its target reported back with a dull *spack*. Still perched on Moth's shoulders, she glued a hook to the arch above her head, detached the reel from the gun, and connected the cable to the hook. Then she affixed a second reel to her rifle, Moth took a couple of steps to the side, and she shot out another cable. Two parallel cables stretched down the corridor, spaced three feet apart, taut as guitar strings.

From a pocket, Cassie produced a folded square of Mylar. She hooked it on to one of the cables and let it unfold. The bottom edge was lined with lead weights, making the Mylar curtain hang flat. It was a perfect mirror surface. She hooked another curtain to the second cable, and then Moth finally let her down.

Grabbing rods sewn onto the leading edge of each curtain, Daniel stepped out, pushing the curtains forward to extend them. Together, he and his crew progressed between the curtains down the corridor.

The Hyakume was a beast made of eyes. Three dozen vat-grown eyes were planted into sockets in the wall, wired through optic nerves to a security station housed deep in the catacombs. The eyes kept a constant vigil, staring straight ahead. They had no lids to blink. As a surveillance system, they were almost perfect. But they were stupid, mesmerized by their own mirror reflections in the Mylar, and as the crew walked the mirror curtain down the corridor, the eyes saw only themselves.

Once the crew made it to the end of the corridor, Jo handed Cassie a white paper bag. She peered inside.

"Oh my god. I don't believe it." Cassandra showed the contents of the bag to Daniel. "She actually brought tacos."

"I didn't think Daniel would plan a lunch break, so I came prepared."

Emma raised a disapproving eyebrow. "Really? Tacos? Now? You're what Otis calls the finest thieves in his employ?"

"We're not in Otis's employ." But Daniel confiscated the bag and stuffed it in his backpack. "For later."

Armed with friends and a sack of tacos, he led his crew into the shadows.

They paddled an inflatable raft through a tunnel of bone. The ceiling was a basket weave of human ribs and ulnas and tibias, the gaps joined by smaller wrist and hand and foot bones, the remains of thousands of dead. This was merely one surviving tunnel of what used to be miles of them. In more prosperous times, before Daniel's father was born, the underground was an amusement park for the kingdom's elite. The banquet halls and movie palaces and playhouses were built in spaces excavated by the Hierarch's magic, and eventually brought down by the Hierarch's earthquakes. Except for this one last canal, which had served as a kind of elaborate dumbwaiter between the private offices of the catacombs and the Beverly Hills delivery annex.

"Can I ask a sensitive question?" Moth said, drawing his paddle through the ink-dark water. "Who did all these bones belong to?"

At the raft's prow, Emma peered ahead, into the darkness. "Not everything in Los Angeles was built on magic alone. Some of it was built with slaves. With prisoners of war. They built the tunnels with their own bones."

The sounds of traffic and pump works above filled the darkness with a low, eerie rumble, like the hushed conversations of giants. There were still three miles to go before the cistern and the workshops, and then the Ossuary itself. That's when things would get difficult.

Emma deserved credit for getting them this far. She'd provided the map and identified alarms and surveillance for Cassandra to disable with screwdrivers and magnets and wire cutters. But Emma's reliability only made Daniel more uneasy. He didn't like being dependent on her.

They passed into a chamber. Ragged and moldy tapestries hung like cobwebs before walls plated with scapulas. Femurs, arranged in fluted columns, soared to a domed ceiling, the remains of boys from Sacramento and San Francisco and Fort Bragg, and Kansas and Nebraska and New York and Connecticut, and Chumash and Cupeño and Mohave Indians from

California, and all the enemy captures from the Hierarch's wars. Places like this were where the Hierarch flung his toothpicks.

Daniel dug his paddle into the water. "Faster," he said.

In an hour, the raft bumped against the bricked-up wall at the canal's terminus. Beyond this point was another world, the occupied catacombs beneath the Ministry of Osteomancy headquarters. There would be experimental workshops and storehouses and offices and restrooms and a cafeteria for the workers. There would be alarms and surveillance and live guards. There would be employees.

Emma turned around in the raft and regarded Daniel. "If you're having second thoughts, now would be a good time to abort."

"Anyone?" Daniel said.

"Was having second thoughts part of the plan?" Moth said.

"I don't recall," Jo said. "There were some shitting-in-our-pants parts of the plan, but not second thoughts."

Daniel laughed. "Cassie?"

"I have second thoughts every minute I hang around you guys. But I'm good to go."

"Okay," Daniel said. "Let's Jacques Cousteau this shit."

Swimming was glorious. Daniel knifed through the water, thirty feet down to the bottom of the ruined pump works. Beneath dolphin-smooth skin, a layer of fat kept him warm, and the only thing dragging him down was the pack looped around his waist, containing his gear and clothes. He could barely see through the dark and murk, even with a miner's lamp strapped to his head, but he could detect the location and movements of his crew, as if the contraction of their muscles sent electrical signals to some new part of his brain. He hadn't changed shape, but the essences of sea creatures were strong enough to make him feel as though he had.

They reached a monstrous nest of pipes and valves. Twisted rebar reached from a pile of debris like the tendrils of some great, frozen anemone. A fur of algae coated everything. The crew spread out, searching for the portal Emma said was down here. Jo flashed her headlamp twice, and they swam over to see what she'd discovered: a circular grate the size of a manhole in the terminating wall.

Moth and Cassandra unpacked their handsaws, impregnated with firedrake-scale dust. They went at the grate, the screech of their saws bounding off the walls. After several minutes, they cut through the last bar and let the grate rest in the muck. Daniel took the lead, swimming into the gloom. If Emma's map was accurate, the tunnel ran twenty yards before ending at the bottom of the cistern.

Pressure squeezed his chest. Troubling aches built up in his legs. He checked his watch. They'd been underwater almost sixteen minutes, and his lungs were remembering they liked air. In a little while, they'd be screaming reminders at him.

He sensed movement ahead. Emma had said to expect carp or catfish. And she'd cautioned that down here in the dark, with traces of osteomantic residue at the bottom, the fish may come in odd forms.

Daniel turned to signal a warning with his headlamp when blades came down in front of his face.

His first thought was he'd run into a bear trap big enough

to take off his head. Scrambling to get away, he caught sight of teeth in the narrow beam of his light, incisors the size of pizza slices, and empty eye sockets in a skull three feet across. What the hell was this? Some kind of big, fucked-up, osteomantic coelacanth?

He pulled his leg back, not quick enough. The fish had him. Its teeth tore into his calf and shin, all the way to bone. It thrashed, jerking him around like a dog with a chew toy. The water turned red. With a dull crack, his knee popped out of its socket, and the air rushed out of his lungs in an explosion of bubbles and a gargled scream. He reached for his headlamp, hoping to signal his crew to turn and swim away, but the lamp wasn't there.

His only hope was to kraken-shock the fish, and his fingers were already tingling when sense took hold through the pain. He remembered he was underwater. Releasing electricity might stop the fish, but conducted through water, it would also electrocute his friends.

The fish jerked its head, teeth still grinding down on Daniel's leg. His vision tunneled, and he ran down his options, and the only one that promised any hope of success was to stop struggling. Maybe while the fish was busy eating him, his friends could escape. This was a dismal plan and it probably wouldn't work, because his friends would never leave him. They would stay with him underwater, even if it meant drowning. They loved him.

Something sliced through the water near his face, cutting a trail of bubbles. Moth's arm came down, swinging a length of rebar. Moth struck the side of the fish's skull and it cracked like a dinner plate. Another blow, and shards of bone separated and fell amid the storm of blood and bubbles. Half the fish's upper jaw and a dozen teeth were still embedded in Daniel's leg, but he was free.

He fluttered away, and the fish opted not to pursue. Instead, it turned toward bigger prey: Moth.

Daniel kicked to reverse course and intercept the fish before it could get to him, but he was too sluggish. Fast as a spear from a gun, the fish fell upon Moth. Again and again Moth hammered the fish's teeth with his rebar, shattering several of them with each blow, but the fish was undeterred. It lifted its head upward, raising its remaining teeth high like the knives of a dozen assassins.

The fish brought its jaw down, and six-inch teeth sank into Moth's neck and back. He trailed blood like a cape as he slowly sank.

Bursts of orange light fired all around Daniel, and he braced for an attack from a new source, but the light came from calcium flares lit by Cassie and the others. Cassie had already assembled her cable gun and was taking aim. She fired, and a hook on the end of steel cable whizzed over Daniel's head to strike the fish in the spine. Half a dozen vertebrae cracked apart into nuggets, but even damaged, the fish zeroed in on her.

With awkward flicks of its tail, it moved slower now, but it still gained on Cassie as she swam away. She dropped the cable-reel gun and scrabbled in her pack for something to help her, but she had nothing useful against the fish.

Jo and Emma converged on her, trying to pull her from the fish's path, or distract the fish, but they were getting tangled up with each other, like a giant bait ball.

Daniel held perfectly still. He closed his eyes and examined his cells. He looked even deeper down, to the cells that were in the process of reverting to their customary, human configurations. He was an osteomancer. His father had altered him and trained him to be a vessel for magic. Osteomancy wasn't just a family of drugs that gave him new abilities for a short period of time. Osteomancy was his fuel, his building material, a force that he could master.

The panlong was a water dragon, sleek and smooth and graceful. Kolowisi, from fossils excavated from the bottom of the Rio Grande, was a creature of the black depths, honored by the Zuni Pueblo. The essence of bagil, smuggled from the Northern Kingdom, lent the speed and ferocity of the great crocodilian creature.

Daniel had blended these elements for underwater swimming. Now, he drew upon their full power.

He surged forward with a speed that should not have been possible with the anatomical structure of his legs. His teeth were still the small, pebbly things evolved to chew soft meat and plants. His fingers were still delicate instruments evolved for tool use. But osteomancy transcended his physical form. He reached the fish and grabbed hold of its spine. He twisted, and its bones shattered with the sound of snapping wood boards. The fish turned toward him, opened its great mouth wide, and Daniel thrust his hands into the its eye sockets and ripped its skull apart as if tearing a loaf of bread in half.

In just a few seconds, he'd broken the fish into a puzzle of bone fragments that sank into the murk.

As the last of the sea creature magic faded, his leg thundered with pain. He opened his mouth in a silent scream, and his starved lungs threatened to burst through his rib cage.

But in the glow of the calcium flares, he saw the faces of his crew.

They were okay.

Things would be okay.

The job was still going okay.

He broke the surface in a stone-vaulted cistern, heaving for breath. Dripping water echoed through the vast space of pillars and shadows.

Moth dragged him onto a floor of ice-cold stones.

"You're hurt," Emma said.

"What gave it away?" Daniel gasped. "Was it all the blood?"

"Your face is the color of cottage cheese." She looked down her nose at the rivulets of blood streaming from his leg and *tsk*ed. "Well. What are we to do about this?"

"Move," Cassandra said, shoving Emma aside. Daniel could tell by the look on her face that it was bad.

"Everyone else okay? Moth?"

Moth peeled off his shirt. He held it up, displaying huge puncture holes. "Lost a lot of blood and tore a couple of nerves. Five minutes and I'll be fine."

"Daniel," Cassandra said, and then she stopped talking.

"Can you see muscle?"

"I can see bone."

"Oh, come on."

"Okay, not a lot of bone." She unpacked her medical kit.

"Just bandages," Daniel said. "No hydra."

"You need the hydra."

Hydra regenerative could stop bleeding and speed tissue regeneration, and even though Daniel had cooked every last ounce of it from the bones in Otis's stores, it wasn't enough to fill a perfume sample bottle.

"Save it for later, in case we need it," he said. "Just bandages."

. Ignoring him, Cassandra daubed a few drops of the white oil onto a gauze pad. "You can give me orders as soon as I'm no longer looking at your exposed tibia. Until then, shut up."

Daniel surrendered, because he knew she was right. In the water, drawing on the magic of the sea creatures, he could swim. On land, he was crippled.

He bit back screams as she wound bandages around his calf. After a few minutes, the pain receded to a cool tingling. The hydra regen coursed through Daniel's blood, filling him with warmth and well-being. He accepted Cassandra's hand and got to his feet. Gingerly, he put a little weight on his leg. He felt like he could kick a soccer ball to scraps.

"So the competence-porn part of this job has clearly come to an end," he said. "Which means we're officially underway. Next phase. Jo, make your face."

They all stripped out of their wetsuits and back into dry clothes. Jo changed into the midnight-blue uniform of a catacombs guard. Daniel held a mirror for her as she molded her face into a new configuration. Pressing her hands against her cheeks, she flattened and widened them. She hooked two fingers into her right eye socket and grunted softly as she pulled it an eighth of an inch to the right, and again as she pulled her left eye in the other direction. She spread her front teeth apart to form a gap. While she reshaped her face, she expanded her belly and broadened her shoulders and lengthened her arm and leg bones. Her hair shortened and curled. Her skin flushed and then paled, finally settling to a freckled, olive tone. Wiping sweat from her forehead, she donned a baseball cap with guard insignia, and she was someone else.

"Break a leg, kid," Daniel said, kissing her stubbled cheek.

"Thought you already did that."

They rounded the walkway bordering the cistern and hunkered in the shadows against the wall. On the other side of an arch, a guard paced back and forth. She was a small, slight woman, but Daniel could smell short-faced bear sweating from her pores. In terms of strength and ferocity, she was a monster.

Jo gave Daniel a thumbs-up, removed a handkerchief from her pocket, and crossed the archway, into the chamber beyond.

Daniel chewed his lip. He would only be able to hear and smell what happened next.

"Sir?" the guard said, startled.

Jo blew her nose into the handkerchief. "How's the watch, Tomasi?" She made her voice thick and gravelly. Emma had been able to get a photo of the guard captain Jo was impersonating, but not a voice recording. The common-cold trick was one of Jo's standbys.

"Nothing to report, sir," Tomasi said.

A *harrumph* from Jo. "You heard about the situation with your relief?"

"No, sir."

"He failed his inspection. He won't be relieving you."

"I can stand his watch, sir. It's no problem." Tomasi sounded so jaunty and happy. Anything for Team Hierarch.

"I don't think you're understanding me. He won't be making tomorrow night's shift, either. Or the night after that. He won't be making his shift for a long, long time. He failed his inspection."

"Oh."

"Oh?"

"I mean . . . Oh, *sir*."

"That's marginally better. I've had to shuffle personnel all over the catacombs. I need you in Annex B, third level."

"Isn't that a restroom?"

"I'm sorry, is that beneath you? I think you'll find many guards would be happy to stand watch at a restroom. I think your relief would be happy to stand watch there. I think he'd be happy if he ever stood again."

Daniel could practically hear Tomasi's lips moving as she worked it out.

"Of course . . . I didn't mean . . . When do I report, sir?"

"Immediately. I'll cover your watch here."

"Yes, sir. Thank you, sir."

A few echoing footsteps as Tomasi headed off.

"Tomasi!"

"Sir?"

"Your keys. You won't be needing them in Annex B."

The jingling of metal. "Should I sign them over?"

"I'll take care of the key roster. Report to your watch. And while you're up there, you may want to review procedures and protocols before *your* inspection."

"Yes, sir. I will, sir. Thank you, sir."

A tense silence, and then footsteps again as Tomasi retreated with haste.

Daniel waited a full minute in the shadows with the others until Jo whistled the all-clear.

She beamed as Daniel hugged her.

The morgue was constructed of stone, mortar, and human bone. Steel cabinets, with drawers large enough to contain bodies, were built into the walls. There were hundreds of them.

"Welcome to one of our kingdom's dirty little secrets," Emma said, her breath fogging the air.

This was where dead magic users were warehoused. Not the osteomancers, or even high-level consumers, but just average users with trace amounts of osteomancy in their systems. Some were homeless, scooped up off the streets. Others died in clinics and hospitals. Some were dug out of their graves. From here, they were transferred to the catacombs' leeching workshops, and once all remaining osteomancy was reclaimed, the bodies were incinerated.

Emma changed from soft-tread boots into heels and threw on a long lab coat. Meanwhile, Jo changed outfits again, this time into the plain gray coveralls of a catacombs worker. She gave no thought to modesty. "An actor doesn't fear exposure," was one of her favorite sayings. Daniel suspected she simply enjoyed exhibitionism.

More modest than Jo, Moth used a blanket for cover as he stripped out of his clothes and lay back naked on a gurney. The metal joints creaked under his weight.

Daniel stood over him. "Not too late to back out, man."

"Shut up and kill me," he said.

Sometimes Daniel couldn't escape the conclusion that Moth liked pain. He'd earned his nickname when he was a small kid, holding his fingers over a cigarette lighter flame for as long as he could stand, which was longer than it ought to be. He got into fights not so much for the pleasure of punching other kids, but because he liked taking their punches in return. Maybe it wasn't the pain he liked, so much as the feeling of resilience. He liked proving he could get up off the playground asphalt for more. He acted as though he were invulnerable, but he wasn't. Not until Daniel changed him.

Daniel had come for a visit at Moth's squat and found him clubbed so badly his face was barely recognizable as a face. And whoever had done him had used knives. It wasn't the worst thing Daniel had ever seen done to a person, but it was awful enough.

Daniel begged Otis to help. He knew how much hydra regen and eocorn Otis had locked away. Enough for Daniel to save Moth's life. But Otis wouldn't relinquish it. He had a customer for the materials, and he wouldn't spare it on a talentless kid like Moth. Daniel asked a second time, was denied. He didn't ask a third time. He knew which safe Otis kept the stuff in.

He used it on Moth. All of it. And when Moth awoke with even his oldest scars gone, he was different.

Daniel gave Cassandra a nod. She loaded her gun with a needle painted bright red and yellow, like a venomous snake, to make sure she wouldn't confuse it with any of the others in her arsenal.

She kissed Moth on the forehead, then put the tip of the gun to his neck. "Not too late to back out, man."

"Cass, I swear to god—"

"Okay, okay. We've just never killed you before. Excuse us for asking."

Moth closed his eyes and took a breath, but before Cassandra pulled the trigger, Daniel covered her hand with his own. "Wait."

Moth's eyes popped open. "What's wrong?"

"Nothing. Just . . . I'll do this. Let me have the gun, Cass."

Moth looked worried, but Cassandra understood. Reluctantly, she gave Daniel the gun.

The things I ask my friends to do for me, Daniel thought. He could bring himself to ask Moth to die, but he shouldn't ask Cassandra to kill him. If something went wrong, Daniel should be the one to bear it.

"Close your eyes, Moth."

"Uh-uh. I'm watching you. Don't fuck this up, D."

Selfish of him, telling Moth not to look at him. He had a right to see what was happening to him. He had a right to see who was doing it to him.

There was a puff of air, and the needle penetrated Moth's neck.

Daniel resisted the urge to hold Moth's hand. Moth had made it clear during planning that he didn't want anyone to make a big deal out of his deaths, and Daniel wanted to respect his wishes.

Moth took half a breath, and the blood drained from his face. His lips parted slightly, and his eyes remained open, but now they stared at nothing. This was different than watching someone fall asleep. This wasn't sleep, nor paralysis, nor coma. There was an absence in the room now, and a mournful horror that Daniel didn't expect. He swallowed and told himself that, when next he spoke, he wouldn't betray any of it.

He pulled the blanket over Moth's face.

Wearing the form and clothes of a low-level catacombs worker, Jo pushed the gurney into the extraction workshops. Emma walked beside her, with an air of contemptuous confidence that she didn't have to feign.

Emma Walker was permitted to be here, and policy allowed her one attendant, so that was Jo's cover. Moth was a corpse, and this was a morgue. But Daniel and Cassandra needed a way to pass through.

Daniel reached back to his sense memories of sint holo. Vapors of confusion and elusiveness emanated from his cells. "Take my hand," he said to Cassandra. She pressed her warm palm to his, and together, they vanished.

He trailed several yards behind Jo and Emma, keeping enough distance to avoid casting his sint holo magic on them. With his invisibility miasma extended to include Cassandra, she was in the most danger. She was in a ghost world, incapable of forming coherent thoughts, of making good decisions. It was as though she were invisible to herself, and her hand felt insubstantial in Daniel's iron grip.

They entered the maze of lab benches in the leeching workshop. Bodies hung by chains from overhead racks. Drip pans below them collected fluid, transported by pumps and tubes to holding tanks for further processing. Workers took bodies apart with long knives and saws and files and picks and shears and scrapers. Some workers kept framed pictures of their families on shelves above their workstations. One had a WORLD'S GREATEST GRANDMOTHER coffee mug. Piped-in soft rock played amid the noise of suction and scraping and blood plinking into the pans.

Daniel was struck by the dense smells of magic. He caught

whiffs of flight, of muscle power, of searing flame. The floors and walls and workbenches here were infused with layers of magic. Over the decades, the finest mists of ground bone hung in the air until gravity brought them down, coating the surfaces. As Daniel moved through the atmosphere, his cells thrummed.

Guards patrolled the workshop, prowling like cats, occasionally peering over the workers' shoulders to make sure nobody tried to palm a tooth or a rolled bit of intestinal tissue. The guards' own magic smelled complicated and potent. The Hierarch invested resources in them. Smilodon for speed, and Colombian mammoth for strength.

Jo pushed the gurney right into a guard's path.

The guard dipped her chin in a neutral greeting. She was a plump woman who didn't appear physically intimidating, though her aroma told Daniel otherwise.

"Good evening, Dr. Walker," she said to Emma, ignoring Jo. "I thought you were on vacation."

"I got back early."

"Mazatlán, wasn't it?"

"Cancún."

The guard nodded and *hmm*ed. "We usually don't see you this far from the core complex."

Emma waved her hand over Moth's corpse. "This one's part of a special research project I'm working on and I want to make sure he arrives in one piece."

The guard seemed offended. "You don't have to worry about that, doctor. I can't speak for other parts of the catacombs, but I don't have a theft problem here."

Daniel could almost hear Emma's superior smirk. She offered her clipboard to allow the guard to inspect her paperwork: a requisition for Moth's corpse, and internal clearance passes for both her and the attendant Jo was impersonating. The guard seemed to read every word of every page. Finally, though, she handed the clipboard back to Emma and stepped aside to let her pass.

Daniel gripped Cassandra's featherlight hand, and they trailed Jo and Emma through the chamber of precision butchery. They'd almost reached the exit when the guard stopped them.

"Dr. Walker?"

Emma turned. "What?"

"Why did you come back early from Mazatlán?"

Emma exhaled slowly. "On Monday a large area of low pressure developed southeast of Jamaica, with increased concentration by Tuesday afternoon, moving southwestward. A confluence of warm-water temperatures, favorable upper-level environmental conditions, and reduced wind sheer led to gradual convection organization with rapid deepening."

The guard blinked. "Doctor . . . ?"

"It was raining," said Emma. "And it was Cancún."

She and Jo moved on.

FIFTEEN

L os Angeles was beautiful when it burned.

Gabriel cowered in an alley behind a trash bin and watched the deepening orange of the setting sun, swirling with grays and purples from the smoke gathering over Silver Lake. With sirens wailing, fireboats struggled through rush-hour traffic down West Sunset Canal, and Gabriel couldn't help but spontaneously devise better ways to organize the canal system and emergency services such that there might be a chance of putting the fire out before an entire neighborhood was consumed. It didn't take magic to run a city. It took administrative skill.

And it had taken skill to get this far away from Fenmont Szu's downtown office without being captured. Max's skill, mostly. He'd had steered them away from hound patrols and pulled them into alleys and bushes when he sensed cops too near. Both of them were filthy, their clothes still damp with canal water and reeking of diesel, and Gabriel had lost his shoes.

Szu's people would have searched the dockhouse below the skyscraper and noticed that the bomb he'd planted in

Gabriel's boat hadn't blasted Gabriel and Max to blobs of charred meat and paste. But Szu wouldn't stop there. Gabriel knew Daniel Blackland was alive. And he wasn't supposed to know that.

Navigating side roads and canals, he and Max made it to Silver Lake and avoided the cops, who threaded through clogged traffic on water cycles. Smoke rose above his neighborhood, two miles away. Gabriel liked his condo, at the top of a wooded bluff with views of the Ivanhoe Reservoir. And he liked his neighbors. They were right now losing their homes and everything they owned, and choking on smoke, and being clubbed by Szu's agents as they ran from the flames, and then tortured needlessly for information they didn't have. He turned and voided sour liquid from his empty stomach.

Crouched beside him, Max wrinkled his nose. "That smells."

Gabriel wiped his sleeve across his mouth. "Sorry."

"Try not to emit odors," Max said. "The hounds can trace it."

"Let's keep moving. Just a few more blocks to Hyperion. There's stuff I need at the coffee shop there."

"This is not a good time for a caffeine break. What stuff?"

"Cash. IDs. Travel papers. With those, we can make it north into the Valley. I know some people there who can hide us."

"You keep things like this at a coffee shop? What kind of coffee shop is this?"

I know a barista there, and she keeps my things in a locker."

"A barista—"

"A person who makes and serves coffee."

Max sniffed. "I know what a barista is. I'm a smart dog."

"Sorry."

"You trust this barista?"

"I used to go out with her. I think she likes me."

"Oh, love. Well. I suppose you've never been betrayed by someone who loves you."

Gabriel swallowed the sour taste in his mouth. He didn't look at Max. "I never said 'love.'"

They crossed Hyperion, just a block away from Intelligentsia Coffee Bar—a red stucco storefront with wrought-iron chairs and tables clustered around a small patio. Across the canal, a dozen black-and-white water cycles swarmed from the El Pollo Loco parking dock. The cops pulled up in front of Intelligentsia, dismounted, and with cleaver-clubs raised, descended on the customers.

It started with people being ordered to step away from the tables where they'd been sipping their espressos and tea and reading books and writing screenplays. A college-age kid in a beret was up against the wall, being frisked. A man with a push broom was being questioned as though carrying a broom was a crime. Then came the screams and shattering glass.

The cops put a girl's head through the plate-glass window. She sat on the ground, blood cascading down her face, rocking and bawling amid glittering shards. Nobody even bothered to arrest her. The cops turned over tables, smashing ceramic cups. They grabbed customers as they tried to flee. Some were cuffed. Others, simply beaten. The sharp crack of bone rang out like a gunshot when a cop struck a pleading man across the face with his cleaver-club. Three cops tackled a man who tried to run. A girl, restrained in a choke hold, reached out to an unattended stroller. One cop had an old woman on the ground, his knee in her back. He zip-tied her wrists and yanked her to her feet. Not once did her face register emotion. Not once did she cry out. She was old, maybe she'd been through scenes like this before.

Gabriel had seen brutality. He'd participated in it. Presided over it. Sometimes a baron would displease the Hierarch, and the police would fall upon his holdings, burn his houses, raze entire blocks of shops and restaurants to deprive him of his income. Or the Hierarch would order a purge, and an entire generation of osteomancers would be lost.

What Gabriel was witnessing seemed at once both more random and more personal. For the people being hurt, there was no cause. For Gabriel, it was a message: Surrender yourself or we'll terrorize everyone you've ever known.

"What are you doing?" Max snarled. He sensed Gabriel's intentions before Gabriel could even act on them.

"I'm going to turn myself in."

"They'll kill you."

"Not right away." He took a step down the sidewalk, toward Intelligentsia. Max gripped his shoulder and spun him around.

"You don't have to come with me," Gabriel said, calm, despite the painful pressure of Max's fingers. "While they're busy arresting me, you can hide."

Max tightened his grip. "I have no friends. No money. No place to go. Without you, I'll be tracked down and killed. With you, I have a chance. A very small, sad chance. I need you."

A muffled blast. They were firing gas canisters into the coffee bar's open door.

"Those people are already lost," Max said. "It's too late for them."

Gabriel clenched his jaw tight.

The barista. Maddie Wilson. She was studying aquaculture at USC. They dated for seven weeks. Still did, from time to time. All she wanted from Gabriel were the usual things. A little companionship, a little fun, a little passion. She didn't ask for much. All Gabriel wanted from her was someone he could trust enough to hold a bag for him and never open it.

Was she on shift? It was Wednesday, and she normally only worked Friday through Sunday. But maybe she'd changed her schedule.

To die in a storm of bullets and fire was a horrible thing. The sound of gunshots was lost in fire. The crack of burning wood and collapsing masonry could drown out everything, even screams. Gabriel had seen his mother shot dead in the formal dining room of their house. She was the Hierarch's niece, but it didn't save her during the Third Correction. They'd shot her in the back of the head, which was a mercy, because they'd set fire to the house and her nightgown had caught and she was burning.

Gabriel wasn't an osteomancer himself. He'd never been fed magic. His mother hadn't wanted that for him. So the Hierarch's men let him go. His father, too, though he was stripped of all the position and privilege being married to Gabriel's mother had afforded. He died in a retirement home at the age of fifty-six.

Gabriel studied. He made himself useful, but not conspicuous. He worked very hard and fought back urges for vengeance with a desire to survive and be useful. He hadn't heard his mother scream, so he kept quiet, too.

He turned and hurried away with Max, the distinct crackling of wood chasing them as the coffee bar burned.

———

Water and Power headquarters on Hope Canal was a mid-sixties-era high-rise of glass and steel strata. It looked like a machine, something that converted raw materials into energy. Gabriel paused before the doors, knowing this was one of those moments in life where the next move you made might save you or destroy you. Luck favors the bold, they said. They were idiots. Going to Fenmont Szu was bold, and now Gabriel was more than half destroyed. His neighbors were dead or jailed, his neighborhood razed.

There was no luck. There was no fairness. There was no justice. There was the Hierarch and Szu and the Ministry of Osteomancy, and there was the Department of Water and Power.

Gabriel and Max entered the building. Even barefoot and battered, Gabriel managed to talk his way past the public reception desk, past a midlevel manager, and up to some department head before hitting a roadblock.

Revealing his real name, and the fact that he was grand-nephew of the Hierarch, got him another rung up the ladder, to a junior water mage. And then, to get past her, he used the name Daniel Blackland.

A man in a very fine blue suit escorted him and Max to an unmarked elevator. Gabriel's stomach sank as the car descended. There were no lit numbers to tell him how far down they were going. When the doors finally opened again, he smelled algae and rust.

"This way," the escort said. He took them to a dark chamber, webbed with pipes the width of tree trunks and valves beaded with condensation, like some mechanical rain forest. The soft roar of a hidden river pervaded the space. The only source of light in the room was a pool the size of a basketball court, glowing like a blue jewel. Water lapped in steady rhythm against the sides.

From the shadows, a voice rumbled: "You must be brave to come to me. You must be a very brave boy."

The voice was deep and old and faintly monstrous. It belonged to William Mulholland, the ancient water mage of Los Angeles. The escort in the good blue suit left Gabriel alone with it.

SIXTEEN

Jo and Emma pushed Moth's corpse on the gurney, and Daniel followed. Once in Emma's laboratory, he pulled over a chair and helped ease Cassandra into it. She blinked slowly, like someone coming out of anesthesia, as they both emerged into visibility.

He rubbed her hand. Physical sensation would help reanchor her in the world.

"Do you know where you are?"

He watched recognition creep into her face.

"Emma's lab?" she said sleepily, and she pulled her hand away. Reluctantly, Daniel let her fingers slip from his.

"Yeah, we made it."

If he'd had any lingering doubts that Emma was a high-level osteomancer, her lab dissolved them. Black marble columns towered to a domed ceiling, decorated with carved wyverns and griffins. One wall contained the largest library of osteomancy texts Daniel had ever seen. Not just books, but also scrolls and loose pages framed behind glass and clay tablets etched in Akkadian and older pictograms.

Daniel was even more impressed by the oak specimen cabinets. The shelves were packed with fine powders of ground bone and horn, and oils and pastes of refined magic, and even more magic in raw bone.

Emma's instruments were no less striking: gleaming precision scales and a vast pegboard of handcrafted tongs and calipers and an exotic zoology of glasswork. Gas jets connected to a maze of pencil-thin brass tubes rose to the ceiling. With an assortment of valves and dials, Emma could summon any kind of flame, like the master of a clockwork dragon.

There was magic all through this room, blending to a thick, fragrant wall of power. It poured into Daniel's lungs. It soaked through his skin. His fingers tingled, as though he'd summoned kraken electricity, and his breath was hot.

"Are you all right?" Emma asked.

"I'm great."

He went to the gurney and pulled the blanket back from Moth's blood-drained face. He put his ear to Moth's mouth and felt no breath. He could find no pulse in Moth's throat.

Jo combed her fingers through Moth's hair. "Where is he now?"

"What do you mean?" Daniel said.

"I mean, where has he gone?"

"He's right there. You're touching him."

"His body's here. But you told us it wasn't like he'd be sleeping. It's not like he's in a coma. He's *dead*. So . . ."

"He's safe, Jo. He's done this before. Come on, we need to get our gear ready for the next phase." Daniel had asked Moth this same question once. Moth didn't want to talk about it. And when he pressed and pressed and wouldn't let Moth escape,

Moth stormed out. Daniel didn't see him again for a month. So Daniel stopped asking.

Emma was less eager to brush off Jo's question. "I think when we're killing people, it's appropriate to question the well-being of the soul. The Hierarch actually ordered us to look into it once. We developed a chamber electrified with a battery built from an oni demon. The hope was to euthanize test subjects and store their spirit energy in the chamber. Unfortunately, we weren't able to conclusively prove the existence of transphysical manifestations. Though we did manage to kill a lot of test subjects. And that is how progress is made."

"You know what?" Jo said. "You're a monster."

"Yes, I am. And you all killed your dear friend without understanding what you were doing. But since his corpse provided the cover story we needed to be here this time of night, it's all fine."

Cassandra rose from the chair. "I don't mind when you act superior to us," she said, "because I suspect it's nerves talking. It's scarier for you to sneak around in the dark than it is to kill people inside magic bottles, isn't it?"

Emma's smug smirk slid into sour. "In any event," she said, "Moth's chest is moving."

Indeed, Moth's great, continental plate of a chest rose and fell, at first shallowly, then deeply as he drew breath. It seemed a gentle awakening, but then his eyes popped open and sat up with a start. He leaped off the gurney, sending it rolling into Emma's desk. Like a cornered bear, he took in the crew, eyes darting wildly.

"Moth?" Cassandra said.

Moth bared his teeth.

"Moth, honey? You're scaring me."

Some of the tension eased from his muscles. The savagery left his face. He coughed.

"I'm naked," he said.

Jo fanned herself with her hand. "Oh, my, yes, you are."

"Who's got my clothes?"

Daniel tossed him the bundled clothes from his pack. They exchanged a look, and what Daniel saw made him understand that on this job, he wasn't just stealing from the Hierarch, but from his friends as well.

"Any problems while I was dead?"

"None worth mentioning. And you're just in time for back-breaking labor." Daniel placed a shovel in Moth's hands.

Fifty feet of stone wall stood between them and an access point into the Ossuary proper, and the stone was impregnated with a preparation of dragon scale hard enough to blunt diamond.

"Onward," Daniel said. But he couldn't hear his own voice, because he had burst into flames.

A halo of blue fames rose from his hands and from the center of his chest, searing hot. He screamed and dropped to the floor and rolled. The flames didn't go out. But, he realized after a few seconds, neither did the flames burn.

He sat up and held his hands up before him. The flames completely surrounded him now, obscuring his view of the room, and of his friends. He was somewhere else.

A full yellow moon took half the sky. He rode a jet stream of cold, thin air, slicing through clouds like a knife and leaving them roiling in his wake. His eyes were situated on either side of the long fuselage of his skull, and he saw a hundred and eighty degrees around him, everything in sharp focus. He meant to whoop in exultation, but it came out as a roar that sent dwarf pronghorns and mastodons and griffins running for shelter among the junipers. He turned and sighted a giant ground sloth browsing the shrubs. Daniel beat his wings, and the sloth issued a panicked grunt and lumbered helplessly toward a water hole. Or so the sloth thought. Beneath a thin layer of dark water lurked viscous, sticky tar. The sloth was heading for a trap.

Flames flared before Daniel's face, and when they died, he was sitting on the tile floor. His crew surrounded them, Cassandra kneeling before him.

"What the hell was that?"

"You tell me," he said. "What did you see?"

"You kind of flamed on for a second," Cassandra said.

Jo waved her hand under her nose. "And stunk up the room, too."

"Methane," Daniel said.

He stood and examined his hands and the front of his shirt. No burns.

"Anything you want to tell us?" Emma said.

He didn't want to tell them anything. Something strange had happened, and he didn't understand it, which meant he wasn't in control. On a job, his role was to be in control. But there was too much at stake to deny it.

"I've been feeling odd since we entered the catacombs," he admitted. "Energized. Powerful. For a minute there, I was another creature."

Emma nodded, as if he were just confirming what she already knew.

"You were absorbing osteomancy in the morgue. And you're metabolizing the firedrake processed in this room. You're drawing magic from stray vapors and dust particulates.

I've only heard of one other osteomancer who can absorb raw magic that easily, and that's the Hierarch." She stared at him as though he were a marvelous specimen. "You're a piece of work, Mr. Blackland."

Daniel struggled to tamp down a swell of delight. He couldn't deny how great he felt. If he jumped high enough, he'd take flight.

"I've never gained osteomantic abilities from breathing rough magic before. Why now?"

Emma frowned as though solving a math problem.

"Maybe you've never been surrounded by so much. You're like a device that's been getting by on low-voltage batteries. Here, you're plugging into your full power. And we're still in the catacombs. Once we break into the Ossuary proper . . . I might have to learn to be afraid of you, Mr. Blackland."

"So you're all nifty with power," Cassandra said. "But are you *okay*?"

"I feel fine. Let's keep moving. Dig." He unpacked his folding shovel. Cassandra gave him a lingering look before getting out her own.

The shovels were treated with seps and grootslang and could dig through nearly everything and turn the spoil to microscopic particles, but it would still take at least two hours to mine their way to the HVAC control room standing between them and the prize.

Two clicking footsteps, and a woman stepped from behind one of the marble columns. She exuded powerful aromas of flame and earth and deep magic.

She was Emma, only older. Her face was more lined, the neck looser, the chestnut hair gone gray, but otherwise, Emma.

Cassandra snapped into marksman posture, her finger curled around the trigger of her needle gun.

Queasy dread chilled Daniel's stomach. They'd crossed a barrier. On one side, the job was under control. On the other side, things spun out into chaos and were never going to snap back into order. He had felt this way once before, on a job: when Punch had gone back for the monocerus. It was the only time he'd lost a member of his crew.

"Three seconds to tell me what's going on before you both die," Daniel said to the Emmas.

"I thought you were on vacation," said the younger Emma.

"Cancún was rainy," said the older.

The older Emma leaped across the distance to the crew. Cassandra squeezed off a shot, but her needle went wide, striking a column with a sharp ring. Older Emma dropped down on her before she could fire again. Cassandra folded as if a bear had fallen on her. She managed to swing her leg in a sweeping kick that Daniel had seen her use to shatter jaws of men twice her size. Older Emma absorbed the blow across her face and spat blood. With one hand, she lifted Cassandra off the ground by the throat. Cassandra's cheeks puffed out, her flesh turning the color of a plum.

Moth got to her first. He drove his foot into Older Emma's knee. It should have crippled her, but he might as well have kicked a steel pole. With her free hand, she drilled a punch into Moth's solar plexus. He crumpled, unable to even gasp. She took his wrist in her slender white fingers.

Daniel saw the way she was holding it, what she was prepared to do. "Don't," he said. But with the barest motion, she turned Moth's wrist, and Moth shrieked.

She lifted Cassandra another inch in the air. The veins in Cassandra's temples bulged. She was struggling less.

"Why did you leave me?" Older Emma said to Younger Emma.

"Put her down," Younger Emma said. "Put her down right now."

"Why did you leave me?" Older Emma repeated.

What was this? Some kind of family drama? Daniel couldn't see a way to work it in his favor. With Older Emma in physical contact with Cassandra, he couldn't kraken-shock her without electrocuting both of them. And Cassandra didn't have much time left. Daniel was already calculating how much eocorn restorative and hydra regenerative it'd take to heal her. Assuming that any of them survived.

Older Emma released her grip, letting Cassandra crash to the floor. Jo went to her.

Daniel gathered his electricity. Sharp jolts shot down his arms.

"Why did you leave me?" Older Emma said again.

"Because I won't be kept like a gallstone in a jar," Younger Emma answered.

Older Emma blinked welling tears. She nodded, resolved. "Then I free you."

Her lips parted. A lick of blue flame played over her tongue.

"No," Younger Emma said, and she stretched her jaws wide. With a roar, blue fire rolled in a wave across the floor and washed over Older Emma. The flames climbed her legs and she howled and raised her arms, as if in surrender, desperate to keep them away from the heat.

Younger Emma's head and shoulders swayed in the slow, sinuous motions of a cobra, and this way she controlled the flames, entwining Older Emma's torso in a swirling embrace. Then, Younger Emma snapped her jaws shut and Older Emma collapsed to the floor. The flames guttered over her charred and blistered body, and her movements were the involuntary convulsions of the dying.

The air was thick with bitter ash and cloying sweetness and methane. The stench was sickening, but Daniel also smelled wondrous things. As Older Emma smoldered, she released magic into the air and the chamber filled with the speed and strength and agility of saber-toothed cats and lions and hippogriffs. Daniel smelled cerberus wolf and black dragon and firedrake, and his cells drank it in, and he was ashamed for savoring it.

Emma cocked her head to the side and regarded her victim. Her brow furrowed. She turned to Daniel. "I suppose you'll want an explanation."

Red bruises striped Cassandra's throat. Her breaths came in shallow gasps. Jo knelt, supporting Cassandra's head, and stroked her hair with one hand and aimed her needle gun at Emma with the other. As Daniel prepared an ampoule of hydra regenerative for Cassandra, he was very conscious of Emma standing behind him.

"Down the hatch," Daniel whispered, squeezing the thick hydra oil in Cassandra's mouth.

When he was satisfied it was going down, he left her in Jo's care.

"So, let's have it," he said, facing Emma. "Who was she? Your mother?"

"My mother was a glass jar," Emma said, unconvincingly chirpy.

Sparks of kraken snapped beneath Daniel's fingernails.

"Don't test my patience, Emma. Not now. You kept something from me, and my friends are hurt because of it. They're willing to die for me. And I'm willing to kill for them."

Emma rubbed her eyes. She looked drawn. "Your father invested parts of himself and parts of you in the Blackland sword. But Emmaline Walker did one better. She crafted a whole, complete, external version of herself. A living replica. Emmaline Walker had a golem. She had me."

She curtsied.

Threads of kraken electricity arced between Daniel's fingers.

"Why make a golem? What purpose does it serve?"

"It serves the Hierarch, of course. If magic is so finite that the Hierarch's taken to eating his own mages, then how useful to grow mages in a bottle. To fill the ranks of his armies. Or the platters on his dinner table."

A physical memory struck Daniel like sudden pain from a phantom limb. He remembered the thing that had gone north with his mother. The boy, that incomplete, broken version of him, wearing his clothes. Holding his mother's hand.

It wasn't just a thing that looked like Daniel. It was closer than a twin. It was made from him. His father had harvested bits of Daniel and made a broken version of him and his mother took it along as a decoy. He was in the boy's head when it knelt in the strawberry field.

What kind of people did that?

"You led us right to the real Emma," Moth said in a low, menacing whisper.

"I thought she was in Cancún," Emma said with a shrug.

The electricity sizzled over Daniel's palms now, and there was heat in his mouth, and the stink of methane in his nose.

"What's in the Ossuary, Emma? What do you want?"

Emma regarded the burnt remains of Emmaline Walker. Her body still simmered with magic, and Daniel could not stop drinking it.

Emma massaged her temples. "I'm not the only Emma that Dr. Emmaline Walker has made. The seeds of us are kept in the Ossuary. I won't see them served on the Hierarch's plate. Not any more of them. You get into the Ossuary to get your sword. I get there to free children."

Emma sighed. She looked tired. "And there's something else. Emmaline Walker wasn't the Hierarch's only golem-maker. There's enough of you in the Blackland sword to grow another Blackland. If you don't want any more little brothers running around, you won't abort this job."

Moth flexed his fingers. "My wrist's feeling better. Should I crush her head?"

Wounded and lied to, Daniel's friends still looked to him, waiting on his word.

Crackling with magic, he'd never felt more powerful and more unsure.

SEVENTEEN

The glyph of Fenghuang, king of birds, marked the door. Depicted in brilliant reds and blues and golds, the chimera bird spread his wings, as if to beat winds powerful enough to bend the mightiest trees. Beyond Fenghuang's door was the Ossuary's heating, ventilation, and air conditioning control room.

The room was guarded by four sentries, now slumped on the floor with needles in their necks. As Moth dragged them away to stash them in a broom closet down the corridor, Cassandra worked the locks. The last of seven magical wards fell, and the crew was inside the concrete-block room.

Daniel surveyed the pipes and vents and ducts and fans. Not wanting to raise his voice above the roar of the air handlers, he gestured to a vent near the ceiling. He seldom used air ducts. Crawling through sheet aluminum was noisy as hell, and he'd had a bad day once in a shoe warehouse when the duct he was creeping through collapsed under his weight and he'd dropped onto a load of counterfeit high-tops. But the Ossuary's ducts were built out of stone. The Hierarch made sure his own structures were sturdy enough to withstand his punitive earthquakes.

The crew slipped on knee and forearm pads in preparation for the long crawl. The more comfortable they were, the less chance they'd betray themselves with a fatal grunt.

Daniel stepped into Moth's interlaced fingers, and Moth boosted him up to the vent grill. After four squirts of grease and many rotations of his screwdriver, he pulled the grill off and stowed it in the vent. The breeze flowing into the duct rustled his hair. He didn't like the feeling. It was too much like being inhaled.

With Moth's help and a little struggle, he climbed into the duct.

His flashlight showed a clear path down the shaft, so he signaled the others to come up after him. Moth's bulk barely fit in the tight space. Daniel wondered if he should have packed a tub of margarine to lube the way for him.

Daniel took point. Twenty feet ahead, branch right, thirty feet, branch right again, another few dozen yards, then take the middle of three branches. He came to a stop at another vent and looked down into a dungeonlike chamber plunging a hundred feet to a stone floor.

If you were sickeningly wealthy, thought Daniel, and possessed so much gold that even the room in which you stored your gold bricks was made of more gold bricks, you might have something in common with the Hierarch.

The Ossuary was the size of an airplane hangar. Stacked mammoth femurs lined the walls. A chandelier of eocorn horns, white as snow, hung from a ceiling of mammoth tusks. The floor gleamed with a mosaic of claws and delicate vertebrae and bone fragments.

Tall shelves with railed library ladders occupied most of the space, arranged in dozens of narrow aisles. There were museum cabinets and steel safes the size of Daniel's living room. Chain-link cages housed fully articulated skeletons: a serpent at least forty feet long, a feline-shaped skeleton the size of an elephant. Mounted on a far wall, a rack held kraken spines as long as javelins.

The aromas should have overwhelmed him, but he smelled nothing. The negative-pressure maintained by the HVAC system meant no magic exited the Ossuary without the Hierarch's express command, not even smells. The system pumped air inside, and outventing air was captured by a filtration system to catch magic-bearing particulates and gasses. Whenever the filters were changed, the old ones were processed to recover the trapped magic, which was then condensed and presumably sent back to the Ossuary for storage. The filters themselves were worth a fortune.

Below, the Tireless Guard stood watch. Decked out in livery like Christmas nutcrackers, they numbered at least two dozen. Each guard was equipped with a shoulder-holstered machine pistol and a lance tipped with a serrated basilisk fang. A good osteomancer could cook the fangs down to a quart of weapons-grade venom with higher street value than a bucket of diamonds, assuming the osteomancer could get his hands on it without being reduced by a well-magicked sentry to a puddle of cooling sludge.

Changes in guard shifts were usually the best time to execute a job, but the Tireless never required relief. They never broke watch, never changed shifts, and according to Emma, didn't even need piss breaks. Watching them through the vent, Daniel detected not a twitch, not a blink, not a breath. Compared to these guys, the Queen's Guard at Buckingham Palace were a bunch of spastics.

Cassandra squeezed in next to him and looked out the vent. Her gun was already assembled, a custom-built dart rifle with an air canister half the length of the barrel. She licked her lips. The shot was total Annie Oakley stuff, through the vent, a hundred and thirty feet to her nearest target. She sat with her legs folded awkwardly, shoulders hunched and head bent. She couldn't even extend her arms all the way. Five shots, and each one had to hit, because her ammunition was precious and rare.

She slipped the barrel through the grid of the air vent and teased the trigger with her index finger. She licked her lips. When they'd first started running jobs together, Daniel had interpreted the lip-licking as nerves. Now, he knew it was just eagerness.

She squeezed the trigger five times, tracking left to right, each shot punctuated by the hiss of high-pressure air release. Five darts struck the floor, glass capsules shattering and mixing catalyst with gorgon essence. Yellow vapors billowed in the space below.

Two of the guards looked up. One reached for his holster, but his hand went cement gray, and his face froze into a rigid mask. Like the others, he was still as stone.

Daniel tugged his goggles and filter mask in place. He lowered the chain ladder to the floor and began the descent. All the while, he envisioned being impaled by a flung basilisk lance, and all the magic in his flesh-and-blood cauldron squirting out.

With every rung of the ladder, the air seemed to grow thicker.

He felt like a deep-sea diver, moving into zones of increasing pressure. It was the presence of so much magic. It enveloped him, this hyperbaric osteomancy, pushing wind and muscle and fire and force through his pores, into his bloodstream. For a moment, he regretted gorgon-freezing the Tireless Guard, because he thought there was a chance he could take them head-on.

You're losing it, he admonished himself. That kind of thinking was just crazy cakes.

He reached the floor, unscathed. Before signaling the others to follow, he wanted to make sure the gorgon was working, so he brought electric tingle to his fingertips and stepped up to one of the guards, edging closer as cautiously as a postman approaching a growling dog. He aimed the pencil beam of his flashlight in the guard's eyes. The guard's pupils didn't change. Either the guard was playing possum, or the vaporized gorgon extract worked perfectly.

Daniel's crew joined him on the ground. They spread out through the Ossuary in a choreographed dance to relieve the guards of their pistols. Using cable saws, they detached the basilisk fangs from their lances. The entire process took two minutes, and at the end of it, the crew had made its first score of the heist.

If Daniel called off the job right now, they could tunnel their way out, and he could bring the room down with an earthquake to cover their tracks. He could break through to the surface near the dockhouse at Wilshire and Fairfax, and everyone could go home. If Otis fenced the basilisk fangs for as much as he promised, they would all walk away from the job wealthy. They'd encountered no barrier they could not breach. They'd tripped no alarm. They'd faced no guard who could stop them or call an alert. They'd overcome unknowns—the coelacanth, and Dr. Emmaline Walker. If they got out now, they would be the first ever thieves to infiltrate the Ossuary and walk out with treasure.

Crime of the century. One for the ages. History.

But Daniel hadn't come here for the fangs.

The gorgon vapors should have been sucked through the vents on the far wall by now, so Daniel pulled the filter mask away from his nose and sniffed.

He staggered. The osteomancy was so strong he couldn't believe the aromas weren't visible. The eocorn chandelier blazed with renewal and optimism. The griffin skeleton burned with flames of raw power. In their rack, the kraken spines gave off an entire ecosystem of scents, so much darker and more potent than the tiny sliver Daniel's father had fed him on the beach.

This is what Sebastian Blackland had prepared him for. Daniel was a cauldron, a sponge, and he grew more powerful simply by standing here. He wanted to remain in this room forever and merely breathe.

Moth and Cassandra both reached for him.

"I'm okay. It's just . . . There's a lot of magic here. Keep your protection on. I don't want you running into a pocket of bad air."

Moth and Jo assembled their digging tools and headed off for the east wall.

"We get the sword first," Cassandra said to Emma, her voice muffled by the mask. "Your agenda is strictly optional."

Emma turned crisply on her heel and made right for a black, glass-doored cabinet. Inside were stored a dozen glass jars, about the size of baby-food containers.

"If you would get this open for me, I could address my agenda right now."

Daniel went over to the cabinet, waving off Cassandra's protests.

Inside the jars were lumpy, flesh-colored things the size of his thumbs. They had the beginnings of eyes, dark little indentations covered by onionskin film. Not so much like fetuses. More like blue-ribbon county fair oddities, potatoes taking on human form. They should stay in the jars, he thought. They should stay locked away with the lights out, so that they'd never become something else. A golem had once been made from Daniel, and it died in a strawberry field, asking for its mother. For Daniel's mother.

"Open the cabinet, Cassie."

Cursing, she examined the wards with her jeweler's loupe. It took her three minutes to get the cabinet open with lock picks made of sphinx tooth.

Emma carefully placed them in a padded casket from her bag. "Thank you," she said, her voice shaky.

"The sword," Cassandra said, anxious to get on with it.

They dove into the aisles. The plan had been for Daniel to locate the Blackland sword by scent. More than leading the crew, this was supposed to be his major contribution to the job, the one thing he could do that nobody else in Los Angeles was as qualified for. And, indeed, the trail couldn't have been clearer had it been spray-painted in red and marked with neon signs. He smelled his father's aftershave, and his electricity, and his intelligence and discipline and knowledge of deep magic. He smelled libraries. Chinese ink on old paper. Workshops full of centuries-old wood and glassware. Unexpected tears filled his eyes. These weren't mere sense memories. This was his father, or what was left as him, as fully present as he would ever be. He smelled the house in Laurel Canyon with the eucalyptus and jacaranda trees and his father's blood and sharp chemical pheromones of fear. And he smelled himself. His hair clippings and nail trimmings and baby teeth, and his own childhood magic.

He blinked his eyes dry. "Here," he called, standing before a single-drawer cabinet.

Cassandra crouched to examine the lock on the front of the drawer.

"I'm not smelling sphinx," Daniel said.

"Yeah. It's not sphinx. It's a nhang lock."

Emma bent forward for a smell. "I don't smell nhang."

Cassandra rummaged in her kit. "If I say it's nhang, it's nhang."

Daniel consulted his watch. "Clock's ticking. Can you do it?"

"Maybe if you two stop quacking at me."

She brought out a bone chip the size of a domino. Its texture was like modeling clay, and she began flattening it between her palms while ordering Emma to aim her flashlight into the lock. Daniel was glad Jo wasn't nearby for this. The key was fashioned from the remains of a human shape-shifter.

"Keep working," Daniel said. "I'm going to check on Jo and Moth."

"Quacking," muttered Cassandra.

Daniel ran clear of the aisle. Across the floor, Moth was neck-deep in a hole, which had already swallowed Jo. Their shovels cut through stone and concrete and packed earth as though it were soap. Given another ten minutes, they'd be through to the building's foundations, and from there they'd tunnel out to safety. Then Daniel would cover their tracks with the Jinshin-Mushi beetle he'd gotten from Sully in Ocean Park, and they'd be home free. They had the basilisk fangs for the cash score, Emma had her jars of potato people, and if Cassandra had anything to do with it, Daniel would have the Blackland sword in hand.

"You guys doing okay?"

"We are digging a hole to a world of beauty and class," Moth said, not even breathing hard.

Daniel got back to Cassandra just as the nhang lock sprung open with a satisfying click.

Cassandra stepped back from the cabinet to make room for Daniel. "Just in time to take all the credit for my work."

"Quack," he said.

He slid the wide, flat drawer out. The smells of the sword curled into the air. But there was no sword inside.

A tuft of black hair, bound in string. A small molar filled with silver. Firedrake dust, hardened like a sugar cube. Sint holo, wavering in Daniel's peripheral vision. And part of a human skull's face, the tobacco-brown cheek and orbital.

The smells swirled over Daniel like ropes, binding him, pulling him down.

"What the hell?" said Cassandra.

The lock of hair was Daniel's. The tooth was his. The skull fragment was his father's.

No, not the sword. Just samples of the ingredients that Sebastian Blackland had invested in it.

Daniel had thought he was so smart. He thought he'd come up with a brilliant plan and half a dozen alternatives and backups in case things went to shit. Alarms and locks and wards. He'd prepared himself and his crew for everything. Except for this.

He was vaguely aware of Cassandra standing beside him with her hand on his arm. "Daniel—?"

He slammed the drawer shut so hard the cabinet rocked. He raced down the aisle, Cassandra and Emma trailing him.

"We have to go," he roared to Moth and Jo, still digging their hole.

Moth poked his head up like a gopher. "What's up?"

"Trap," Daniel said.

The contents of the drawer smelled exactly like the Blackland sword. They were a lure, and Daniel had come all the way to the Hierarch's Ossuary to bite.

Moth gave him a bitter smile. "What's the new plan?"

Daniel unscrewed the cap on the bottle of Jinshin-Mushi flakes and sprinkled them into his mouth. He tasted molten rock and heat and pressure, and his jaw fractured into rubble and tremors ran through his skeleton, and his ribs splintered and his pelvis cracked. But these were just sensations. This was just the flavor of magic. This was sorcery, and it would either destroy him, or he would master it and be an osteomancer.

He directed the seismic power to his hands. He didn't know quite what to do with it.

"The plan, Daniel? What's the fucking plan?"

Daniel's hands began to shake violently.

"Get out of the hole."

Moth boosted Jo to the cracked stone-mosaic floor and scrabbled after her. He coughed fine-powder dust, and with the others, watched Daniel to see what amazing new act of cleverness he'd conjure to save them all.

Daniel just stood there with quaking hands, wondering if he could pull this off.

He knew about plate tectonics and faults and fissures. He knew how to create tremors. If he could direct that energy into the beginnings of the tunnel Moth and Jo had dug, to push the earth away and complete their escape route in seconds instead of minutes . . .

White light flashed, and the air stank of unfamiliar magic. It was old and deep and enormous, and it drove Daniel to his knees.

He screamed for his crew to run. Or he thought he did. He couldn't hear himself, and he couldn't see anything but a figure striding toward him. He blinked spots from his eyes and tried to bring things into focus.

To his shame, he was just as terrified of the Hierarch as he'd been that day, ten years before. His father had been so strong, yet the Hierarch devoured him. He devoured his father and in a sense, devoured his mother. He devoured Daniel's life, and as powerful as Daniel was now, with the osteomancy of the morgue and Emmaline Walker's workshop and the magic Otis had given him and that Daniel had stolen and traded for, he felt like nothing more than thin broth.

It wasn't the Hierarch. He recognized Fenmont Szu from television. In person, he was taller. His hair was blacker. The drape of his suit, more impeccable. His face was a little too symmetrical, his cheekbones tapering in sculpted S curves. Cosmetic osteomancy. It was all a little grotesque.

Twenty guards accompanied him, armed with assault rifles. Daniel put his hands in the air.

The Shinjin-Mushi beetles crawled beneath his skin. If he could free them, he could bring the ceiling down and crush the pillars and the cabinets and the guards and Fenmont Szu, flattening them under tons of rubble and bone.

But he couldn't do it without also killing his friends.

Szu regarded Daniel like a violin teacher judging his student's fingerings and shook his head with disappointment. He took a single, small step forward. A crushing weight drove Daniel to the floor. On his back stood a mammoth. That's what it felt like, and he smelled the mammoth's strength and mass, paralyzing him.

He wondered if he'd black out before his spine splintered. He tried to say he was sorry, to Cassandra, to Moth and Jo. He wouldn't waste words on Emma. No doubt she'd helped engineer this trap.

He should have been smarter.

A single spark of kraken electricity flared over his knuckles. It sputtered out.

EIGHTEEN

They put Daniel in a room with no light, except for a weak nimbus leaking from the bottom of the door. He was splayed on his back atop a rubber mat, wrists bound by rubber straps to rings in the wall. His hands were sealed in rubber bags, secured with duct tape. He'd been insulated to nullify his electricity.

Silver spikes of pain radiated from the center of his spine, but at least he could feel his legs and even wiggle his toes if he didn't mind gasping.

He tested the straps, but only out of some sense of obligation to resist captivity. Moth might have managed to yank hard enough to rip the rings from the wall, or else rip his own arm out of its socket. Jo could resculpt her wrists and make them slender enough to slip through. Cassandra could dislocate her thumbs. But Daniel was a sack of useless magic.

The job could have gone better.

The door opened and Daniel lifted his head. He made out the silhouettes of at least four guards out in the hall before the door shut. With the click of a switch, harsh yellow light stabbed his eyes, and he found himself alone with Fenmont Szu.

Szu moved with a confidence that must have required dance lessons. His suit seemed to flow around him, never bunching, never creasing. Was that magic or merely good tailoring? Only the left pocket of his jacket bulged conspicuously.

Daniel coughed. "How's your day going?"

"Pretty well, thank you," said Szu in a voice like cream.

"Are you in pain?"

"I wouldn't mind an aspirin, if you're offering."

A chuckle from Fenmont Szu.

"You're being very brave, Mr. Blackland. An aspirin. I stepped on you with the weight of a mammoth."

Again, the chuckle. Fenmont Szu was a chuckler. Daniel hated chucklers.

"Are we going to have the kind of conversation where you just make fun of me? Let me save you the trouble. I walked right into the Hierarch's trap and you kicked my ass. It was amateur hour. A clown show."

"You're being too hard on yourself, Mr. Blackland. Dozens of would-be thieves have entered the catacombs, but only a rare few make it all the way to the Ossuary. You really did quite well."

"Nice of you to say. Is Otis working with you guys? This whole time it's been a con to get me here?"

Szu dragged a chair from the corner and placed it at Daniel's feet. He sat, crossing his long legs, hands folded on his knee. He had the fingers of a concert pianist.

"You're quick to figure it out."

"You don't have to blow sunshine up my ass. It's all pretty obvious, when you stop to think about it."

Otis was a businessman. What was the most valuable commodity in his warehouse? Daniel. And who was his richest possible customer?

"Otis gets, what, the fangs and the sword?"

"What makes you think there's still a sword?"

"Because if there's not, I'm going to feel really, really bad about myself. I mean, even worse. So, when's dinner?"

From his jacket pocket, Szu removed a pair of thick, black rubber gloves. He pulled them over his graceful hands, and suddenly his musician's fingers looked like crude implements of torture. Also from his pocket came a pair of garden shears. The blades were serrated, the grips coated in more black rubber.

"Let my accomplices go," Daniel said, not capable of concealing his desperation. "They're not osteomancers. I'll cooperate with you. You can do whatever you're going to do to me."

"You have a bleak sense of humor, Mr. Blackland."

Szu walked beside Daniel's outstretched body. He crouched and took a gloved handful of Daniel's hair, grabbing it close to the roots, and squeezed.

I can handle this, Daniel thought. But he couldn't handle wondering what was being done to Moth. To Jo. To Cassandra.

"I'll work for you," Daniel said. "I have all my father's power, plus power of my own. And I'm the best thief in the kingdom, you practically said so yourself—"

Szu placed Daniel's nose between the blades of the shears.

"I am here to do one thing," Szu said. "To make sure you really are Sebastian Blackland's son. Otis isn't the most trustworthy of partners, I'm sure you'll agree. So I need a piece of you for testing. If you are Daniel Blackland, then the Hierarch will eat you. If not, I'll dine on you myself. And on your friends."

"They're not osteomancers." The shears pinched Daniel's nostrils, and his voice sounded nasal. Comical. Hilarious.

"That's all right," said Szu. "Not every meal needs to be nutritious."

Szu squeezed the shears, and Daniel reached desperately for kraken lightning, for sint holo, for seps serpent, for firedrake. All he could smell was Szu's deep magic.

The sharp pressure of the shears went away.

"I'm just playing with you, Mr. Blackland. Your nose is far too interesting an instrument to damage with pruning shears."

"You have a bleak sense of humor."

"Indeed."

In a swift movement, he grabbed Daniel's left hand and gripped his little finger through the bag. The blades of the shears cut rubber and broke skin and crunched bone, and Daniel's finger was off.

I can handle this, thought Daniel, and he wailed.

Szu left him there. No food, no water, no sense of time. Just a tiny finger gone. The pain thundered. He bled, filling the bag over his hand. Pretty clever, the bag. It made sure no blood got spilled. His blood was too potent to waste. How much magic had his father lost to the Hierarch's cutlery before he was dead? Did he whine? If he had, Daniel couldn't hear him over the sound of the Hierarch's chewing.

His head felt bloated and hot. Feverish. What were the odds that Fenmont Szu sterilized his pruning shears before amputating Daniel's finger?

Fenmont Szu was an asshole. Everyone was an asshole.

Daniel moaned, and the room drank his voice to silence.

Once upon a time, Daniel could fly. He was not a man, then, nor even a boy. He was a sleek creature the length of a gondola-bus, and he cut through air with beats of his steel-scaled wings, and anyone who dared hunt him—feathered Garuda, Fenghuang, packs of chengrong dog-birds—died in flame and ash. He was once this creature, not long ago, for a bare few seconds. But now, except for the faint flavor of methane on his tongue, he was not.

He composed a list of people he'd make suffer.

Otis was at the top. Obviously.

Then came the Hierarch and Fenmont Szu.

Emma Walker.

He closed his eyes and imagined their names, written in elaborate script on parchment, like a proper recipe, bursting into blue flame.

The biggest name on the list was his own. Someone had to pay for Moth and Jo and Cassandra. And for Punch.

Punch was the wrong nickname for Pauline Moana. She did her work with pressure points and jabs. But with red hair from her incarcerated Scottish mother, and coloring and facial features from her Tahitian father, the rules of the schoolyard deemed it inevitable that she'd be known as Hawaiian Punch.

On the eve of Punch's last job, she sat in a booth in the back corner of Ship's Diner on La Cienega with Daniel and the rest of the crew. Daniel liked Ship's. Every table came with its own toaster, and he found that neat. As he created the entire toast spectrum, from flour white to tar black, he asked each member of his crew what they would do if they had all the money in the world.

Jo went first. "I'd buy my own theater. Just a little playhouse, maybe two hundred seats. One-woman shows, maybe some improv workshops, some banned plays. Mostly just art for art's sake." She spread jam on toast with an elegant flourish.

Moth, by contrast, had a list of coveted possessions. A diamond toilet brush would not be the most ostentatious of his purchases.

Cassandra, her arm hooked around Daniel's, revealed only that she would buy a few things but invest most of it. "Someone's got to be a responsible adult," she said.

"What about you, Daniel?" Punch said, passing him a plastic container of strawberry jam. She knew strawberry was his favorite.

Daniel thought for a moment. Not about what he'd do with a pile of money, but about how much he wanted to reveal. And then he decided he was being silly. This was his crew. These were his friends. His family. He could tell them anything.

"Guess I'd use it to get out of town," he said. And because this was his family, they knew exactly what he meant. They knew why he wanted to leave the Southern Kingdom. Of course. He lived in fear that one day, someone would figure out who he really was, and then he'd be hunted. And they knew that if he ever had enough funds to buy his way over the border, they'd have the choice of coming with him, because he wouldn't leave them behind unless they wanted him to.

"What's it going to be for you, Punch? Champagne swimming pool or gold dirigible?"

Punch moved a blob of strawberry jam over her toast. She met nobody's eyes, just stared at the wood-grain laminate table as she spoke. "I think I'd give my money away to whoever needed it most."

For the rest of the meal, everyone but Daniel laughed and talked about the Punch Moana annual telethon for the needy.

Daniel didn't laugh because he knew Punch meant she'd give all her money to him. And he should have wondered why. He should have looked deeper. Instead, he just accepted. She loved him. Cassandra loved him. Jo loved him. Moth loved him. He didn't question it. He just accepted. He just took it.

"You mope too much."

Daniel craned his neck forward. A girl sat at Daniel's feet in Fenmont Szu's chair. He recognized her round, brown, freckled face, and the tufts of red hair jutting from beneath a black beret.

"Hey, Punch," he said. "You can't be here."

"Why not?"

"Because you're dead."

She rolled her eyes. "I know that, Daniel. I was there when I died." She began pointing at places on her body, her arms and shoulders and belly and breasts and temple. Those were the places the bullets struck her during the botched monocerus job.

"I know you're not here, Punch. I can't smell you."

"I can't smell you either. Does that mean you're not here?"

"That's hardly the same thing. You're dead."

"We haven't seen each other in years, and you're so hung up on me not being alive you can't even say, 'Hello, how ya been?' "

Pugnacious, but with hurt in her eyes. So very Punch.

"I'm hallucinating you. I think Fenmont Szu gave me tetanus."

Punch stood and examined the room, walking along the

wall. Her boot heels tapped against the concrete floor. "Fen-mont Szu is an asshole."

"Duh," Daniel said, letting his head fall back.

So, okay, he was hallucinating his old, dead friend. This didn't have to be a crazy moment. Daniel didn't believe in horoscopes, in the predictive power of tarot cards, in the ability to divine lit-eral meaning from dreams. But that didn't mean those things weren't useful. They could be tools for self-reflection. And when one was in pain, locked away in an enemy's dungeon, what bet-ter time to self-reflect?

"Why'd you go back for the monocerus, Punch?"

"You know why."

He did, but he hoped he was wrong, and he wanted Punch to give him another answer. He wanted her to tell him she went for the bigger score because she got stupid and greedy. But he knew better. She went back for it because she thought she could fence it herself and wouldn't have to give Otis a cut and then she could give Daniel a big sack of money and he could add it to his escape-from-LA fund.

Why would she tell him any different? She was a ghost, and alleviating him of his massive guilt would be the antithesis of a haunting.

"Can you untie me?"

"No."

"Didn't think so," Daniel said, unsurprised yet still disap-pointed.

"I'm sorry I'm not more useful to you."

"Why are you here?"

She leaned over him, her face entering his field of vision. "The same reason the others are here. The same reason I pulled jobs for you. The same reason anybody does anything for you. Because they love you."

"That's really heartwarming."

Punch drew back. The flat impact of her footsteps circled him.

"We all love you."

Daniel sighed, and the ravaged stub of his finger leaked blood. "Why?"

"You haven't figured it out yet?"

"My mind's been occupied."

"I think you have figured it out, but you don't want to admit it. It's like, if you say it out loud, the people who love you will disappear and you'll be alone."

"I'm alone now, Punch. Fenmont Szu cut off my finger with a dirty garden tool and now I'm sick and I'm hallucinating."

"Thieves steal more than just things," said the whisper of Punch's voice. "And you're not alone."

There were no more footfalls and no sound of the door, but Punch was gone.

Daniel closed his eyes for a time. How long, he couldn't say.

A scream of metal jolted him back to awareness. A blade punched through the door like a knife through a wad of tissues and drove a chasm straight down the middle of it. Cassandra's head emerged through the gap, like a baby being born.

"Hey, quit screwing around," she said. "We gotta go."

He could see it in her face, the love Punch was talking about, that she usually did such a splendid job of masking. Her scent was possibly the most beautiful and most real thing Daniel had ever smelled.

"But I'm so comfy here."

With blows of the groot-coated shovel, she hacked at the door until the gap was large enough for her to squeeze through.

She ran to his side and sliced the rubber straps. When she pulled the bag off his left hand, she gasped.

"Oh, god. Your hand."

"I'm okay. Hey, you know I always really loved you, right?"

"Is this the best time to be talking about this?" Gently she helped him to his feet.

"Sully was saying some stuff in Ocean Park about love potions."

Cassandra gave him a grim look.

"And then Punch said some stuff—"

"You're delirious. Come on, let's get you out of here."

He nearly toppled, but Cassandra caught him. She was good at catching him. His thoughts felt slippery, but he understood this was a breakout, and not keeping his head together was bullshit.

"How're the others?"

"I got the others out, plus most of our gear. The guards were divvying it up. Spoils of war or something. I need something for your hand. Your kit wasn't with the rest of our stuff, but maybe we can find some hydra regen somewhere."

She looked miserable and desperate.

"What about Emma?"

"She helped us with the guards. Otherwise, we'd be in a world of fuck-all right now."

"We're not in a world of fuck-all?"

"Even bigger fuck-all," said Cassandra.

"As long as we're together."

In the corridor, Jo and Moth were searching the pockets of the unconscious guards.

Moth turned his head, and Daniel winced at the sight of Moth's left ear. It was just a hole, streaming blood.

"Damn, Moth."

Moth grinned, wicked and mad. "What's that, stumpy? A little hard of hearing right now."

He wasn't the only one wounded. Blood ran from a six-inch-long gash in Jo's forearm.

"Jo . . ."

"I'm okay," she said, biting her lip against the pain as she pinched her claylike flesh to mold the wound shut.

Daniel caught the metallic whiff of her blood, but also other smells that confused him. Akhlut? Colo Colo? These were shape-shifting creatures, but not the specific ones that gave Jo her ability.

Maybe his nose was off.

With the sight of his friends alive and mostly whole, and with neutralized guards sprawled on the floor and cleaver-clubs scattered about, it was tempting to hope that everything was okay now. But his crew were all high-value prisoners, Daniel especially, and the Hierarch wasn't going to let them bash in some heads and run away from the Ossuary.

Proving him right, klaxon bells rang out.

"Back to the air shafts?" Cassandra asked.

Emma came tearing around a corner, a twist of smoke curling from her mouth. "No. They know how we came in. The shafts will be guarded and blocked. But there's another way. Follow me."

"Don't trust her," Jo urged.

"If you want to get out of here, you'll have to," Emma said.

Everyone looked at Daniel, waiting for his decision. Jo looked tortured. Daniel was in no shape for this. His head burned, and the world seemed tilted sideways, and everything smelled funny, and he could feel magic streaming from his stump.

"Get us out of here, Emma," he breathed.

Emma took them down a row of more cells. They were unoccupied, but a choking stink of suffering lingered outside them. After some more twisting passageways, she delivered Daniel and crew to yet another shut door. Footfalls approached behind them.

"Through here," Emma said.

Cassandra and Daniel performed a hasty inspection for osteomantic wards and mechanical booby traps, and before being fully satisfied it was safe, Daniel told Moth to take the door.

Moth's shovel tore into three-inch steel, filling the space with metallic shrieks. Flechettes of debris flew through the air and clanked on the ground. Moth was making quick work, but not quick enough.

Guards came down the corridor, guns drawn. Daniel moved to put his body between the guns and his crew, and the only thing saving him from being cut to shreds by bullets was the fact that the Hierarch didn't want his meal contaminated with dirty projectiles. The guards widened their positions to shoot around him, and Daniel raised his bloody left hand.

His lightning traveled a jittering web down the ceiling and walls. In the instant before it struck, Daniel glimpsed the patch sewn on the windbreaker of the guard at the front of the pack. The patch was embroidered with the wings-and-tusks emblem of the Hierarch's security apparatus, as well as with the guard's name: Lopez. Daniel was killing a person named Lopez, and reverberations from this death would travel out in countless unseen directions, like a swarm of Jinshin-Mushi beetles creating earthquakes and toppling buildings in places Daniel would never see.

Lopez shrieked and fell back, and the stench of melting rubber-soled boots and cooked meat bloomed in the air.

Daniel shot more lightning and hit the advancing guards. Hot blue arcs leaped from body to body. A guard in the rear leveled her rifle, and Daniel sent a bolt from the ceiling into her gun. She coughed out a scream and fell.

That was easy, thought Daniel. Why was that so easy? His control had never been this good. Maybe because he'd been exposed to kraken particulates in the Ossuary. Or maybe he'd inhaled some of his father's skull when he opened the drawer. Or maybe he'd just never been so afraid and so angry at the same time.

"We're through," Moth hollered. Daniel turned away from the guards, sprawled on the floor, smoke rising from their backs. A few were moving. There were some groans. Most were still, and Daniel felt sick and powerful.

He joined his crew and slipped through the remains of the door. Moth slammed an inner door of decorative wood behind them.

From a place of klaxons and screams and steel and concrete, they had passed into one of order and contemplation. The walls of the long, narrow room were paneled in rich wood. Light from shaded glass lamps cast a warm glow. There was a bar, with a silver ice bucket and crystal decanters. Leather-upholstered club chairs. Oil paintings, including what looked like a van Gogh. Jo didn't even give it a greedy glance.

Deeper in the room was an oak table, long enough to seat twelve on a side. The chair at the head of the table, topped by a carved wooden dragon emerging from a wooden scroll of waves, was grand enough for a throne.

This was a dining room, and Daniel knew what fare was served here.

They continued on, through another door at the far end. Here, a Persian carpet ran down the center of the room, little more than another corridor with glass walls, behind which, hanging on hooks and racks, were human bodies in various stages of butchering. There were bones, from knuckles to complete, articulated skeletons, most of them tar-stained from osteomantic consumption. There were strips of skin, stiff like rawhide. Joints and slabs of meat. On shelves sat jars of eyes and bits of liver and stomach and brain and tongue, and cans whose contents Daniel could only guess.

The glass windows were bordered by rubber seals, but the scents pushed their way into Daniel's head. The remains belonged to osteomancers. This was the Hierarch's meat locker.

He wanted to look away but found he could not. The drawer he'd expected to find the Blackland sword in had instead held a small part of his father's remains. Maybe there were more. Maybe the Hierarch hadn't consumed the rest of him. Daniel's gaze passed over every scrap of what was once a human being, wondering if he was looking at his father.

Emma was saying something, but it was just background noise until she yanked his arm hard enough to get his attention. She was pointing at something on the carpet.

"Dig here," she was saying. "It drops down to a utility canal. Swim north fifty or sixty yards and you'll see a bricked-up airshaft. Go up the shaft until you hit ceiling, and then tunnel up."

222   GREG VAN EEKHOUT

"Why does it sound like you're not planning to come with us?"

He didn't get a chance to press Emma further. The potent, now-familiar aroma of Fenmont Szu's magic washed over him. "He's coming for you. Tell your friends to start digging."

Daniel nodded, and Cassandra and Jo and Moth dug into the floor with their shovels. They broke the skin of the carpet, tore through wood, and began tossing up scoopfuls of concrete as though it were beach sand.

"I still haven't figured you out," Daniel said.

Emma smiled, wry and enigmatic. She handed him her bag, containing the casket of potato people. Her sister golems. "Take this to 5022 West Pico Canal. Give her the bottles. Tell her I sent you. They're your best chance of seeing another sunset."

"Why don't you just come with us?"

"You have a better chance of surviving on the outside. I have a better chance of holding off Szu. Deliver the casket."

"To who?"

Emma turned and headed off to meet the redolent wave of Fenmont Szu's magic.

"Emma!" he called to her retreating figure.

Moth and Cassandra and Jo were already knee-deep in their new tunnel.

"Cassandra, take this," Daniel said, handing her Emma's bag. "I'll be right back."

"Where are you going?"

"Szu's coming. Emma can't take him alone."

"He'll kill you." Cassandra's voice lacked inflection, and her face betrayed no emotion, and that's how Daniel knew she was terrified.

"Keep digging, okay? I'm counting on you."

"Daniel—"

"I can handle this."

He caught up to Emma in the dining room. Fenmont Szu still hadn't arrived, but his magic was already there, a mass of roiling dragon and thundering mammoth herds.

"Don't let the smell unnerve you," Emma said. "He's not unlimited, and every particle of magic he's exuding on scent means less magic he can use for his attack. He's just trying to intimidate us."

"You think we can beat him?"

Emma laughed. "We've got no chance. But I'm going to delay him, and you're going to go back to help your friends survive."

Her breath smelled of damp fungal caves, with a strain of sulfur.

"So your plan is to die here while we dig a hole?"

"Either I die here, or your friends do."

"We can hold him off together." He brought electricity to his fingers. The arcs were weaker from recent use, but he could still fight.

"There are worse places in the Ossuary than the parts you've seen, Mr. Blackland. There are worse things than butchery. You have the gifts to do something about them. One day, you might also have the strength. 5022 West Pico Canal. Tell her what happened down here."

"Tell who?" he asked her again. "What are you talking about?"

The floor shuddered, and Fenmont Szu came thundering down the long dining room floor. In appearance, he was still himself. But his smell, his aspect, his essence, marked him as something else. Fenmont Szu wasn't merely using magic. He *was* magic.

Daniel had seen power like this once before, in his father's living room, when the Hierarch appeared with his fork.

Emma smiled. "I'll attend to this. Shoo."

She turned toward Szu and opened her mouth. Flames wavered on her tongue.

The glasses behind the bar jingled and the paintings on the walls rattled as Szu drew close. Emma widened her mouth and vomited cascades of flame. Waves of heat seared Daniel's face and eyes, and through tears and heat-blurred air, he watched Szu slow and stagger.

Szu took three more crushing steps forward.

Emma roared. Everything in her path vanished behind the erupting flames.

Daniel threw an arm across his face and ran back to Cassandra and Moth and Jo.

He helped them dig.

NINETEEN

The police boat's searchlight probed the ice-cold water. From six feet under, at the bottom of the canal, the light seemed to bend unnaturally. Was this just simple refraction, or was the light source osteomantic? Daniel flattened, forcing his chin deeper into mud and algae slime as the boat made its achingly slow pass. Languid horntail and coontail fronds waved in the current. When the plants grew still, Daniel peered toward the surface to make sure the boat was gone.

He'd managed to tease more aquatic magic than should have been possible from the last of the kolowisi, bagil, and panlong sea-creature extracts, but he and his crew had been huddling on the bottom of the canal for nearly half an hour now, and soon they'd be terrestrial creatures again and would have to surface.

Moth gave in first, launching himself up through the darkness for air. After that, there was no point in delaying the inevitable. Daniel's face broke the surface and he filled his lungs with oxygen and diesel fumes.

He swam for the bank and crawled up among rusted buoys and shopping carts and milk crates. He was tempted to collapse in the mud and sleep. It had taken them hours of tunneling to get out of the Ossuary, with Daniel using Jinshin-Mushi beetle to collapse the tunnel behind them.

With a groan, he rose to his feet and helped Cassandra to hers.

"Worst job ever," she said, her voice shuddering with the cold.

Like him, she was soaked and caked in mud. They helped drag Moth and Jo up, and Daniel led his battered crew through shadowed alleys.

They spent the dark morning hours camped beneath a flume-way overpass. A homeless man threatened to knife them unless they found another place to sleep, but when Moth flexed the ridiculous muscles in his forearms, the man retreated back to his nest of blankets and garbage bags and cardboard boxes. Another man offered them a swallow from his jug of Wolfskill, which only Moth accepted.

Before daybreak, Cassandra went off for some badly needed supplies. Daniel's watch ticked off a tense fifteen minutes before she returned with clean clothes, first-aid supplies, bottled water, wet wipes and towels, and a bag of granola bars, half of which she gave to the man with the Wolfskill.

"Thought you'd ditched us," Moth said, changing into a grass-green tracksuit.

"You wear XXXXL pants, dude. Took me a while to find a big-and-tall store to break into."

"I think you added an X there, dear."

Daniel hissed while she treated the hideously ragged stump of his little finger with alcohol and applied a gauze dressing.

"There's a whole zoo of canal microorganisms in there," she said. "You're probably going to grow a second head."

"I don't care, as long as it's as pretty as you."

She punched him in the neck, but very lightly.

Things felt normal. Trading quips. Moth wearing stupid clothes. It was as though they were only bruised and bloodied instead of hunted and wounded.

Jo wasn't having it. She sat off on her own, with her back to a concrete pillar, her knees drawn up, staring a thousand-yard stare.

Daniel kicked aside broken glass and a rusty nail and sat beside her.

"We're going to have to move on in a few minutes. You okay?"

She took a long time before answering. "I don't even know what we're doing anymore. It wasn't supposed to go down like this."

"I know, Jo. I know it was supposed to go different. I'm sorry."

Having spoken the words, and hearing how inadequate they sounded, he wished he hadn't spoken at all.

"Every cop in the city's looking for us."

"Well, I'm used to that. That's my life. But look at me. I'm still the crazy free spirit you know and love." He held up the throbbing wad of gauze packed around what remained of his little finger. "Okay, minus half an inch, maybe."

"It's not funny," she said, too loud. "Maybe we can hide from the cops, but we can't hide from Otis. He sold you. You were supposed to deliver yourself. You know what happens when Otis makes a deal and the other party doesn't deliver. He'll grind us up and sell us as dog food."

Moth walked over and put his finger to his lips and shushed her like a librarian. "Easy, kiddo. Worry about the Hierarch. The boss can deal with Otis."

Jo shot to her feet. Her eyes looked wet and bruised. "Oh, really? How's he doing so far? We got no sword, we're hiding like rats, and we got no place to go. But you're all still licking Daniel's ass like it's ice cream."

"Maybe you should lower your voice," Cassandra said.

But Jo wasn't done. "I say we go back down, and we finish the job we were hired for. That's the only way we get out of this with an inch of skin left. If we don't, Otis will—"

"Jo," Cassandra said with chilling calm. "Lower your voice."

Jo swallowed the next part of her rant, but her clenched fists boiled below the skin. Her cheeks fluttered. Daniel had never known her to shape-shift in response to emotion, but she was losing herself now. And it was his fault.

He drew her away from the others, his hand on her shoulder. Her could feel her shoulder blade shifting beneath her shirt.

"I screwed up," he said.

Her lips thinned, deflating. "Yeah. You really did."

"I didn't figure out what Otis was doing until it was too late. He knows I'm too slippery to let myself get bagged in an alley, but I'm dumb enough to walk into the Hierarch's trap under my own steam."

"Dumb," Jo agreed.

"But here's the thing. This is still a job. It has to be a job if we're going to make it out the other end. The objective's the only thing that's changed. The score now is staying alive."

"You have a plan on how we're going to manage that?"

"Not much of one. But Emma gave me an address. She said there'd be help there."

"An address. From Emma. That's your plan. Please tell me you have a Plan B."

"I'm working on it," he said.

"Then let me help you with that. Let's go back underground, get the sword, and deliver it to Otis. That way, not only do we survive, but we get rich. Sure, there's still a guard presence. Sure, maybe Fenmont Szu's still alive after whatever Emma did to him. But they're looking for us here on the outside, not in the Ossuary. They'd never expect us to come back—"

"Right, because going back would be stupid."

"—and you can pulp them with your earthquake-beetle trick. Pulverize the whole place, kill most of the guards. Between your nose and our digging tools, we can still find the sword."

"We don't even know if it's being kept in the Ossuary," Daniel said. "We don't even know if still exists."

"Emma believed in it, and she turned out pretty square."

"Maybe we'll consider that Plan F."

A fresh red stain bloomed on the bandage covering the gash in Jo's forearm. For the second time, Daniel smelled unfamiliar shape-shifting essences coming from her.

Something was off.

"Better have Cassandra take care of that," he said.

Cassandra stole a pontoon van and drove it to the five-thousand block of West Pico Canal, a neighborhood of mechanics and used furniture stores and a day-slave market behind a hardware store. Armed men in uniforms checked slaves in and out of the fenced pens, but they were private security, not cops or Ministry security. They wouldn't be looking for Daniel and his crew.

Cassandra tied the van off beneath the shade of a dusty

palm tree, and Daniel led the crew down cracked sidewalks. It was a short but nerve-jarring walk, especially when a pair of black-and-white water cycles zipped down the waterway, but it turned out the cops were only escorting some baron's luxury yacht downtown.

"Aw, can't we have breakfast, at least?" Moth moaned as Daniel rushed them past Roscoe's House of Chicken N Waffles.

Cassandra made a face. "I find the combination dubious."

"The waffles are substandard," Moth allowed, "but the chicken is delectable. They elevate each other."

Cassandra would not be convinced. "I don't believe chicken and waffles can mate and produce viable offspring."

Jo glowered.

They arrived at a two-story corner building with bars over the windows. A vacuum cleaner shop occupied the first floor. It wasn't quite 7 A.M., and the sign on the window was flipped to CLOSED. In the unlit shop, upright vacuum cleaners stood in ranks, like soldiers.

Out of habit, Cassandra examined the door lock. "Want me to break in?"

"Let's try it legal for a change," Daniel said. He rapped his knuckles against the door glass.

A light in the back of the shop went on, and a figure wove a path through the vacuum cleaners to stand a few feet back from the door. She wore a belted bathrobe, the pale skin of her face and neck standing in soft contrast to the darkness of the shop. Tall and slender, she appeared not much older than her mid-teens, with large, pale-gray eyes, and a delicate finger curled around the trigger of a shotgun.

"She doesn't seem friendly," Cassandra said.

"Or like someone who can help us," added Jo.

Daniel moved his face closer to the glass. "Emma Walker sent us."

The face changed, so quickly Daniel almost missed it, but for a flash the girl's eyes grew hard as diamond, and the fine features sharpened to hawklike intensity, and Daniel no longer knew what the fierce thing on the other side of the door was, other than that it was osteomantically potent.

Then she resumed being what she'd been before, at least in appearance. She unlocked the door.

"Come inside," she said.

They followed her through the showroom and upstairs, to the second-floor apartment over the shop. There was a living room and a sparse kitchen. The furnishings were high-quality thrift-shop finds, mostly black-lacquered wood and red silk upholstery of Chinese design. The only books in view were a copy of the Yellow Pages and a stack of soap opera digests. At the girl's invitation, Daniel and his crew took seats, looking like admonished burglars invited in for tea.

The girl told them to wait while she put together some re-freshments. Daniel protested that it wasn't necessary, but she acted as though she hadn't heard him. She returned bearing a tray of tea and a plate of shortbread cookies. She left the shot-gun in the kitchen.

Moth helped himself to cookies as she poured the tea. Her manner was serene and courteous, and Daniel wondered if he'd imagined her transformation behind the door. He smelled Oolong, but no magic.

He saw it then in the shape of her nose, in her jaw, in her eyes: She was a younger version of Emma.

"Tell me what happened to her," she said.

"We met in Chinatown," Daniel began, remembering that, during their first encounter, they'd drank Oolong, the tea of black dragons and great sorcerer-kings. Without telling her the specifics of the job—the place or the score—he admitted that Emma had been helping them with an illegal enterprise, and the last time Daniel saw her, she was helping them escape a powerful osteomancer.

He watched her face as he spoke.

"But you already knew all that, didn't you?"

The girl set down her teacup and closed her eyes. She seemed prayerful.

"Yes," she said. "Most of it. Emma took you into the Ossuary. Where else would she have gone? The sorcerer who killed her? Was it Mother Cauldron?"

"Fenmont Szu."

"The Hierarch's scalpel and truncheon."

Daniel still clung to the hope that she'd somehow survived. He didn't want any more sacrifices to him in his ledgers. "Are you sure she died?"

"It was Fenmont Szu. Of course she died."

His lungs tightened, a physical manifestation of his guilt. He wasn't sure the guilt was warranted—Emma had used him to get into the Ossuary, after all—but the guilt was there, regardless. It did Emma no good.

The girl returned to the kitchen. Daniel watched her carefully. She took up the shotgun. "Come with me."

Daniel stood. "You guys stay here. Finish your tea. Enjoy your cookies."

"All of you have to come," the girl said. "You're being pursued, and your scent leads here. I'm going to have to abandon this place."

Moth stuffed a handful of cookies in his pocket, and they all followed her into what turned out to be a complex warren of rooms, closets that led to other rooms, sliding panels opening to more passageways, and then down a staircase. The girl lit the way with a flashlight, revealing walls of wood and plaster, giving way to brick as they descended, then to stone blocks and mortar, and finally to undressed granite. They were below canal level now, and when they reached the bottom of the steps, the girl took them through a stone tunnel with a ceiling so low, Moth had to bend to avoid scraping his head. The low hum of canal water flowing behind the walls made Daniel feel as though they were walking through the city's circulatory system.

"Where are we?" he asked the girl.

She stopped and turned, her face ghostly white in the halo of her flashlight beam.

"Have you ever seen a map of the canal system?"

Daniel was a thief. He'd seen a lot of maps.

"When the canals were first built, they called it Mulholland's Mandala," she said. "A mandala is a—"

"A maze," Daniel said. "A labyrinth."

"Right. Osteomancy isn't the only kind of magic. Los Angeles is driven by trade and consumption, so osteomancy dominates here. But labyrinths hold power everywhere. You'll find them in cathedrals in Europe. You'll find them on Celtic stones passed from mother to daughter. And on the petroglyphs of the Hohokam. Theseus found a wild man in the center of his labyrinth. Look at an old map of the canal system—a true map—and you'll see the mandala. The byways of Los Angeles vibrate with power. Enough, maybe, to challenge the Hierarch."

"So why doesn't he bring them down? He can't read a map?"

She turned again and resumed walking. "Not all things are down on maps. Some fingers in Mulholland's Mandala remain dry. When the water mage decides it's time to topple the Hierarch, he'll turn his valves and let water fill all his empty spaces and complete his power circuit. But until then, my family and I hide in the empty places."

"So you're allied with Mulholland?" Daniel wasn't thrilled at the idea of throwing his lot in with another old sorcerer.

"He doesn't know we're here. We're allied with ourselves," she said.

The passage widened, and the moist air warmed, and they came to a grotto of sorts, with water trickling down the walls from a great height and collecting in black pools. The space was filled with cots and sleeping bags and some proper beds, and even a four-poster. Plastic lawn chairs and loungers and dinette chairs with orange, sparkly plastic cushioning completed the furnishings. Strings of white Christmas lights sagged overhead, and in alcoves, the flames of votive saint candles flickered. Frogs croaked.

A woman stepped out from beneath a lintel fashioned from a railroad tie. Her nose was long and elegant, her face lined but attractive.

Other than her short, dyed red hair, she was Emma.

She pinned Daniel with a frank stare. Her lips parted, and blue flames licked the air.

Some two dozen people lived in the grotto, ranging from toddlers to people in their fifties. There were a few singletons, but most were twins or triplets. They hauled buckets of water, sorted groceries, swept the floors, and attended to the electrical wires that hung from the ceiling like mangrove roots. By the smell of it, there were stores of magic here, too, though they were kept out of sight.

"I owe Emma thanks," Daniel said. "She gave her life for ours."

"I would have chosen differently," the older Emma said. Wisps of blue plasma flashed behind her teeth.

"We have to respect her decision," the younger Emma said.

"I'm not so sure we do," the older said, "since it resulted in exposure of her purpose. Not to mention her immolation."

That sounded like something the Emma Daniel knew would say.

"What was her purpose?" Cassandra asked. Daniel noticed the way she'd subtly positioned herself between him and the older Emma, always guarding him. It was something his friends did so often, so naturally, that he'd stopped making note of it. They were always prepared to take a hit for him.

The young Emma swept her hand in a gesture encompassing everyone in the grotto. "All of us here are mirrors. Or, golems, if you like the cruder term. My sister and I, like the Emma you knew, are spawns of Dr. Emmaline Walker, who is . . . was . . . one of the pioneers in this kind of work. All of us were born in the Ossuary. The Emma you knew was not the first to escape, nor the first to evade the Hierarch's hounds. But she was the first who went back, time and time again, to liberate as many of us as she could. She freed dozens of us."

"So you see," the older Emma said, "while you were after profit, our sister was a liberator of slaves and test subjects. And now she's a pile of ash, and here you are, asking for our help. I think I'd rather roast you."

"Maybe this will change your mind," he said. He unzipped

his bag to show the Emmas the casket of jars Emma had freed from the Ossuary. He opened it.

Proto-golems, mirror-spawn, whatever they were properly called, it was wrong to use them as currency. But Daniel was still a thief, which meant he took things and used things he had no rightful claim to, because that was how he and his friends survived.

The younger Emma bit her lip and reached for the jars, but Daniel stepped back and closed the casket.

He was becoming a monster. "This is a transaction."

In exchange for the jars, the Emmas agreed to use their underground network of safe houses, conductors, and shepherds to get Daniel and his friends out of Los Angeles, as far as the Sierras, the eastern border of the Southern Kingdom. They'd have to survive the mountain passes, where the Hierarch was rumored to keep bands of living gigantopithecus and herds of griffins. Whether or not that was true, there'd be border guards to contend with. And if they were lucky enough to make it down the Nevada side of the ranges, they'd have to survive one of the vastest deserts in North America, only to throw themselves on the mercy of the United States government.

It wasn't exactly his dream of defecting to the Northern Kingdom, with bales of cash for new identities and bribes and start-up funds.

"I'll need to talk it over with my friends," he told the Emmas.

The young Emma took them through the tunnels to a large,

dark room serving as a graveyard for shopping carts. The Emmas needed time to get messages to their sisters on the outside, and there was nothing to do now but rest.

Jo barely waited for the Emma's footsteps to recede before airing her objections.

"Exile? We go up a fourteen-thousand-foot mountain, come down into a United States desert? Maybe we end up in a refugee camp, or maybe a prison? That's what Emma calls help?"

"It's not ideal," Daniel admitted. "But I think it's our only option. What do you want to do, Jo?"

"I already told you. Let's finish the job we started."

"That's what Punch said at the warehouse in Saugus. She never came out."

"We got our asses kicked down there, Daniel. We got lit on fire. And there's one thing you don't do when you're on fire. You don't run. We're still the best thieves in this kingdom, and the only thing that's going to save our lives is being thieves. The Blackland sword is still in the Ossuary. Otis is still expecting it. If we deliver, he can do for us a thousand times better than these Emmas. And if we don't, we're dead, whether we're in Los Angeles or Las Vegas."

Cassandra gave the rebuttal. "You're talking about the Ossuary where we almost died. The home of the Hierarch, a wizard whose reach touches even Otis. And Otis may not actually give a shit about the sword when his real game is delivering Daniel."

Cassandra's arguments were overwhelmingly better, but Daniel was still willing to put it to the vote.

Cassandra and Moth stood with him.

Jo stood alone.

She sat cross-legged on her blanket, grasping her own hands, and smiled her sad smile.

"Okay," she said.

"You sure?"

She lay down and covered herself in a blanket. "Of course I'm sure. Friends till the end."

TWENTY

A whisper in the dark: "Dude, get up."
    Moth lurked over Daniel like a giant gargoyle.
    Cassandra was curled up in the corner, snoring, and
Jo lay buried beneath a mound of blankets.

"What's up?" Daniel whispered, following Moth to the door.
Moth put a frankfurter-sized finger to his lips.

He took Daniel through the Emmas' maze of rooms and hall-
ways, through the network of attics and hidden panels connect-
ing rooms to other buildings, and finally up the long, rickety
stairwell that led to the surface. They came up between two
garbage dumpsters in the alley behind the vacuum cleaner shop.
The sun tinged the purple-gray sky with dawn. A few pigeons
picked at the greasy remains of a Chinese takeout box. Out on
the canal, a garbage scow rumbled.

"What's going on?"
Moth rubbed the back of his neck, reluctant. "It's Jo," he
rumbled. "She ain't herself, is she?"

No, she really wasn't, and Daniel was relieved he wasn't the
only one to notice. It was more than just a case of Jo suddenly
questioning Daniel's decisions. He didn't mind that. He'd led

them right into Fenmont Szu's jaws, and he *should* be questioned. But Jo was fixated on the idea of going back into the Ossuary, and that made no sense.

"I think she might have gotten a little broken down there," Daniel said. "I'll try to make it up to her, somehow. I'll try to make it up to all of you."

Moth stood with his hands in his pockets and looked at his boots as though they were the most fascinating objects he'd ever seen.

"What are you not saying, Moth?"

The big man sighed. "Here's the thing: I'm not sure Jo's wrong."

"You want to go back? To the Ossuary? The sword might not even be there. We don't know if it ever was. And we barely escaped the trap Otis and the H-Bomb set for us."

"It's not a great plan," Moth admitted. "But I like it better than hiking into Nevada. I like it better than leaving Los Angeles. I've got some people here, you know."

Daniel was ashamed he hadn't considered that. If Moth and Jo and Cassandra were with him, then everyone he cared about was accounted for. But they all had other friends. Family. Loved ones.

"What if just you and me went back?" Moth said. "It'll be like old times, like when we used to heist slushies from the Mi-T Mart in Culver City."

Daniel thought about it.

Then he smelled akhlut and colo colo.

"That sounds swell. But there's just one little problem with that, old buddy, old pal. Your forearm is bleeding again. Jo."

Jo looked at the arm she'd reshaped to look like Moth's. A

ruby stain leaked through the sleeve of Moth's jogging suit. She sighed through Moth's wide nostrils.

Her hand came out of her pocket, holding a revolver.

Daniel gaped at it. It was not the first time he'd had a gun pointed at him. Only the first time it was held by someone he loved.

"Put it away, Jo. Please."

"We're going back down. Just you and me. Your nose, your earthquake magic, my shovel. We're going to get the sword."

"We're not."

She raised the gun a fraction of an inch.

He felt like weeping.

"You can't wave a gun around and expect me to go wherever you tell me," he said. "It's not a magic wand. It's not a remote control. It's a gun, which means I have to believe you'll shoot me if I don't play along. Are you going to shoot me, Jo?"

Maybe it was an alteration of her smell, or something in the tension of Jo-Moth's shoulders, or something in her expression. But Daniel knew she was going to pull the trigger—maybe to scare him, or to graze him—and with gouging sadness, he raised his hands like a symphony conductor and electrocuted his friend.

When she fell, she was no longer Moth. And to Daniel's astonishment, she was no longer Jo.

A man in his early thirties lay at Daniel's feet. His head was shaven, his cheeks pockmarked, his teeth yellow and crooked.

Daniel let the electricity die. He plucked the revolver from the ground and dropped it in one of the dumpsters.

"Who are you?"

242   GREG VAN EEKHOUT

The man angrily wiped away a tear. "My name doesn't matter."

"I'm going to torture you if you don't answer my questions. And I'm very angry right now and won't feel bad about it."

"Fuck you—"

Daniel shocked him again, delivering about half an amp. The man lay on his belly, gagging.

"Who are you?"

"Steven Baker," he choked out. "You don't know me."

"No," Daniel said. "That's right, I don't. What have you done with my friend? Where's Jo?"

"I don't know."

Daniel shocked him again, and he screamed.

"I don't know, you asshole," the man said, shuddering. "Ask your uncle."

"Otis?"

The man, Baker, nodded. "He's got her somewhere. I really don't know."

Daniel's anger at Baker drained away, replaced by new anger at himself. He should have known, from the second in the Ossuary when he'd smelled Steven Baker's wound. It was an entirely different mix of shape-shifting essences than Jo's. He should have put it together.

"How long have you been posing as her?"

"I replaced her the night before the job started. Otis was prepping me while you were prepping your crew."

"And he wanted control over me in the field, so he installed his own inside man."

Steven Baker coughed and nodded. "You win the balloon."

It made sense now—Jo balking at leaving the Ossuary, arguing that they should go back and finish the job. Because

Otis had promised to deliver Daniel to the Hierarch, and as things stood, he'd reneged on that promise, so Daniel had to go back.

"You should have tried harder to keep me down there," Daniel said. Electricity sizzled at his fingertips, the sound of flies dying on bug zappers.

"I wanted to. But Otis underestimated your loyalty magic."

Daniel squinted at Baker. "Loyalty magic? What are you talking about?"

"You know, the spell your dad put on you. That makes people willing to follow you." Baker seemed confused by Daniel's lack of comprehension. "Come on, you really don't know?"

The pins and needles in Daniel's fingers strengthened to knife jabs as he gathered more kraken electricity.

Baker glared at Daniel with contempt. "Your friends love you. They would do anything for you. They would die for you. They *do* die for you. But you never wondered why? Did you think it was your personal charm? Because you're such a great guy? No. It's because your daddy gave you an osteomantic gift that makes people loyal to you. Because he knew one of the best protections he could give you was the love of your protectors."

"Otis told you this?"

Baker nodded.

"He lies," Daniel said.

"Eocorn horn, heated to seven hundred degrees, melded with *Panthera atrox* and terratorn coprolite. That sound familiar?"

Those were the ingredients Sully had long ago sold to Daniel's father. He'd said they were the makings of a love potion.

A reality of friends, of love, of things Daniel thought given to him out of generosity, dissolved like cotton candy on the tongue.

Baker shook his head with a laugh of disbelief.

"I've only had short exposure to you, but even now, I almost want to join your gang for real. Even after everything's gone to shit, I almost want to be your best pal. I almost want you to take me out to the malt shop. How fucked up is that?"

"Did you hurt Moth and Cassandra?"

Baker shook his head. "The worst I did to them was stealing Moth's tracksuit. I don't think he'll miss it."

Electricity webbed between Daniel's fingers. "How much is Otis paying you?"

Baker smiled bitterly. "He's not paying me. He's holding my daughter hostage."

Jo, Steven Baker, and Baker's daughter. Three more people with the misfortune of tangling their fates with Daniel's. It took a particular kind of genius to compromise Daniel's crew and somehow make it Daniel's fault. Otis was good.

"Get up," Daniel said. "We're going for Moth and Cassandra. If you're lying about them, I'm going to kill you from the inside out."

Steven Baker rose gingerly to his feet. "You're getting more violent, Daniel. You were a nicer guy when I met you."

"If things work out, I'll help you get your daughter back. I promise. But you're going to have to work with me."

With a spasm, Baker bent over and clutched his belly. Guttural sounds emitted from his throat, ridiculously like a seal struggling to bark. He jerked with convulsions. Daniel took a quick step back, ready in case this was just a ruse. But Baker looked at Daniel with wide eyes, not just in pain, but with accusation, as if Daniel had betrayed him and was doing this to him. He fell, striking his head on the pavement, like the crack of a cue stick against a billiard ball. Blood puddled beneath his head.

From the alley's mouth, a voice: "Dammit, I told you not to kill him."

"Sorry, Mr. Argent, I didn't mean to. His physiology was weird."

Four men stood at the alley's mouth. Two of them, including the one who'd apologized, wore Department of Water and Power uniforms. A third man, tall and thin, took in the air with flared nostrils. He was pointing like a gun dog, waiting for his master's release.

The final man, about Daniel's age, wore a nice suit and stared at Daniel with sober resignation.

"Daniel Blackland," he said. "You are under arrest."

Daniel raised his hands.

"Okay," he said. "Okay. No problem."

Electricity crackled over his fingers, and he decided not to feel sorry for these men.

A seizure of pain gripped his abdomen, and he doubled over, just as Steven Baker had done before he fell and died.

He never lost consciousness, but the pain was too great for him to do anything but groan softly as the DWP men wrapped his wrists, hands, feet, and ankles in rubber and clamped a bag over his head. They hauled him into a boat. Everything seemed muffled and distant as it pulled into traffic.

"You're not injured," said a voice. It belonged to the man who'd told Daniel he was under arrest. One of the DWP guys had called him Mr. Argent. "Your friend would have been fine if he'd kept to his feet, but the head injury he sustained when he fell was fatal." His voice thickened. "I really am sorry."

"Accidentally killing someone takes a special kind of incompetence," Daniel said through the bag. He smelled nothing but rubber and his own hot breath.

"The people I'm with are water mages, and I'm not very familiar with water magic. I'll be more careful next time."

"That'll be a great comfort to my friend's family." Silence followed. "Who are you and what do you want with me?"

"My name is Gabriel Argent. I'd like to say I've been looking for you for a long time, but it only seems that way."

Daniel detected a bitterness in his voice. "Well, congratulations. How'd you do it?"

The boat stopped, probably at a traffic buoy.

"It wasn't easy," Argent said. "Your trail went dead right outside the Ossuary. But I figured you had to go somewhere. The canals seemed reasonable."

"A lot of canals around the Ossuary."

"Tell me about it. I took samples from over two thousand locations. You know what's in the canals?"

"Shit?"

Argent sounded tired. "Everything's in those canals. If I enumerated it all, it'd induce cramps. But my techs isolated a mix of osteomantic essences. And my associate here, Max, identified that mix as being particular to you."

Max said nothing, but Daniel knew what he was. He'd encountered hounds before.

"So you knew I was in the water. That doesn't tell me how you traced me here. Not even the Hierarch's security is that good."

"They could be," Argent said, "with better organization. But you're right. I'm not working for the Hierarch. I'm working for someone else."

"I'm getting boat sick with this bag on my head."

"Sorry."

Firedake rose from Daniel's gut and filled his mouth with heat and pressure. A blast hot enough to melt the rubber would burn his own face, unless he became even more firedrake, with the dragon's armor of impervious scales. He could do that. He saw himself throwing his wings back in a dive, plunging through a volcanic eruption of his own making.

Then something gurgled in his belly, and he writhed in pain on the boat deck. He reached for lightning, and the pain bent him in two.

The boat came to a stop and Daniel was frog-marched to an elevator that dropped a long way into cold and damp. The doors opened to sounds of rushing water, like a room full of waterfalls.

"I'm going to have them take the bag and the restraints off," Argent's voice said, low near Daniel's ear. "For your own sake, don't do anything stupid. You're outclassed here. Just listen to what the man has to say."

The rubber bag clung to his sweating cheeks and forehead as it was tugged off. The rubber sheets and straps over his hands and shoes came away. His escorts surrounded around him in the damp space. Gabriel Argent faced him.

"Take my advice, Daniel. You can't win down here."

Daniel gave him no response.

"I'll be back for you later," Argent said, as if he were trying to sound reassuring. He and the hound and the two DWP goons withdrew to the elevator.

Daniel was left alone in a cavernous chamber, where the incessant, soft roar of fluid made him think of a vast ear canal. Saturated air coated his skin. An intricate network of pipes and spigots and valves rose from the stone floor to a domed latticework of plumbing. In the gloom, Daniel made out water-wheels, turning with unfathomable purpose.

"Please step forward, Mr. Blackland. I have bad eyes."

Daniel moved toward the only light source in the room, an Olympic-sized pool, glowing turquoise. A broad steel desk rose from the center of the pool, like an island. Hunched behind it in a voluminous white suit was William Mulholland. His blue eyes twinkled like a sun-dappled pond.

"Thank you for coming to meet me."

Daniel forced a laugh. "You mean thanks for being assaulted and kidnapped? I guess you're welcome."

Mulholland hummed a chuckle. "You remind me of your father."

"Do I? Or is that one of those obligatory things old men say to the sons of other old men?"

"Your father was an elegant man," Mulholland said. "He was educated and graceful. You are not."

"He was a tall Anglo and I'm a short brown guy, you mean. That's kind of racist."

"Ah, but you did inherit Sebastian's recklessness. That's not necessarily a bad thing. I started out as a ditchdigger. If I'd been afraid to take risks, I'd have probably died with a shovel in my hands."

"And now you're the kingdom's most powerful plumber."

Mulholland and the Hierarch had risen to power together. Without the Hierarch's life-extension magic, Mulholland would have died half a century ago. But without Mulholland, Southern California would still be a desert.

Mulholland's chuckle sounded like digestion. Great, another chuckler. "Most people go through life with a severe misconception about the nature of water. They think water gives. That it flows around obstacles. The Hierarch once thought that of me."

"He was wrong?"

"In 1941 I brought down the Sepulveda Dam and let the Los Angeles River kill three hundred and forty-eight of the Hierarch's citizens. I do not give." He coughed, liquid gurgling in his lungs. When he got it under control, he smiled kindly, like a grandfather. "Your heist into my old friend's Ossuary went dreadfully wrong, didn't it?"

Daniel saw where this was going. One way or another, he was headed back to the Ossuary, either as merchandise delivered to the Hierarch, or as a thief to pick up something in there Mulholland wanted. Death sentence either way. But if it was the latter, maybe he could get a reprieve.

"I've had better days," Daniel said.

The water mage rose and moved around his desk, stepping out onto the pool and walking on water toward Daniel. By Mulholland's pleased expression, Daniel knew he'd betrayed an instant of awe.

Mulholland stood before him now. He wasn't a physically impressive man, just a sagging container of flesh filled with magically preserved innards. But he was ancient and mighty.

"This kingdom runs on magic, Mr. Blackland. But it's the wrong kind of magic. Osteomancy. A consumable. A nonrenewable. Europeans stumbled on these shores, looking for gold and magic, and like they did all over the world, they found it being used by the people who'd lived here since before the invention of history itself. It was only a matter of time before a man like the Hierarch decided to take it all and kill anyone who got in his way, and he dug out every last bone in every last tar deposit. Bones that had been lying in the earth for millennia, bristling with magic, pried out and ground up and smoked away in decades."

He motioned Daniel to follow him into the dark forest of humming pipes.

"The water running through my network is even more ancient than the bones that came from the La Brea Tar Pits, or the bones imported from Japanese islands and the Gobi Desert. Some people reckon all the water on earth came from space. Bombardments of magic, over billions of years, originating out there, from the deepest closets of mystery. From space to sea to cloud to rain to earth to sea. Ancient. Eternal. But here's a secret." He leaned in close to Daniel, like a hideous wave about to crash down. "Southern California has no water of its own."

He took Daniel deeper into the pipes, a rain forest of snaking copper tendrils and condensation falling in fat droplets. "The Hierarch's wars with Northern California aren't just about territory, or osteomantic spoils. It's about water. Our war with the United States cut us off from the Colorado River. The Pacific Ocean gives us a near infinite supply, but my desalination plants are old and crumbling to rust, and I can no longer replace them without the Hierarch opening his purse, which he is increasingly loathe to do. And yet the canals still flow. The flumeways still push traffic. Water still comes from the taps. By magic. My magic, which I expend every day, with fewer and fewer resources."

He stopped, the lines in his face like the cracks in a dry lakebed.

"Without water," he said, "we have no food. Without water, we have no transportation. Without water, we have no industry. The Hierarch murdered your father."

The shift in topic was so abrupt, Daniel could only laugh. "He really did. Killed him, cleaned him like a fish, and ate him, right in front of me."

He wondered if men like Mulholland and the Hierarch had fathers. Maybe they were hatched from eggs.

"And you never sought vengeance?"

"Living well is the best revenge."

Mulholland made a soggy cluck. "And are you, Mr. Blackland? Are you living well?"

"Every minute you don't kill me is the very best moment of my life, Mr. Mulholland."

Mulholland's face darkened.

"I must have water. The Hierarch won't give it to me. So he must be washed away."

Daniel shut his eyes. Hadn't he always known it would come to this? Not because he was the vengeance-obsessed son of a great wizard. He was not. He'd never been. He'd found a different way. Maybe he hadn't lived a moral life, and he'd never freed himself from the web of power and exploitation he'd been born to, but he'd found a way to survive, and he'd found people he cared about, who, maybe against their own will, loved him back. But somehow he'd always known he'd be used regardless of his intent. Sebastian Blackland had stirred him and sculpted him to be a weapon, and in this kingdom, a weapon was too useful a tool to be left alone.

"If I do this for you, it's just me, alone," Daniel said. "I don't want anyone else involved."

"You are referring, of course, to your friends."

Daniel knew what Mulholland was going to say.

"They are already involved," Mulholland said. "Gabriel Argent took them into custody hours ago. If you successfully complete this job for me, they'll live. If not . . . Well."

Mulholland straightened his jacket and withdrew into his wet jungle.

Argent was waiting for Daniel in the elevator. His face was the color of newsprint, with shadows under his eyes. He didn't look like he slept much. The doors shut, and the car rose out of the sodden dark.

Something occurred to Daniel. "Argent's your name? Any relation to Rose Argent?"

"My mom."

"My father mentioned her once. Haven't heard the name since."

"Third Correction."

"Yeah," Daniel said. "That happens."

"He's going to kill your friends anyway," Argent said. "And you, too."

Daniel already knew that. Mulholland wanted his rival out of the way. Anyone who killed the Hierarch would automatically become his new rival.

The doors opened.

"I can fix this," Argent said. "We should talk."

And so they did.

TWENTY-ONE

The Los Angeles Museum of Art sprawled across twenty acres of plazas and landscaped park, less than a mile west of the La Brea Tar Pits. In a black business suit, Daniel got in line at the box office. He clutched a briefcase in his right hand. It contained a rubber ball, some wire, a few rolls of duct tape, a gun, and several plastic souvenir snow globes.

His left hand was wrapped in cloth and elastic bandages. A skiing accident, he was prepared to say, if anyone asked. The throbbing pain of his finger stump still radiated all the way to his collarbone. The aching fatigue of the last few days came in waves. His eyes felt sandblasted and his thoughts came sluggishly. Not good working conditions. So easy to make a mistake.

He smelled hound, and sure enough, stationed around the plaza were half a dozen dogs and handlers. Sint holo was always Daniel's most reliable magic, but even though Gabriel Argent assured him that very few hounds were trained to detect sint holo, Daniel wasn't willing to risk it. He couldn't chance being identified by his osteomancy. He wouldn't use kraken or firedrake or any other kind of magic. Not until he faced the Hierarch.

He purchased an all-exhibits pass with cash and entered the museum through the Ahmanson Building, which, in addition to the European, Islamic, and modern art collections, housed the People's Gallery, currently closed for a new installation.

At the front desk, he picked up a museum map.

"Please let me know if I can help direct you," said a man in a blue blazer, sitting behind the desk. He was regular museum staff. The woman standing behind him, also in a blue blazer, was not. Her penetrating gaze lingered on Daniel's face, and he resisted the urge to make sure his fake mustache was on straight.

He spent a few hours admiring dance paddles and ancestor figures from Rapa Nui, Turkish dishes and Iranian tile, paintings by Cézanne and Degas, and he memorized the locations of all the cameras tucked in the corners of the galleries behind smoked plastic domes in the ceilings. He sat on benches to rest his feet and watched the comings and goings of art lovers and docents and security guards. It would be different at night, but if anything, security would be lighter then, with the crowds gone. Unfortunately, the patrol posts and patterns would be different, too, and Daniel wouldn't have a chance to observe them.

At 5 P.M., he had an expensive BLT and a sparkling water in the café.

At 7 P.M., an hour before closing, he attached himself to a docent-led tour group and followed them to the second floor. To his right was the German Expressionism gallery. To his left, restrooms and a drinking fountain. And directly in front of him, a desk manned by a pair of guards.

Daniel parted company with the tour and entered the bathroom. He washed his hands and checked his mustache, and when a man at the urinal went away, he stepped into a toilet stall. Forty seconds later, he lay in the crawl space above the ceiling, spread-eagled to distribute his weight. With the way his week had gone, he was pretty sure he'd come crashing down through the ceiling tiles. He waited and listened and tried hard to stay awake and keep his mind off bad thoughts.

At 7:56, he heard the rustle of plastic garbage bags and the slosh of a mop.

He waited until the janitor left.

Nobody else came.

He slid some panels aside and dropped down into the stall.

From his briefcase, he took the rubber ball and a coil of monofilament wire. Reaching as far down the toilet bowl as he could, he pushed the ball in until it was firmly stuck. He flushed and used the monofilament to tie the flush handle in the down position. In less than a minute, water was sloshing over the sides of the bowl and spreading across the floor.

Fuck Mulholland's water magic. *This* was water magic.

Back up into the crawl space he went.

It took seven minutes before he heard the restroom door. Then, a voice:

"Do I look like a plumber to you?" said a female.

A woman. Dammit, why did it have to be a woman?

"You're maintenance, right?" answered a second, male voice. "So, get in there and maintain."

"I thought I was a broom pusher. That's what you rent-a-cops are always saying."

"Christ, lady, will you just get in there and fix it, before it floods one of the galleries? Call another broom pusher if you can't handle it."

Again, the pneumatic hiss of the door as it closed, followed by muttered cursing and the splash of footfalls across the wet floor.

Daniel was crouching on the toilet when she opened the stall door.

She was not a small woman, and Daniel was not a large man. It would work.

He raised the gun Steven Baker had aimed at him. In his other hand he held a roll of duct tape.

"I promise, you're going to be fine," he said. "I just need you to answer some questions about the staff here."

She blinked at him.

"Also, I'm going to need your shirt."

In the dark green shirt of museum custodial staff and the black pants that went with his suit, Daniel approached the security desk. The man on duty was distressingly large and well muscled.

"Hey, Chao, what's up?"

The guard gave him a noncommittal smile. "You guys get that toilet fixed?"

"Yeah, but we need help cleaning up. There's shitty water spreading toward American Contemporary."

"What do I look like, a mop?" Chao laughed at his own humor. He was a humorous man.

Daniel chuckled. "A mop, yeah, that's a good one. No, thing is, the super's not answering his radio."

"Why not?"

"Probably forgot it while he was beating off to the Greek statues. I need you to call his office."

Chao looked from Daniel to the phone on his desk and back to Daniel. "What's the matter, your hands broke?"

Daniel held up his bandaged hand, which concealed the taped stump of his missing little finger. "Actually, yeah. Skiing accident. And this one," he said, holding up his right hand, "touched a bunch of toilet water. But if you don't care about germs, I can manage—"

A family-sized bottle of hand sanitizer stood like a gel-filled tower on Chao's desk.

"Fine," Chao grumbled. He lifted the receiver and went to dial. When his hands were visibly away from the alarm button on the underside of his desk, Daniel slipped a Knott's Berry Farm souvenir snow globe from his pocket.

"This is a bomb," he said. "Put down the phone and keep your hands where I can see them or you die on fire. Don't look at the camera, and slide your chair away from your desk."

Chao froze. "That's not a bomb."

"I'm an osteomancer and I'm telling you it's filled with fire-drake saliva, and if I so much as shake it it's going to be raining the ashes of your ass."

Actually, if he shook it, little glittery flakes would swirl around and descend on a tiny, plastic frontier town diorama. It was just a snow globe.

Chao cradled the receiver. "What do you want?"

"Um? To steal some art? Stand up. You're going to walk me down to the first floor and let me into the video room."

"Or you shake Knott's Berry Farm?"

"You catch on quick, Chao. Maybe I'll bring you on as my apprentice. Let's go. We'll take the stairs."

Daniel followed him to the stairwell on the opposite side of the lobby. Chao took the steps gingerly, as if he was afraid to step on a mine.

"You made me leave my desk without checking in first," Chao said. "My friend in the video room will know something's wrong."

"That might be true, except everyone knows you've got a thing for Sanchez, who stands watch in Modern, and you can't go twenty minutes without stepping over to flirt with her."

Chao looked over his shoulder at Daniel. "Who's your inside man?"

"Right now, you are. Keep walking."

On the first floor, Daniel guided him to a room with a door marked STAFF ONLY.

"Inside."

"I gotta be buzzed in," Chao said, somewhat smugly.

"I'm going to coach you, then." He told Chao what he wanted him to say. "And here's your pep talk. Firedrake saliva is really evil magic. And it's sensitive. Shake it hard enough, and it will go off. And by go off, I mean flames. But it burns in firedrake-subjective time."

"I don't even know what that means."

"It means you'll be ash in seconds, but it will seem to you like it's taking an entire week. So, think about that while you're talking to whoever's behind that door."

Chao swallowed and thumbed the intercom button on the wall.

"What do you want?" came a fuzzy voice through the speaker box.

"Let me in."

"Why?"

"I'm out of hand sanitizer."

"Man, you're not supposed to drink that stuff. Seriously, what do you want, and who's that with you?"

"You don't know Guice? From maintenance? Everyone knows Guice. How long you been working here?"

Daniel smiled and gave a little salute for the benefit of the camera that was no doubt trained on him now.

"I don't know Guice," said the fuzzy voice.

"He's here to fix the toilet upstairs," Chao said.

"Yeah, I saw the water coming under the door. What's he doing down here if the busted can's upstairs?"

"I think there might be water leaking into Modern," Daniel said, too loudly, like someone unaccustomed to speaking into a microphone.

"So, what are you bothering me for?"

"You know the regs, Parvis," Chao barked, sounding authentically irked. "He can't go in there without a work order. He just wants to check your monitors to see if there's water coming in."

"I don't see anything in Modern," Parvis said. "Except that hottie, Sanchez. Hoo boy, can she stuff a guard uniform—"

"Parvis, if you don't shut your cake and let me in—"

"Okay, okay, a guy can't even have fun on the graveyard shift?"

The door buzzed, and Chao pushed it open with the fervor of a bull hoping to gore a matador.

Parvis turned out to be a pasty white man with a hand of solitaire cards spread out before him, along with a half-empty pizza box and a two-liter of Orange Crush. A dozen TV monitors loomed over his desk. Behind him, video recorders buzzed and hummed in a rack.

"You gotta get a sense of humor, Chao," he said, taking up

a slice of mushroom and black olives. "It's called camaraderie. Esprit de corps. It's being a team player, and, oh, man, Sanchez just bent over! Will you look at her—"

"This guy's got a bomb and he's going to blow us all up instantly, only it'll take forever. It's both instant and forever, and painful both ways, so do whatever he says."

"Thank you, Chao." Daniel held up the Knott's Berry Farm snow globe. Very carefully, he set a second snow globe, this one from Disneyland, on Parvis's desk.

Parvis looked like he'd just seen a turtle wearing tap shoes.

"You're going to blow shit up with Snow White's Castle?"

"It's dragon spit," Chao said, helpfully.

"Take this," Daniel said, handing his duct tape roll to Chao. "Bind his ankles together and tape his hands to the arms of his chair."

"They are so going to fire you for this," Parvis said when Chao completed the job.

Again, gingerly, Daniel picked up the Disneyland globe. "Open your mouth, please."

Parvis refused to comply. For a guy who looked like captain of the AV club, he was pretty cheeky. Daniel was actually developing a fondness for these guards. They weren't Fenmont Szu. They weren't storm troopers. They weren't henchmen. They were just guys, probably underpaid, hired for the boring task of making sure nobody stole stuff they themselves couldn't afford in five lifetimes.

Daniel showed Parvis his gun.

"It's either open your mouth or I shoot you in the eye."

With a glare of contempt, Parvis opened his mouth.

Daniel slipped the Disneyland globe between his teeth. "Don't spit it out, or you'll slosh it and ignite the firedrake. I wouldn't scream, either. It's sound-sensitive. Your watch relief comes on in two hours. I'll be out of here by then."

He inspected his work. Tiger kidnapping, fake mustache, duct tape and tourist souvenirs.

He went to the door, then stopped and looked back. "Parvis, I know you're having a bad shift, but don't blame Chao for this. I'm responsible. Everything that's gone to shit . . ."

He found himself thinking bad thoughts.

"Everything that's gone to shit is all on me."

The world was beautiful. Everything was gardens of misty roses, and wheat fields of soft gold, and clean, white sails, drifting over glassy blue water.

French Impressionism occupied two galleries and was patrolled by a single guard who paced between them. In the passage separating the two galleries, Chao peered around a corner and signaled Daniel to follow him. He took Daniel through the north gallery when the guard was in the south gallery, and by the time the guard returned to the north gallery, they'd slipped into Dutch Golden Age.

Before the Ossuary job, the idea of hitting the Los Angeles Museum of Art would have been too ludicrous for Daniel to consider. Now, he saw it was relatively easy. Or, it would have been if he'd had his crew. Cassandra would have dealt with the cameras and alarm systems. Jo would have impersonated a guard, and Moth would have dealt with anyone they couldn't scam their way past. Also, Daniel might have gotten a little sleep first.

He just had to keep Chao in line. And what if Chao led him

right into a guard patrol, or triggered some hidden alarm switch, or decided he no longer believed in the threat of the Daniel's gun and Knott's Berry Farm snow globe? Would Daniel shoot him? Would he electrocute him? Who was he willing to hurt to protect his friends?

"You're doing fine," Daniel whispered. "Just tell me this: How's the People's Gallery guarded?"

Chao stopped. He turned and looked at Daniel in disbelief.

"The People's Gallery? You're hitting the People's Gallery? That's the *Hierarch's* gallery."

"I know."

"His personal collection."

"I am aware of this fact."

"You steal his shit, and he will flay you."

"I am comfortable with my choices," Daniel said. "And keep your voice down. How many guards?"

"Four outside the entrance."

"And inside?"

"Nobody gets inside. I thought you already knew the layout."

"Are you talking shit? Don't talk shit to me. Just tell me about the guards."

"The guys in there aren't like me and Parvis," Chao said. "They're armed to the teeth with magic."

"I think I mentioned I'm a badass osteomancer. Take me there."

"You're going to die, and you're going to take me down with you." But Chao resumed, leading Daniel through a cloud of aromas—three-headed wolf, mastodon, Pacific griffin—until they came to the source of the smell. Four guards stood before a timber door, a massive thing, banded with black iron, like the entrance to a castle. These guards wore special uniforms, of royal purple, with gold-braided sleeves and epaulettes.

"The epaulettes are too much," Daniel said.

The guards struck poses with their trident-fang lances, leveling them at Daniel's belly. Daniel removed the last of his snow globes from his pocket, this one from Universal Studios, and placed it on the floor.

"Tell them what I am, Chao."

Chao sighed. "He's a badass osteomancer."

"That's right. The globe's filled with the amniotic fluid of a wyvern. Same stuff is packed in my molar. Move or speak and I'll bite down and destroy you and the stuff you're paid to protect. Lay down your arms and open the door."

A pause long enough for a bead of sweat to trickle down the back of Daniel's neck.

"Do it," one of the guards said.

Two of them drew back the great iron bolt lock, and all four pushed the door open for him.

"End of the line for you, Chao," Daniel said.

"And for you, too."

"We'll see. By the way, your girl in Modern Art? Sanchez?"

Chao glowered. "What about her?"

"I think she likes you."

Chao's face beamed like the sun emerging from clouds.

Hope must be a nice thing, thought Daniel. He entered the People's Gallery.

The guards shut the door behind him and slid the bolt back into place, and Daniel went forward into a chamber dedicated to the Hierarch's majesty. There were gifts from foreign governments: a jade teapot and rice paper scrolls and a brick from a Mayan temple. There were bronze sculptures of the Hierarch on horseback, and a B-52 tail section hanging on wires. The most splendid piece was a billboard-sized oil painting dominating the eastern wall. The Hierarch strode across the water from Catalina Island. Seas churned and foamed at his feet, and gray whales leaped from the water, like eager dogs. He seemed to smile down on Daniel, and the smile was threatening in its paternal indulgence. A brass plate identified the work simply as ARRIVING IN LOS ANGELES. Nobody actually knew where the Hierarch had come from. Some said he came in the 1880s from China on the deck of the frigate *Prometheus*. Others said he came up from the deserts of Mexico. Still others had him sailing an iceberg down from the Bering Sea.

The Hierarch had been in this room. He'd spent his time, wandering the gallery, admiring himself, and leaving behind osteomantically charged air as thick as tar. Daniel understood now why Mulholland had instructed him to break into the museum, to come here, to breathe the Hierarch's air.

It wasn't to assassinate the Hierarch.

Daniel was being fattened for the kill.

If he actually did manage to assassinate the Hierarch, then good for Mulholland. If he failed, then Mulholland was no worse off.

Beneath the painting was a modest tunnel opening. Mulholland had told him that this tunnel was the Hierarch's private gallery entrance, but even without the water mage's intel, Daniel would have known where it led. A familiar essence wafted from it, one Daniel had not smelled in ten years.

He breathed deeply of the Hierarch's magic and entered the tunnel.

TWENTY-TWO

Gabriel took a Department of Water and Power service boat to the former location of his neighborhood coffee bar. From the passenger seat, Max sniffed the air. If he detected magic, Gabriel didn't want to know about it.

In a short time, Gabriel had secured a position in Mulholland's organization. He could requisition a boat. He could requisition water mages. He had a future at the Department of Water and Power. Patronage. Someday, maybe real power. All he'd had to do was deliver Daniel Blackland.

He killed the engine and let the boat drift. Canal lights cast wan yellow light over the black water. A few days ago, this was a vibrant place of galleries and restaurants and shops. Now, all was quiet. The current rippled, and Gabriel let it carry him along, like an amusement park dark ride.

City workers had already erected a construction fence around the charred ruins of the coffee bar. In a few days they'd have the wreckage cleared, and in a few weeks the property would be granted to someone else, and something new would be built on the site and it would be hard to remember what had stood here before. Property in Los Angeles was a revolving door.

Gabriel valued documentation and reports and spreadsheets. Records were history. Even bureaucratic records. And history was important. He flipped open a notepad, got out his pencil, and wrote, "Former Uses of 3922 W. Sunset Canal."

He took a moment to consider before writing anything down. He liked his reports succinct.

People used to come here to drink coffee.

They played chess and checkers and backgammon and bridge and hearts.

They read *Variety* and the *Hollywood Reporter* and the *Los Angeles Times* and the *Chinese Daily News* and the *La Opinión* and the *Herald Examiner*. They read the official hagiographies of the mages. They read westerns and detective novels and *fotonovelas*.

They wrote poems and plays and novels and screenplays and manifestos.

They did crossword puzzles and sketched and doodled. They met for first dates and blind dates and for immoral and unethical affairs. They fell in love.

They were beaten with clubs and shoved through plate-glass windows. They were arrested, and they bled, and they burned.

"Max. Tell me why you killed your last handler. The true reason."

The hound tucked his chin into his chest, as if he were trying to avoid a foul odor.

"I already told you. I wasn't lying."

"I don't think you told me the whole truth. Tell me now."

"He had power over me. I was tired of people having power over me. So I killed him."

"Don't I have power over you?" Gabriel asked.

"Obviously."

"But?"

"Is there a but?"

"I'm still breathing, so there must be."

"You never made me wear a leash," Max said.

Gabriel had taken off Max's leash because he thought he could get better work out of him that way. There was no kindness in the act, only utility.

"And that was reason enough to kill? Because you didn't like someone having power over you?"

Max gave him a look, innocence combined with irritation. "Is there a better reason?"

"Fenmont Szu called me a risk taker," Gabriel said. "I was insulted. I took some risks because I didn't see any other choice. Now I'm about to take another one. A big one." He glanced over at Max, in his fine gray suit and lavender tie, the profile of his nose carved sharp against the canal lights. Here was a man who had been used as a tool most of his life, and when Gabriel looked at him, he couldn't imagine him as a boy or an adolescent. It was as if he'd come this way out of the box.

Gabriel started the engine. "If you want to leave, now would be a good time."

"Where would I go?"

"I could get you to the desert. I have a cousin there. She could help you get out of the Southern kingdom."

"She could? But would she?"

"She's rich and she likes me. We used to stick gum to the bottom of pianos."

Max sniffed. The tinge of soaked wood and smoke still hung in the air.

"I think I'll stay with you," Max said. "This cousin of yours would sell me back in less time than it'd take to soften a wad of gum."

Max was probably right about that. Blood ties didn't mean much. Nor did personal history.

Gabriel threw his notepad in the canal. The pages darkened, and his neat, precise writing blurred, and the pad sank below the surface of Mulholland's canal.

Most of the great powers in Los Angeles kept private prisons in their strongholds. Disney's was said to be sunken beneath his haunted house, but Gabriel didn't know. Maybe he dressed his prisoners in international costume and forced them sing that "Small World" song.

William Mulholland kept his prisoners in tanks.

The room where the tanks were kept was not called a prison or a jail or even a detention facility. It was simply called "Tank Room 17." Gabriel took note of the high number.

Tank Room 17 was chilly and damp. The floor, walls, and ceiling were lined with mint-green ceramic tiles, like a public shower. It contained a dozen cylindrical glass tanks, each eight feet tall and connected to an elaborate system of pipes and hoses. Inside two of these tanks were Daniel Blackland's associates, Cassandra Morales and the man called Moth, whose real name Gabriel hadn't yet uncovered. In fact, he'd stopped trying.

The prisoners were as lethal in their own ways as Blackland himself, and if not for the water mages Mulholland had loaned him, Gabriel wasn't certain he'd have pulled off arresting them. As it was, the people he'd found hiding with them had escaped into their labyrinth of interconnected warrens and were scattered who-knew-where. Gabriel had lied and told Mulholland he was working on tracking them down, but he didn't think Mulholland cared that much about them.

Stripped naked, Blackland's friends floated vertically in their cells. Cassandra Morales's hair waved languidly, like the tendrils of an anemone. Moth was stuffed in his tank like a pickle in a tight jar. They were given no breathing apparatus, but the water in the tank was rich with perfluorocarbon, which carried more oxygen than blood. They stared hatefully at Gabriel through fluid and glass.

Liquid breathing was the way we were meant to live, Mulholland had proudly declared to Gabriel. He believed man had evolved from aquatic apes, and Mulholland had some sort of mad utopian dream of returning to that natural state. Gabriel couldn't understand why guys with power couldn't be content to make sure people had adequate food, shelter, transportation, education, and opportunity. Why wasn't that ever enough?

A single guard sat behind a steel office desk. He looked hopelessly bored.

"I need a few minutes alone with the prisoners."

The guard wasn't even armed. The tanks were sealed with custom bolts, and it took a special wrench to turn them. That wrench was kept elsewhere under lock and key. There were slots near the top of the tanks through which once a day someone sprinkled food flakes, exactly as though the prisoners were goldfish.

The guard got up and reached over his head to stretch. He yawned. "If you can spot me five minutes, that'd be great. All the water in this place but I still gotta walk through half the building to take a leak."

And suddenly Gabriel was doing the guard a favor instead of asking for one.

"No problem."

He waited until the guard was gone and then approached Cassandra Morales's tank. It must have been awful to be immersed. They must have thought they were being drowned. Mulholland's "natural state" was preceded by terror.

Moth pounded on the inside of his tank with his massive fist. The glass was so thick Gabriel couldn't even hear the impacts.

The door to the room opened, and Max slipped inside. He dropped a duffel bag in front of the tanks.

"Guard went to the john?"

"Yes," Max confirmed.

Gabriel turned back to Cassandra Morales. She showed him her middle finger, and Gabriel showed her what he'd been keeping in his pocket. It was a triangular wedge of firedrake scale, honed to a razor point. Firedrake could cut through diamond. It could certainly cut through glass. Taped to it was a note with detailed instructions for now and for later.

He found a stepladder behind the guard's desk and brought it over to Morales's tank. Standing on the top rung, he dropped the firedrake wedge into her feeding hole. It sank, spiraling down like a fishing weight, and Cassandra Morales caught it in her nimble fingers.

The tunnel from the Hierarch's gallery enclosed a single, narrow canal. The way was dark, but Daniel followed the smells of power until they grew strong enough to drag him along. An hour of walking brought him to a place with walls of cooked brick and a floor of soot. Terrific. He'd delivered himself to an oven. But, no. He pulled aside a curtain of fine iron links, and like a magic trick, found himself in the fireplace of a Victorian parlor. He ducked under the mantel and stepped through, his ash-covered shoes sinking into plush, red carpet. Books lined wooden shelves. Candles flickered in a fussy chandelier overhead. He recognized this place.

Done up like a French château, the Magic Castle used to be an exclusive club for the city's osteomancers, entertaining them with bars and lounges, a dining room, secret passages, stages for lectures and demonstrations. Why would the Hierarch, a man with true magical power, engage in a child's amusements? It was theater. Judges had their wigs and gavels, priests had their robes and candles, kings had their scepters and sparkly hats, and the Hierarch had a castle. So typical of Los Angeles, a city with deep magic in its bones and arteries, to express its power with film-set realities. Like the Hierarch, the city showed her true face to few, and to see it, you had to gouge the surface and dig.

Daniel had been here before. His father brought him as a young boy to meet his colleagues. He'd shaken hands like a grown-up and been weighed and measured. He didn't remember everything. But he remembered how one gained entry past the parlor.

In one of the bookcases sat a pewter owl. Daniel spoke the secret word to it: "Marrow." The bookcase swiveled open to reveal a hallway, and he stepped through.

Mulholland had sent him here to assassinate the Hierarch, which was just funny when you thought about it. But Daniel's deal with Gabriel required something even more difficult of him. He was here to steal the Hierarch's beating heart.

At the end of the hall, he found a small theater with a stage and vaudeville curtains.

"You're here," came a voice from behind the curtains. It was surprisingly mild. Even bland. And very tired. The voice wasn't frightening. What scared Daniel was the complete lack of odor. Everyone smelled of something. Food. Soap. Osteomancy. Something. But not this man.

"You're not very stealthy," said the voice.

"I didn't suppose I'd be able to sneak up and kill you in your sleep. You knew I was coming. Otis almost managed to hand me over to you. And now Mulholland's completed delivery."

"But you came of your own free will."

"I had no choice," Daniel said. "My friends are being held hostage. If I kill you, I get them back. Full disclosure."

"Mulholland promised you that? Do you believe him?"

"I'm really not going to go into great detail about all my business arrangements," Daniel said. "Are you going to come out from behind that curtain? Not being able to see or smell you is freaking me out."

"I'll give you this, then."

Aromas fell upon him in waves. There were things he knew, like mammoth and kraken and wyvern, and other smells he'd never been exposed to, of arctic creatures and things from the center of the earth and things that hinted of plasma and frigid lunar wastes. Daniel staggered and choked and turned to flee, to run long and far and never return, but the bookcase swiveled back in place, closing him in.

"Does that help, Daniel?"

Breathing was no longer an involuntary act. Daniel had to tell his lungs to pull in air. He swallowed. "Really, really freaked out."

"You must care a great deal for your friends, to put yourself through this."

"I like them well enough."

"Maybe you can murder me, Daniel," said the voice. "You're pretty powerful. You breathed in a lot of my magic when you crept through my Ossuary."

"That's what you wanted. You loaded me up on magic to make me a more nutritious meal."

And despite his terror, he did feel powerful. He'd absorbed so much magic since rappelling down from the HVAC vent in the Ossuary that every breath of charged air strained his thin skin. He was an overflowing container. Maybe he could survive this day. Stranger things had happened.

He looked at his hands. Blue aurora danced across his knuckles.

"I'm ready," he said.

"I'm sorry, Daniel. No, you're not."

The stage curtain jingled and squeaked as it drew back, and there, standing on the scuffed boards, was a tall man in a white shirt and black slacks. He was thin, bony, with bent shoulders and hair the color of cobwebs. Daniel had expected the monster in the living room, the thing too hideous and awesome to look at directly, the thing that ate his father with a fork. Nothing about this man suggested a mighty sorcerer. He looked old. A little sick. Like someone who spent too long losing at the greyhound track.

But Daniel had been fooled by shape-shifters, by golems, and by potions that caused him to mistake love stolen through osteomancy for love given freely. He'd been fooled by accomplished liars and by actors and by magic. And Daniel had smelled him. He knew better.

"Abracadabra," said the Hierarch.

Daniel directed lances of kraken electricity at the stage. The flash of his own lightning blinded him. He heard a hoarse scream of pain. Smoke rose from the Hierarch's chest. He opened his mouth to say something, but Daniel wasn't planning to listen. Instead, he stretched his jaws and released a torrent of blue flame.

With the sound of a thousand flags ripping in the wind, a parcel of fire spread out before him. He pushed with his lungs, sending a wall of fourteen-hundred-degree air at his enemy.

The Hierarch reached out, as if to catch a ball. "Stop that," he said.

He squeezed the air.

Daniel's flame guttered. He crumpled under the Hierarch's phantom grip, feeling his ribs bending inward. A raspy whistle emitted from his throat as his lungs compressed, and he fell to his knees. But the kraken lived in the black depths of the sea. Its body thrived under pressure even greater than what the Hierarch was punishing him with, and Daniel was kraken.

He shot to his feet and summoned Jinshin-Mushi beetles. They emerged from his palms and the backs of his hands. They ran down his arms, scuttling out from under the cuffs of his sleeves, from between the buttons of his shirt and from the back of his neck and the front of his collar. The beetles scurried down his legs and spilled, clattering, over his shoes. He vomited beetles. They crawled out his ears. In their thousands, they tunneled through the Persian rug at his feet, through the floorboards, into the earth. Glass chandeliers shattered. The building's joints squeaked and groaned and cracked. The floors buckled and the walls swayed.

The Hierarch leaped off the stage and took three steps toward Daniel before the floor beneath him collapsed. He fell, quick as a man through the trapdoor of a gallows. The ceiling followed in a deluge of wood and plaster chips and dust, and the stage tilted down and slid, joining the avalanche of debris.

After a few seconds, the earth stilled.

Daniel crept up to the edge of the pit and took a breath. Dust and debris settled one floor down. He still felt the beetle manifestations roiling beneath his skin. They wanted to be let out. They wanted to make more earthquakes. And Daniel wanted to let them. He could bring down the entire castle. He could bury the remains in a mudslide. He could go back to the Ossuary and crush the Hierarch's precious treasures, and bring down his Ministry headquarters.

From the hole came soft moans of pain.

Good. He hoped there were bones sticking through the Hierarch's flesh. The thought of him suffering was Daniel's only comfort. All he had done was survive several seconds of confrontation.

He peered over the shattered floorboards. It was about a twelve-foot drop, with no easy way down. He preferred it here on the ledge. Down there was danger. Down there was a wizard who might be seriously injured or just simply angry.

Debris shifted below. There was a cough. Green smells of

regeneration wafted up from the hole: hydra essence, from a creature so resilient you could sever its head and it would grow back. The Hierarch was already healing himself.

A child's voice: "You can't beat him that way."

At the theater entrance stood a boy, seven or eight years old. Shaggy-haired and dressed in an oversized T-shirt and jeans too short for him, his feral appearance reminded Daniel of a slave-wraith. But there was awareness and intelligence in his solemn eyes, which seemed to be appraising Daniel. He exuded a tantalizingly familiar and powerful aroma.

"You won't beat him by throwing fire and poison at him," the boy said. "He's got more fire and poison than anyone. You should run."

Fresh blooms of magic rose from the hole and assaulted Daniel's nostrils. Whatever fear he'd been suppressing came to the surface now.

"Run where?"

From the hole came more sounds. Scrabbling. Piles of wreckage being shoved aside. Climbing.

The floor moved in a queasy roll. The walls undulated, and the earthquake smell tumbled through the building. The walls cracked into webs.

"Burn him," the feral boy said. "Slow him down a little."

Daniel leaned over the pit and loosed a furnace. Swirling flames poured out of him, down into the hole, answered with rising shrieks of pain.

The boy didn't wait around to see the results. He darted down the hall and around a corner. Daniel pursued and caught up just in time to see him scurry up a ladder, through an opening in the paneled ceiling. Daniel went up after him, into an attic.

Rays of grimy light came in through a round, leaded window near the rafters. The space was filled with the mundane storage of a private club: holiday decorations, milk crates full of candlesticks, boxes of paperwork, a mound of junk under a canvas tarp. But there was also a stainless steel operating table, with a drain that fed into a basin on the floor, and a nest of rubber tubes. An array of saws and knives and pincers hung from hooks. There was a copper fork. This was a place in pause, waiting to be filled with screams, more intimate than anywhere Daniel imagined the Hierarch would work his osteomancy, and all the worse because of it.

"Who you are?" Daniel said, his hands tingling with subdued kraken energy and nerves.

The boy reached into his pocket and flipped a quarter at him. Daniel caught it.

"You forgot to call heads or tails."

"Just look at it," the boy said.

Daniel did, first at the wings-and-tusks emblem on the tails side, then the heads side, featuring the Hierarch's portrait.

"See it now?" The boy helpfully tilted his chin and ran his finger down his long nose.

"His son," Daniel said.

The boy shook his head.

"Golem, then."

"Uh-huh. I was supposed to wait inside there."

He pointed to a broken crate.

"You broke out of your box."

"Yeah."

Daniel didn't buy it. "If you're really his golem, you'd be under guard, in a vault. You'd be the fucking crown jewels."

"I *was* under guard." He drew back the canvas tarp. Two

bodies in black uniforms lay curled beneath. Daniel smelled venom.

The boy sniffed the air. "You hurt the Hierarch pretty bad. He's not healed enough to come for us yet."

Daniel had dropped a ceiling on him and breathed enough fire to burn down an apartment complex. "I hurt him. Well, that's encouraging. I guess."

"He'll get better."

"I know. I'm not finished with him yet. Just taking a breather."

"Are you going to kill me?"

The thought hadn't occurred to him, but it should have. If the boy was the Hierarch's golem, he was a threat.

Is this something you're willing to do now? Daniel asked himself. You're going to kill a kid?

"Of course I'm not going to kill you. You should wash your mouth out with soap for even asking."

The boy regarded him, wary and curious. "Aren't you scared?"

"Of course I am. I'm terrified."

"Then why don't you run away?"

Daniel shrugged. "Can't. Won't. What about you?"

"I already ran away once. That's why they crated me."

The Hierarch kept his golem in a box. This is the kind of thing Emma Walker was trying to prevent.

Daniel reassessed the boy's age. He talked older, but he might only be six. Daniel wasn't well versed in kid morphology. "What's your deal, anyway? What's he using you for?"

"When he wears a golem out, he puts himself in a new one. And I'm it, a golem grown from his own, original flesh. From his own magic. The problem is, I'm not mature enough yet. I'm not powerful enough. He'd be stepping into a weaker body. But he's too far gone to wait. So, first he needs to nourish me.

That's what you're for. He calls you a meal fit for a king," the boy said. "I'm the next king."

Like a pipe organist, Mulholland sat before an expansive array of controls: switches and levers and valve-wheels, all accessible from a wooden throne on brass rails. Above the console, climbing all the way to the plumbing webwork in the high ceiling, was a board with hundreds of gauges and dials, and a vast configuration of lights that Gabriel recognized as a map of the kingdom's aqueducts.

Mulholland began to turn valves. "You're just in time. I'm cutting off flow through Pyramid Dam."

Gabriel had been studying. Water flow through the dam drove the turbines of a 1,495-megawatt hydroelectric power plant. Cutting off the water would darken huge swaths of the San Fernando Valley. With the spin of a few valves, Mulholland was throwing lives into chaos. There might be people lying on operating room tables, or on life support, and commuters depending on traffic controls. A few valves, and hundreds of thousands of lives were casually put at risk.

On the map, a light blinked red.

"May I ask why?" Gabriel asked. "Have the people in the Valley erred in some way?"

"Not in any remarkable way. They pay their taxes, they work their jobs, they switch on their televisions and warm themselves in its reliable glow. They turn their faucets and water their green lawns. Their children and dogs leap in the sprinklers, and their goldfish swim endless circles in their bowls. They boil their pasta and rinse germs off their hands and flush their excrement out of sight. Tomorrow, when I give them back Pyramid Dam, their lives will continue as such."

"A demonstration," Gabriel said.

Mulholland nodded, a pleased teacher. He rose from his chair. "It's a good idea to remind people who their magic comes from."

Mulholland looked over his console, where the blinking red light had gone black, and clasped his hands behind his back. He seemed very satisfied.

"I've always been impressed by magic," Gabriel said. "But there's more. There should be more."

Mulholland turned away from his controls and glanced at him, curious. "Oh?"

"There are sources of power that don't rely on bones and mandalas. There is bureaucracy. There is administration. There is the idea of running things for no other reason than things need to be run. There is power fueled by sober responsibility. There is service."

Nerves were making Gabriel pompous. He hadn't meant to make a speech. Speeches got you noticed. But maybe, just this once, attracting attention was a good tactic.

Mulholland frowned. His watery eyes looked into Gabriel's.

"End it," Gabriel said.

A shot thundered, and Mulholland's forehead blew out, along with a great splash of brains. The blast echoed through the pipes of the vast chamber, for so long that Gabriel wondered if it would ever end. He decided that, even if the sound died, the echo would reverberate through the life of every man, woman, and child in the kingdom. There would never be a moment when Gabriel didn't hear the sound of that gunshot.

Mulholland lay on the stone floor, facedown, with a pool of blood expanding from his head.

Max, standing behind Mulholland's body, pocketed his gun.

"We just turned off half of the kingdom's power," Gabriel said. "Let's hope Blackland can turn off the rest."

With his handkerchief, he cleaned Mulholland's brains off his shirt.

The webwork of pipes all around him sang out and groaned, and the earth beneath him shook.

The attic floor rolled beneath Daniel's feet. Wood ground against wood and floorboards ruptured. Deep in the earth, tectonic plates moved with thunderous cracks. The Hierarch was coming for Daniel.

The golem boy vanished behind a rain of dust and cobwebs from the ceiling, and when Daniel summoned a wind to clear the air, the boy stood, facing him, gripping the Blackland sword. The smell was unmistakable.

Daniel felt a pang of embarrassment. The sword *did* exist, and Daniel had failed to steal it. He breathed something between a sigh and a laugh.

The boy took a few wobbling steps toward Daniel. He held the sword out to him, handle first. "Kill me. Cut me open. Eat as much of me as you can. With my magic added to yours, you might be able to beat him."

"Shut up. I'm not going to cut you open."

"It's what I'm for," the boy insisted, his voice rising. "I'm supposed to be eaten."

"Eat you? I thought he was going to become you."

Tears cut paths in the boy's grimy face. "How do you think he does it? He eats. It's all he does. If you don't, then *he* will. He'll eat every last crumb of me. He'll *be* me. And I'll be him. I don't want that."

"I'm not going to eat you," Daniel said with finality. "God, sometimes I hate my hometown."

"It's the only way!" the boy shouted back, so ferocious that Daniel recoiled. He was red-faced now, sobbing. He stripped off his T-shirt and spread his arms out and presented the white flesh of his belly for the sacrifice.

Daniel smelled the power in him. The golem-boy possessed the components of the Hierarch's magic, and Daniel knew he was right. With his osteomancy fueling Daniel's own, maybe he could destroy the Hierarch. Maybe he could just take the boy's heart. And why shouldn't he? Why shouldn't he eat this miniature replica of the Hierarch and use his power to live, to slay the monster and earn Moth's and Cassandra's release? Daniel was an osteomancer. His gift was to gain strength from what he consumed. To take and use magic. To take and use his friends' love and loyalty. Why not take what the boy offered?

The shaking subsided. The swaying settled, and dust motes danced in the air.

"You take the sword," said Daniel. "Take it and haul your ass away from here as fast as you can. I'll fight him off to give you time."

"There is no more time, son," the Hierarch's voice said.

Silently, gracefully, the Hierarch rose, floating outside the shattered attic window with the night sky behind him. His sparse hair moved in a gentle breeze. He smiled in a familiar way and ignited. A corona of osteomantic energy flared around his silhouetted body. He was like a black sun.

The boy wailed. He held the edge of the blade up to his throat and screwed his eyes tightly shut, his intent clear. He would die, and Daniel would feast.

Flames rose around the window frame. They spread to the wall, and the wood blackened and crackled away like paper before the Hierarch's blazing magic.

"Give it to me," Daniel said, reaching for the sword.

"You can't beat him."

Daniel winked at him. "I can. Got a secret weapon. But I need you to do something."

The boy looked up at him, and Daniel felt a strange urge to ruffle his hair. Because whatever else he was, in addition to a magical construct born from the tissues of a cruel and powerful man, he was also a boy.

"When it's over, find his heart," Daniel said. "As much of it as you can. Bring it to Gabriel Argent at the Department of Water and Power."

"I don't understand," the boy said.

"In a way, I kind of hope you never do. But do it for me. That's the deal we're making. You deliver the heart to Argent."

"Okay," the boy said.

People were always so eager to please him.

Daniel turned to face the Hierarch. Leading with the sword, he launched himself through the burning window frame. Charred wood burst into flakes and splinters as he flew into the abyss. He vomited blue fire and embraced the Hierarch. Together, they plummeted.

The Hierarch's heat seared him. Daniel's eyebrows crisped. The heat scorched his eyes, his gums, his sinus cavities. Spinning and burning, they continued to fall toward the canal at the bottom of the hill. With firedrake talons, he gripped the

Hierarch's throat in one hand. In his other hand, he gripped the sword. He imagined wings spreading from his back, larger than the sails of a great yacht. He beat them and arrested his descent.

Three more strokes of his wings, and he shot over what was left of the Magic Castle. Half the roof was caved in, pulverized clay shingles and chimney bricks spilling down the hill along with masonry from the broken walls. Below, on the ledge of the attic floor, the Hierarch's golem looked up in wonder as Daniel propelled himself and the Hierarch over the castle.

"You're forgetting something," the Hierarch whispered in his ear. "You're using the magic I fed you in my Ossuary. *My* magic."

Gravity reclaimed them. They dive-bombed to earth, cratering into soil and manzanita and buckwheat.

They'd impacted in Runyon Canyon Park, a perch of dusty trails and shrubs above the Magic Castle on an eastern ledge of the Santa Monica Mountains. Panicked lizards and rabbits and coyotes skittered for cover in the chaparral. Pain lanced Daniel's lungs as he struggled to draw in breath, but he was satisfied. This was a fine place, far removed from the castle and other buildings and innocent bystanders. This was just the kind of place he needed.

The Hierarch was already back on his feet, brushing off his trousers. "Is that your secret weapon?" he said, gesturing at the sword.

The sword was not his secret weapon. It was just a reminder of what he was, of what his father had designed him to be: a weapon made of his own magic.

The bombs he'd used for the museum break-in were fake, but he carried inside him a real bomb. His body contained kraken and seps venom and wyvern and firedrake and groot. An osteomancer with deep magic became the creatures he ingested, and Daniel was a creature of fire and lightning and acid and earthquakes.

The Hierarch surely knew the magical ingredients Daniel was composed of, but he couldn't know what Daniel was willing to do with them.

Daniel thought, when he came to this point, he'd be reaching inside himself to find rage. Instead, he found himself reaching for warmer feelings. He thought of his friends. He wished he could see Cassandra again. He wished he could find a way to apologize to her. He wished he could buy Moth a chili burger. He wished he could save Jo from Otis. Moth and Cass would have to take care of that. Like so many other times, his friends would have to pick up after him.

"Boom," he said.

There was no passage of time as the substances in his body broke apart. Magical analogs to molecules and atoms released their bonds, and Daniel was the heart of a sun. His energies surged through his body, and he was distantly aware of tremendous agony and the high pitch of his own scream, like that day on the beach when his father gave him lightning. Daggers of white light shone from his eyes and from his gaping mouth and from his pores. He was a weapon. The most powerful weapon Sebastian Blackland had ever crafted. All his life, people had sought to wield him. Now, he wielded himself.

Magic flew out in all directions, physical events of flame and light, backed by the forces that couldn't be described by other physics. He exploded.

———

I t wasn't enough.

The Hierarch looked upon Daniel with curiosity and reached out with his right hand.

The spires of light ceased their expansion from Daniel's body. The shockwave collapsed. The swirling arms of flame radiating from him reversed their course, and Daniel's magic rushed back into his body, like a fire hose forced down his throat. Blood streamed from his nose.

"I'm sorry," the Hierarch said, squeezing, "I know this hurts." Daniel fell to his knees

Blood filled his mouth. It streaked from his ears and down his neck. Tears of blood streamed from his eyes.

The Hierarch smiled fondly, looking out over the expanse of Los Angeles. "I've always liked it up here," he said, making picnic banter as Daniel died. From here, Daniel could see a huge swath of the Hierarch's capital city. The city lights turned the bellies of the low clouds orange. The boats on flumeways sat still, clogged in a late-night traffic jam. The vast basin of Los Angeles glittered below.

Daniel lifted his head from charred earth, and he summoned words, but in the end, the only thing he could croak was "Why?"

The Hierarch's face was thoughtful. "Why I killed your father? Or why I'm going to feed you to my boy? The answer is the same. It's what I want."

"No," Daniel said, forcing the words out through his tortured chest and throat. "Why? *Why* do you need power?"

"Ah," the Hierarch said, just as Sebastian Blackland did whenever Daniel asked a good but unexpected question. "I truly wish I didn't, Daniel. I wish I could stop. But I can't. I can't stop eating. It was simple when we just ate what the Tar

Pits gave us, and what we could sell and trade for. Such rare, delicious bones. But I wasn't the first osteomancer to eat a fellow sorcerer. I'm not that much of an innovator. And I made the decision not to be food a long, long time ago. You're a thief, Daniel. You know if you don't take, you're only waiting until someone else does. I never believed the men who rose to power were the smartest, the most capable, the most deserving. They're simply the ones who made the decision to claim what anyone else could have. If it weren't me, it would be William Mulholland. Or a man like your father. Or poor old Fenmont Szu. It could be any of them." He swept his arm across the entire Los Angeles basin. "You thought you'd broken into my Ossuary. But here's a secret: The entire kingdom is my Ossuary. The people have been breathing my air for generations. They've living in my exhaust, in my soot. They've been walking my pavements, and eating the fruit grown from my soil. My magic is everywhere. My cache of bone is wrapped in their living flesh. They're all treasures."

Daniel let his face fall back into the dirt. He was so tired. And everything hurt so bad. His world tunneled, and if the Hierarch was still speaking, his voice was lost behind the sound of rushing blood in Daniel's head. He could smell his own adrenaline, the lactic acid in his battered muscles, and the endorphins his brain was sending out to help him cope with pain and stress. He smelled the weak remnants of his own magic. His skin was broken. Blood vessels torn. Bones cracked. He had come open to the world, and his magic was draining away.

And there was another smell, so faint, as the Hierarch's footfalls crunched in the earth, coming closer.

It was the smell of everything, coming from all around him.

He was smelling all the magic. Maybe this was just the aromatic equivalent of seeing his life flash before his eyes.

If the kingdom was the Hierarch's Ossuary, then how much magic could Daniel ingest, up here, on this hill? A particle per billion? Even less?

The magic surrounded him. All else was recipe.

He let it soak into his body. He imagined thousands of Jinshin-Mushi beetles streaming up from the earth and burrowing under his skin. He imagined corrosive venom, seeping up from the soil, burning its way into his flesh, burning through his bones, all the way to the marrow. He imagined the thin residue of magic atmosphere growing dense and raining upon him. He was a sponge of magic and pain. He was a cauldron.

He breathed the Hierarch's living Ossuary. He breathed the kingdom.

Beetles digging, fire burning a hole in him like a blowtorch, Daniel gained his feet.

He chose a spot in the center of the Hierarch's chest, and he pushed. The Hierarch shrieked like a horse in a burning barn.

Daniel pushed again, and the Hierarch doubled over.

He pushed, and the Hierarch fell.

"You killed my dad before he made me a true osteomancer," Daniel said. "But he did live long enough to make me a glutton."

It would take some time to kill him. The Hierarch was much older than the body he was wearing, and he was good at staying alive.

But the magic in the earth flowed up through Daniel's body,

and the Hierarch would die on this hill, overlooking his kingdom. Daniel had chosen this.

He wondered what the Hierarch's heart would taste like, and his mouth watered.

TWENTY-THREE

The city didn't yet know what had happened to it.

Traffic flowed on some canals. On others, boats fouled the water with idling engines. Searchlights probed the air, but they were just promoting clubs and bars. Fireboats shot water on the Magic Castle, and white smoke billowed over the hillside.

Stumbling down Sunset in his torn, burned clothes, Daniel was the most interesting thing on the sidewalk. Stares, averted glances, looks of disapproval . . . He must be a fascinating sight. He'd already been passed up by three cabs, but he couldn't blame the drivers. He didn't have any money to pay them with anyway.

"Watch out," the Hierarch's golem said. "Glass."

Daniel stepped around a broken bottle in his bare feet, wondering if his flesh could still be cut.

"Thanks."

He clutched the boy's hand. In his other hand, he held a plastic grocery bag. Inside the bag was a treasure. Or half a treasure. The part that Daniel hadn't eaten. He kept the sword tucked through his belt. He looked like a lunatic.

It wasn't until he passed Sunset Newsstand, west of La Brea, that he overheard someone talking about the fire. The newsstand proprietor sat on a stool, reading the racing report, obviously trying to mind his own business while a man in a fine suit tried gamely to engage in conversation.

"Saw some lightning up there," he was saying. "Weird lightning. Heard there were some fireballs, too. And shaking."

The newsstand man flipped a page. "You don't say."

"Localized tremors like that don't happen naturally. Seismic waves travel, you know."

"Mm-hmm."

"You ask me, it's osteomancy. The castle used to be some kind of private wizard club, and those guys get territorial. You think?"

"I don't think," the proprietor said. "I sell papers, cigarettes, candy, and porn, and I mind my own business."

A safe policy, Daniel thought. The Ministry had spies, and they could afford good suits.

Good Suit gave up on his conversation and took notice of Daniel. He stared into Daniel's grimy face, then at the boy, then back at Daniel. He reached into his jacket.

Daniel wasn't sure what to do about this. He had so many options.

From Good Suit's pocket came a wallet. He passed a note to Daniel as if he were tipping a maître d'.

"Get your boy something to eat and some decent clothes," he said. "And don't drink it." Then he bought a copy of *Hustler* and went on his way, leaving Daniel with the fifty.

It took all of it to convince a cabbie to take him to the Ship's Diner on La Cienega. Daniel set the boy up at the counter and ordered him a bowl of tomato soup and a glass of milk. When the waitress assessed Daniel's appearance and found him wanting, she asked him if he could pay for it. Daniel put on his winningest smile. He promised her a twenty-tusk tip if she'd give him a few minutes to go get some money. More out of pity for the boy than being charmed by Daniel, she agreed.

"I'm going to be just outside," Daniel told the boy. "If anyone bothers you, scream. Loudly."

"A banshee's scream is a hundred and ninety-four decibels. Anything louder than that and the sound wave breaks down. Will that be loud enough?"

"It'll do," Daniel said.

In the parking docks behind the restaurant, he climbed into the front passenger seat of a black stretch outrigger. Gabriel Argent sat behind the wheel. Argent's hound lurked in the back. Back east, this was how they conducted mob hits.

"I wasn't sure you were going to make it," Argent said. "Lots of fireworks up in the hills. God, you look like hell. Should we be going to the hospital?"

"I lived. He died. Give me my friends."

Argent eyed the bag in Daniel's lap. "You brought the thing?"

Daniel opened the top of the bag and let Argent peer inside.

"Max?" Argent said to the hound.

The hound leaned forward and sniffed. "It smells like everything."

"I'm not sure that's helpful," Argent said. But Daniel knew what the hound meant. The Hierarch's heart tasted like it smelled, like liver and beef and like the thousands of different kinds of magic the Hierarch had ingested during his long life.

"It's the real thing," Max concluded.

Argent held out for the bag, but Daniel moved it out of his reach.

"First you free my friends. If you can't or won't, your heart goes into the bag, too."

Argent didn't seem to take the threat personally. "I freed them four hours ago. Look." He pointed out the windshield at the diner's entrance. There, standing on the sidewalk, were Cassandra and Moth. Cassandra looked at her watch, and they went inside.

It felt to Daniel as if steel bands squeezing his chest had sprung loose, as if he could breathe properly for the first time in days, and he spent a moment to gather himself.

"Four hours ago, I hadn't even made it to the Magic Castle yet. But you freed them anyway. Why?"

Argent took his time answering. "I'm not a good man," he began. "I've been involved in some very bad enterprises. I've ordered people hurt. I've killed. I'm the man who removed the head from the Department of Water and Power. But you're the man who stole the kingdom's treasure. And I don't want you as an enemy."

Daniel handed him the bag. Argent opened it and considered the Hierarch's heart.

"It looks like there's only half there."

"Plenty left for you to sell or use or whatever you want. What are you going to do with all that power?"

"What are you going to do with yours?"

Daniel licked the back of his teeth and tasted magic. He opened the door and stepped outside. "You're right, Argent. You don't want me as an enemy." He shut the door and went to meet his friends.

It would be a brief reunion, he knew.

He needed to go see Otis, with whom he did not have an appointment.

Outside Otis's warehouse, Daniel placed his palm flat against the concrete block wall. It was hard to decide what to do. He could secrete seps venom and burn through the blocks. He could dissolve them like talc. With a simple push, he could bring the building tumbling down. He wondered if the Hierarch had paused like this on the night he burst into his father's house.

Daniel decided to go through the back door.

It wasn't even locked.

He anticipated a volley of bullets from Otis's bodyguards. Instead, his footsteps echoed through the empty warehouse. The crates and boxes, the sacks of pet food, the posters for flea collars and kitty litter had been removed. The menagerie of magic-detecting birds and hamsters were gone. The chain-link wraith-slave pens alongside the wall were vacant as well. Even the air smelled empty. Any osteomancy residue had been sucked into vacuum cleaner bags and hauled away.

He continued to Otis's office. The file drawers were pulled out, empty. The hobo clown painting rested on the floor, leaning against the wall.

On the cleared-off desktop rested a white envelope, placed so dead center that Daniel imagined Otis using a ruler and calipers.

Daniel tore it open and read the note inside:

*Sorry for not leaving a forwarding address. I sup-
pose you're the new Hierarch now. Good luck.*
                    Sincerely, Uncle Otis

Daniel read the note again. He concentrated on every word,
every pen stroke. He could see Otis smirking as he folded the
note and licked the envelope and placed it there for Daniel to
find.

How fun it must be, to be Otis.

His fingers grew hot, and pencil lines of smoke rose from
the paper.

"Daniel?"

He turned. Standing in the doorway was the real reason he'd
come back.

"Jo."

She rushed him and threw her arms around his neck, and
they stood that way for minutes, until Daniel pushed her away
and held her at arm's length.

"I'm okay," she said, misinterpreting the way he examined
every contour of her face, every subtlety of her expression. He
smelled the nhang spirit and kitsune fox and dragon's teeth
that gave her shape-shifting, and he still couldn't be sure if it
was really her.

"Tell me something only you and I know."

"Tito's," she said, obeying without hesitation.

"What about it?"

"The first time you told me what happened to your parents,
and the first time I told you what happened to mine, we were
at Tito's Tacos. You complained that the chips were like roof
shingles, but you liked it there, because the old men in the
back knew how to roll a burrito tighter than a cigar."

"Jo," he said, and he drew her back into a hug. "I'm so sorry. I didn't find out Otis replaced you until we were out of the Ossuary."

"You're an idiot," she said.

Daniel gave her more apologies, which she was too ready to accept. In his system was a mixture of eocorn essence, terratorn coprolite, and high-quality *Panthera atrox* that made his friends love him and quick to forgive. He could thank his father for that. And it was a gift he knew he had to rid himself of, even though the thought of casting it away terrified him.

"He gave me a message for you," she said.

"What?"

She hesitated. "He's probably just screwing with you. It's like his hobby."

"Jo. What's the message?"

Wincing, she reached into her pocket and fished out a folded slip of paper. She handed it to Daniel.

The paper was yellowed and brittle. Written in fading ink, the precise, block-printed letters spelled out, "I'm ready. Send my son."

The note wasn't signed, but no signature was necessary. Daniel recognized his mother's hand.

Otis had never shown Daniel the note. He'd never told him his mother had sent for him. He'd kept Daniel all to himself.

Daniel would find Otis. He'd smoke him out of whatever hole he was hiding in and he would kill him, loudly and publicly. He would make a spectacle of Otis, and everyone, the whole kingdom, would know what happened when you pushed Daniel Blackland.

He sighed and folded the note.

"Come on," he said, taking Jo's hand.

Moth sniffled as he carried Daniel's bag. The bag contained little: a couple of spare shirts, some underwear and basic toiletries, an empty picture frame, but Moth still insisted on loading it into the trunk of Daniel's boat. He bear-hugged Daniel, gave him a gentle punch to the chest, hugged him again, and then Daniel got sniffly, too.

"Stay out of trouble," Daniel told him.

Moth snorked and guffawed. "What are the odds?"

"Not so good. Just be careful, okay? I don't know what Otis is planning."

"If he comes looking for me, then he's gonna get his head tore off and shoved so far up his ass it pops out his neck hole and becomes his head again. I love you, Daniel," Moth said.

"I know. My dad didn't give you much choice."

"I don't care about that loyalty-potion shit. I still love you."

Daniel tried to find a joke, but the well was empty. More powerful than he'd ever been, he was empty. "Why, Moth? I'm honestly at a loss here. Why do you love me?"

Moth paused, collecting his words. "Because you, buddy, do have a choice in who you love. And you choose to love your friends." He cuffed Daniel on the side of the head. "Go talk to Cassie."

After a final, huge, spine-cracking hug, Moth lumbered down the dock to give Daniel and Cassandra some privacy.

"Hey," Daniel said. He glanced at her, which was a mistake,

because now he couldn't look away, and he knew at some point he'd have to look away.

"Hey," Cassandra said, her hands in her pockets.

"You won't change your mind and come with me?"

"What do you think, Daniel?"

"I think you should change your mind and come with me."

She sighed. He exasperated her. He always did. "You know I didn't break up with you because I stopped thinking you were cute, right?"

"I know I'm cute," he said.

"I didn't break up with you because I stopped loving you."

"I know."

"I broke up with you because even then, I knew I couldn't stop loving you. I don't mean in a stupid love-song way. I mean . . . I knew I couldn't stop. And I don't know how I knew, but it felt wrong to me. Even then."

"I'm sorry my dad did that to you guys. I really am, Cass. I hope you know I mean it."

She crossed her arms and looked down the canal. Moth was still there, trying to make it seem like he wasn't watching them.

"I know you mean it, kiddo."

She kissed him on the cheek and turned and walked away. Daniel's chest beat with the power of a thousand different osteomantic creatures. It beat with strength, and with power, and with magic, and every beat was slow and heavy. He watched her go, hating the whispering voice that told him to force her to turn back. He could do it, if he wanted to. It would be so easy.

The voice telling him this was not the Hierarch's. It was not his father's. It was all his own.

In the following days, the remaining powers went to war. There was no official statement, and the propaganda machine kept blathering about sports and celebrity news, and the weather reports were noticeably bland and inaccurate, at a loss to explain the lightning cracking the sky apart, and the blue fires that raged in the hills, and the tremors bringing down the mansions of the Council of Six.

Yet the water still flowed, all the way from the downtown center of the kingdom's capital to the last capillaries of the desert outpost of Lancaster, where Daniel traded his boat for a land truck.

As he drove through the night, he left behind the vague orange sky of the city for the dizzying stars. The earth, where all his magic originated, felt thin, without gravity. If Daniel let go, he'd drift, unanchored.

Gabriel Argent had called the Hierarch's heart the kingdom's treasure, and surely it was a treasure. Daniel could still feel the half of it he'd eaten coursing through his veins, filling his cells with its power, and whispering to him, telling him what he was capable of now. The power begged to be used.

The golem-boy slept in the passenger seat, and he was a greater treasure yet. They'd come looking for him: Council osteomancers, aspiring lesser sorcerers, foreign powers and thieves and people like Otis. Maybe they wouldn't try to take him by force. Maybe they'd be willing to negotiate. Maybe if Daniel parted him out, piece by piece, a tooth here, a finger bone there, they'd finally leave Daniel alone.

Daniel would never do that, but the fact that he could even think of it made him push down the accelerator. He was abandoning Los Angeles, but he wouldn't abandon the boy.

Cold air came in through the vents, rustling the boy's hair, and Daniel smelled his fresh magic. He kept driving toward the borders of the kingdom, away from familiar ghosts, toward ghosts he didn't yet know.

ACKNOWLEDGMENTS

As always, my thanks go first to Lisa Will, for every kind of help in every part of my life.

My editor, Patrick Nielsen Hayden, not only made this a better book but repeatedly declared his enthusiasm for the project at times when I needed it most. Caitlin Blasdell ably represented my interests at every stage, from proposal to final manuscript submission and beyond. The team at Tor Books turned my manuscript into an actual book, and I would like to thank Miriam Weinberg, Irene Gallo, Theresa DeLucci, and Patty Garcia, among others, for their skill and hard work.

I haven't yet published a book that wasn't critiqued by members of the Blue Heaven writers workshop. In this case, I relied on Cassie Alexander, Paolo Bacigalupi, Chris Barzak, Tobias Buckell, Rae Carson, Deborah Coates, Charles Coleman Finlay, Sandra McDonald, Paul Melko, Sarah Prineas, and Jenn Reese. They are a solid criminal crew, and it is to them I dedicate this book.

I owe additional thanks to Deborah Coates and Jenn Reese for supportive e-mail correspondence, and especially to Sarah

Prineas for a last-minute read that gave me the stomach to send in my final draft.

Sheila Williams bought the short story that gave messy birth to this novel, "The Osteomancer's Son," for *Asimov's Science Fiction*. And Dave Thompson not only picked the story for the PodCastle podcast, but helped convince me that a novel-length expansion of it might have an audience. Tim Pratt, whose opinion I highly value, also read the novel and gave me a very welcome thumbs-up.

John M. Harris and Sharon Takeshita at the Natural History Museum of Los Angeles answered my questions about the La Brea Tar Pits. And many people on Twitter suggested heist movies and books for research. I should have written down their names. I didn't. I'm sorry. But please all consider yourselves Favorited.

Finally, I would like to thank Tito's Tacos.